THE UNHEARD SONG

by Cary Neeper

Penscript®
PUBLISHING HOUSE

Characters and alien species depicted herein are trademarks of
Carolyn A. Neeper. The Penscript® logo and calligraphy are trademarks and
Penscript is a registered trademark of Shawne A. Workman, DBA Penscript
Publishing House.

Publisher's Cataloging-in-Publication
  Neeper, Cary.
    The unheard song / by Cary Neeper.
    p. cm. — (The archives of Varok ; 5)
    Includes bibliographical references.
    While struggling to make verbal contact,
    the humanoid varoks try to help the aquatic
    ellls build a safer lifestyle and avoid
    overpopulation stress.
    Library of Congress Control Number: 2022931991
    ISBN 978-1-62222-007-6 (trade pbk.)
    ISBN 978-1-62222-009-0 (Nook)
    ISBN 978-1-62222-010-6 (ePub)

    1. NonHuman-alien encounters—Fiction
    2. Extraterrestrial beings—Fiction. 3. Communication—
    Fiction. 4. Overpopulation—Fiction 5.Science fiction. I. Title. II. Series:
    Neeper, Cary. Archives of Varok.

First edition
Published by Penscript Publishing House
San Jose, California.
http://www.penscript-publishing.com

In loving memory of Ma and Pa:
Jessie Hillman Jones Almond (1899–1972) and
Harold Russell Almond Sr. (1900–1993)

CONTENTS

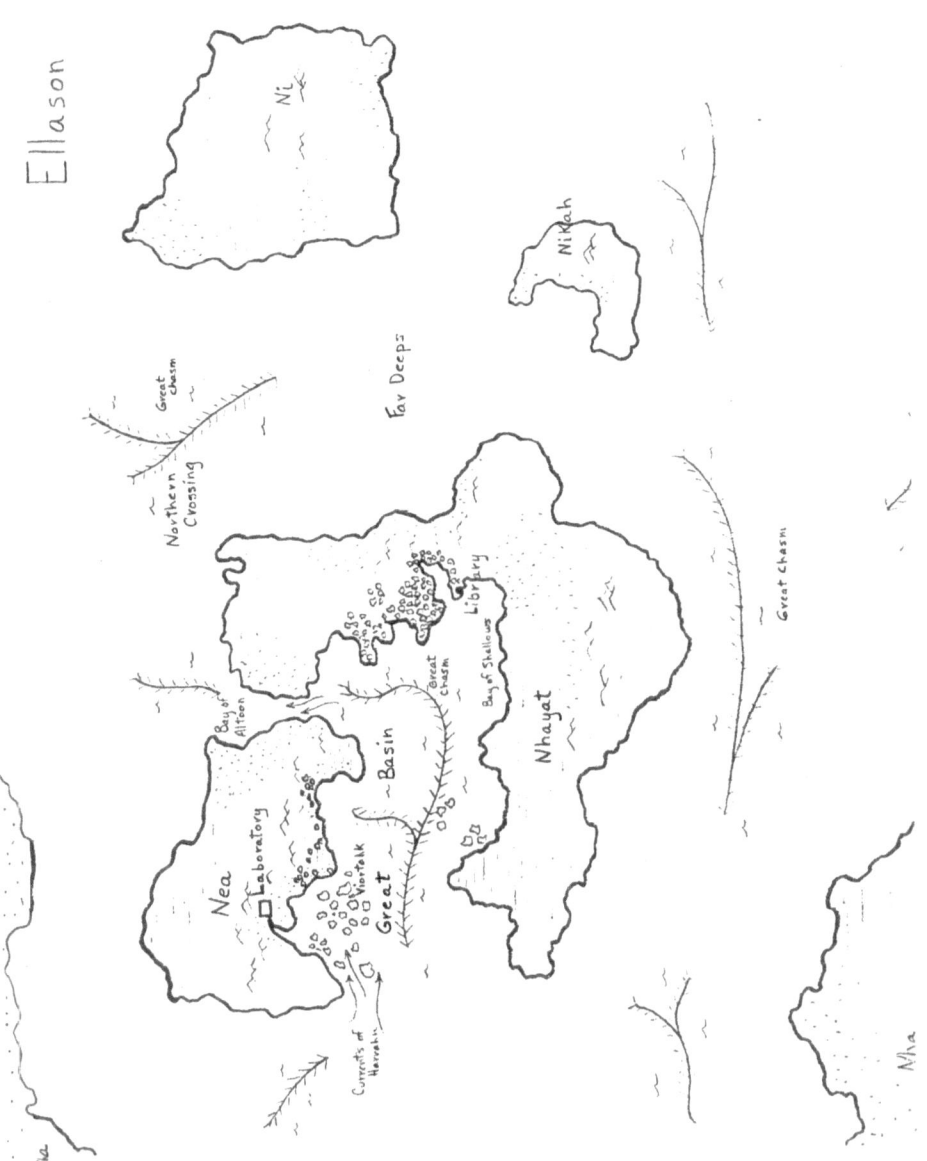

Ellason

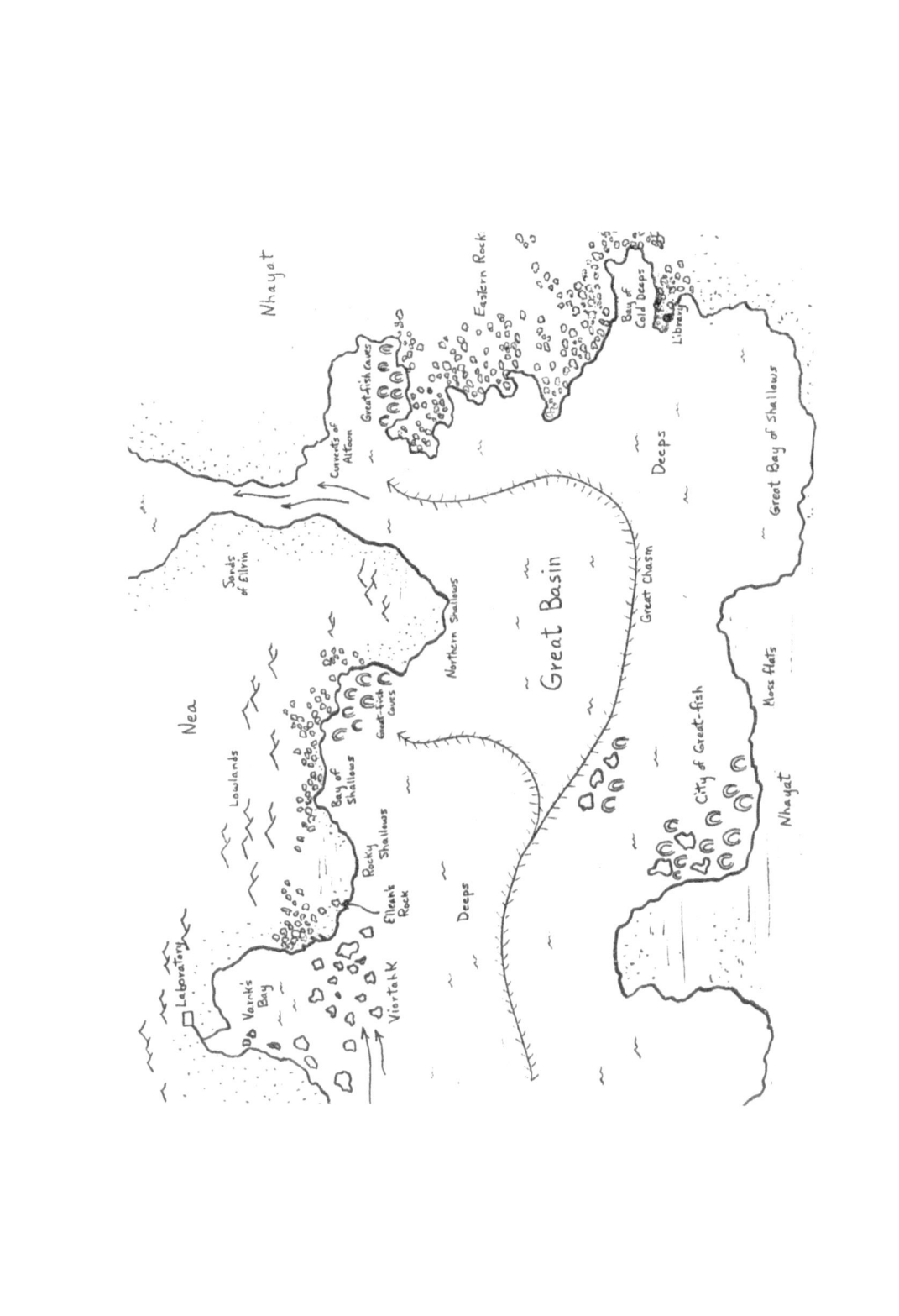

I. The Historical Setting

The time: 3631 *ir* Varokian time (5000 BCE on Earth), soon after we varoks discovered another planet in Sol's system, inhabited by aquatic bipeds who called themselves ellls. At that time, the technologically primitive hominids on Earth were of little interest to us.

The location: Earth's solar system, including Jupiter with its moon, Varok, and eight other planets, notably Ellason, another inhabited world which will not be detected by human beings on Earth until circa 2036 CE. Ellason is an internally heated planet of radius 9026 kilometers in approximately a 1200-year eccentric orbit around the sun. The nearest approach to the sun, near the orbit of Neptune, occurred circa 9929 BCE Earth time, and again in 2071 CE.

—Aman Telariahn (Amantel), Varok, 2072 CE Earth

AN END TO GAMES

Too far from Earth, unseen by human eyes,
There rode a verdant world
With silent lands 'neath thirty moons.
In heavy seas dwelt sentient life—
Fair ellls with webbed hands.

The young varok known as Korad gasped as Ellason came into view. The planet shone like a precious turquoise gem in the dark void of the outer solar system—so different from Varok, his home, an isolated, densely shrouded moon of Jupiter. This place teemed with life, more like the primitive blue planet Earth with its richly clouded skies and wide oceans.

Korad's untamed face of warm sienna shone with wonder. Already he loved this strange watery planet, too rarely visited by Varokian scientists. Astronomers' calculations had predicted its presence in Sol's outer realm, but only recently did they realize how intelligent was the life—great-fish and ellls—that reveled in Ellason's deep oceans.

From the adjoining seat in the space cruiser's passenger section, his varokian mentor Tera adjusted her passenger restraints, then looked directly at the young varok, without apology. Korad (Kor Adtalorian) had won the position of relief scientist to help address a crisis the ellls had made for themselves. He could do the job. This new recruit was a grand mind still exploring its potential, a nearly mature varok, only one Callisto cycle away from graduation in Ellasonian Studies at the Varokian Concentrate.

Dry land appeared through the mist. It spread out below like a gigantic, self-lit map. The outlines of Ellason's continental shores shone with thousands upon thousands of bioluminescent creatures. Sheets of their blue and green lights framed far-flung islands and lit narrow channels. Several moons sent a faint, red-orange glow over all.

Korad's eyes moved over every inlet and bay as he searched the patterns. "There must be ellls in the waters below, Tera."

"Yes," she said, "they are always on the move, schooling or tending their gardens."

Swiftly they flew past broad planes of turquoise light embracing dark land. "That must be Ellason's Great Basin," Korad said. "I have noted great-fish caves in its steep cliffs, and the homes of ellls in its broad shallows."

Tera could see Korad's dedication to the project, but the tone in his words seemed raw and vulnerable, as his person would be, too soon. Ellason was a wild place not yet fully understood.

Korad turned away from the viewport, aware of his elder's thoughts.

"We can save the ellls, Tera," he said, "if we can find a way to communicate with them. I must learn to understand them on their terms—not ours. Surely the Directorate will not overrule my approach. Is that what I read in your mind?"

The fire in his eyes danced with an urgency his mentor found tragic. "We haven't unraveled the ellls' sonic code, Korad, and now we have evidence that they may converse with pressure signals to their body tiles. On Ellason you'll be just another alien with no way to communicate."

"Then I'll find a way."

"I like your confidence, but do beware of your varokian assumptions. We are blessed with minds open to others of our kind, but you may not be able to read the ellls' thoughts, not even their mood, through their tangle of sensory input. We have made mistakes just trying to read their body language. We have been more successful interpreting the gestures of the primitive bipeds near the icy lands of Earth."

For a moment Korad looked puzzled. "I realize that the bipedal Earth creatures are built as we are, but so are the ellls. Why haven't they made more use of their dry land? Is it understood why ellls evolved lungs?"

"Not really. Perhaps ellls who could breathe out of water escaped from ocean predators onto dry land. We know of two large sea-dwelling animals that hunt ellls."

"Were their calls for help recorded? We know that ellls make throat sounds, but their tongues are very long."

Tera laughed. "Indeed they are, but we have no idea how they use throat sounds. Apparently, they don't have a spoken language. We have nothing but reports of brief encounters with ellls. We haven't made any kind of meaningful contact. The ellls taken to Varok didn't fare well. Ellls probably regard us varoks as fearsome creatures."

"Has anyone studied the electromagnetic signals from their tile lines? We understand the lateral lines on Earth's fish, don't we?"

"Ellason is not Earth, Korad, and ellls are not fish."

"Perhaps they communicate with chemicals, like Varok's trees. Do they threaten with toxins?"

"We haven't seen evidence of chemical conversations, and unlike everyone else living in Ellason's oceans, ellls have no bioluminescence. They stay dark, which is probably a good defense."

Korad met Tera's troubled eyes and chose his words carefully. "We are all made of the same elements, Tera. I like to think that there is no such thing as an alien. The word *alien* comes from our failure to recognize that every living being is a person, a conscious entity, no matter how they sense their environment, no matter how they eat or fight or communicate."

"I hope you're right," Tera said. Her respect for the youth grew two notches. Here was the attitude varoks at the lab needed in order to make real progress with the ellls. "Our philosopher—you'll meet him soon—has suggested that we can win the ellls' trust by demonstating respect for them and their planet. Do you believe that?"

The varokian student settled back in his seat as the ship descended into the mists. Smooth flats of clay near giant rocks framed wide laboratory buildings barely visible, for they were made by varoks from the land's natural adobe. "Of course," he said at last.

– Δ –

As the space cruiser settled onto the landing pad near the varoks' study center, Tera sensed with her patch organs that the young varok imagined schools of jolly ellls cutting through the warm shallow waters, velvet green bipeds wearing bright colors in their plumes, laughing at the joke of filling their exoteric planet with life.

It had been a joke all right, Tera thought, a joke on the varoks. They had not suspected that there was another Varok-sized planet in eccentric, 12,000-year orbit in "their" solar system. For decades, their curious attention had been turned toward Earth and its spotty indications of hominid progress. Ellason moved in a huge elliptical orbit beyond the Kuiper Belt at aphelion, too far from the sun to be practical for varoks to visit often. It had been hidden for ages from their technical vision. Now it was at perihelion, close enough to study, in the vicinity of Neptune's orbit. Such an errant planet would not support life—certainly not intelligent life. Yet there it was, teeming with life, its oceans heated with pockets of natural nuclear fission and unrelenting deep-sea volcanism, its lands dimly lit by thirty volcanic moons.

When the varoks made their first journey to Ellason, they found living beings evolved as specialists in bio-luminescence. Ellason also teemed with primitive hemo-synthesizing beasts, whose sulfur oxidation, ages ago, had powered the evolution of intelligence. Some of the most primitive microbes still harvested methane for their energy requirements. With careful biosensing, the varoks discovered the dense undersea farmlands of life-enhancing bipeds, the ellls, and Ellason's more elusive creatures, aquatic philosophers, the great-fish.

So much for varokian uniqueness, Korad thought. *We thought that other life in the universe would be too rare in all of time's vastness to make meaningful contact.*

"And here it is," Tera laughed, "and soon you will meet Amanok, my friend the prophet, Aman Okrahlan, Director of the Elll-watch. He will give you different eyes to see through. His allotted time on Ellason has been extended to a full Varokian half-year. Your assignment will overlap his for several light cycles. His love of ellls is equal to yours. You and he will soon find a way to approach them, if—" Tera sighed and shook her head, "—if you and he together are not overruled."

Ilean

In days gone by, where days do not exist,
Beneath the deeps where varoks dare not range
And human search still fails,
Within the seas of Ellason
There lived an elll thought strange.

While Korad began work at the Varokian Observation Laboratory, a young elll called Ilean in the nearby Ellasonian seas began to realize something was wrong, something about herself, something not elllonian. She loved venturing onto land, where she could stand tall on her two webbed feet. Instead of swimming and foraging with her school, she preferred to be alone and explore the creatures she found out of water. On land she could indulge her own talents and forget the never-ending demands from the school.

Ilean often drifted alone to the farthest corner of a small bay in Ellason's Northern Shallows. One fine moonlit period she swam to a deep, clear inlet where the rocks rose out of the water covered with rich moss-like plants. Small pools shimmered all around her, alive with crawling beings and tiny swimmers. The rocks felt warm. Their silence was welcoming, a respite from the constant buzzing of her school. This area was her favorite haunt, a place of quiet where she could drift undisturbed with her dreams. Here she found relief from swimming with her school of twenty other ellls, where too many noises jabbed at her.

Ilean eased back into the water where a narrow crevice separated two boulders. She flapped her gills for the fun of it. Then she dove and tried making patterns in the muddy bottom, like great-fish did.

They had always been kind to her, the great-fish. They seemed to respect her privacy, but maybe they were just shy. Maybe some day she could tame one, if tame was the right word. Her sponsor Duregal said the great-fish knew more than eyes could see, more than schools of ellls could imagine. Maybe they could tell her why she irritated other ellls. Maybe they could tell her about the bright lights that shone like jewels beyond the moons that lit the night sky.

Ellls could see many more stars than varoks saw, for ellonian vision extended far into the infrared. The patterns of stars noted by ellls had more to do with aesthetics than with their sense of time. Most cared less for the slow changes among stars than for the beauty of their patterns. Some moonlight changes did coincide with biological transitions in the vast seas, like the release of spores from *llaoon* grass or the hatching of an egg chosen for incubation. Thus ellls noted the passage of time, hardly noticing the orbits of the moons and the rotation of the planet.

Above the rocks Ilean's school appeared, feeding on mist-hoppers and beam-fish. She rose above water and inflated her lungs to watch her fellow ellls appear and disappear into the glimmering surface.

She floated still for a moment, watching her blue body plumes rise above the moss green tiles that held them. She dove and explored the hidden spaces between the rocks below. A tiny creature—something edible with a buzzing sound for a name—pulled back into a deep crack lined with sea plants. It lit her hideaway with a pleasant biolumines-cent glow. Her long tongue shot into the crack—too late—and she was glad. The creature had caught her eye. How could you eat something that had begged for its life?

Maybe I'm okay after all, she thought. For one moment she felt like a thoughtful, masterful creature.

Though she was not hungry, she searched for more living treasures in the rocks. She liked to watch them. Her be-finned hands propelled her effortlessly away from the crevice. The crystal water shone with countless microbes signaling to each other in six shades of blue. To en-joy the shimmering light, she extended her long back-fin and balanced over a patch of rock-moss, decorated with a glowing mud-worm.

She examined the deepening blue of her plumage. The cool hues of her branched plumes signaled her approaching maturity. Soon she would produce her first *el* egg. No longer a tad, she would then be free from her obligations to Duregal, her sponsor.

Ilean wanted to feel free from the fear of causing her school more trouble. She would live as an adult alone—on the periphery of elllo-nian life. Her odd waves would no longer wash over the other ellls and disturb their schooling patterns. *Once I produce eggs, no one will care if I swim off in a wrong direction. I will follow the gardeners of land-moss out onto the beaches, or hide among the rocks and chase lohn birds and dig for crawlers.*

"There she is!"

With a flash of dark green plumes, the young male, Ba-ohl, dove toward Ilean and teased her away from her underwater retreat.

Ilean laughed, gulping water and spitting it out, as her friend chased her up to the gray satin surface of the shallows. There the school was feeding on small black fish hiding in the shore-moss.

"What do you want with me, Ba-ohl?"

"Sa-el and I need one more on our jumping team."

"I can't clear the jumping rock. You come at it too fast."

"Sure you can clear it. Come on, Ilean." The gray lights in Ba-ohl's eyes reassured her.

"Just follow us," Ba-ohl said in careful sonar, "and when you see the rock, jump as high as you can. Sa-el and I will do the crossing and the moving patterns through the air. Just go over the rock."

Ilean saw the moss-covered tiles of Ba-ohl's throat continue to move. Why had the barking drum beat of his voice died away? What was the harsh, staccato buzzing sound that took its place? Why did other ellls do that? She hated it.

"I can't understand you," Ilean cried. He should know how the vibrations shook her skull. "Stop it."

"I'm sorry, I forgot," Ba-ohl said in sonic code, audible again. "It's an easy game, Ilean. You'll like it, if you'll only take some time to learn it."

The elll called Sa-el swept up from below and grabbed Ilean's free hand. She didn't like him. His sensory channels ran a bit too swift and deep for her and for his own good. She called for Ba-ohl.

She gasped as Sa-el and Ba-ohl pulled her along underwater. Faster and faster they towed her, until the beamers and glowing mist-hoppers painted a mad blur across her eyes.

In the distance she could barely make out a wall of rock rising from the ocean floor. She knew it broke the surface of the water like a small island—and they were rushing straight toward it.

Panic rose in her throat. At this speed, would she see the rock in time to leap clear? Yet she needed speed to make the jump.

She knew that a second team of ellls was racing toward the same rock from another direction. The game was to leap over the rock in crossing patterns designed to challenge the other team. It was a dangerous game. Adults had told her that split-second timing and last-minute adjustments in air were needed to maintain pattern and to miss the oncoming team of ellls. *Stupid game,* she thought.

The elders of the school officially discouraged the game with knowing smiles. It was excellent training, after all, for young echolocation reactions. "Ba-ohl, I don't know when to jump. Where are we?" Ilean called in a desperate, low sonic voice. "You've got to tell me when."

Ba-ohl heard the panic in Ilean's voice too late. "Now!" he called, releasing the grip on her arm.

Ilean leaped upward as she saw the rock suddenly rush toward her. Her body left the water in a graceful arc but failed to clear the rock's surface by nearly a meter. As if from nowhere, the crushing blow threw her back into the sea.

·

LIFE–MOMENTS

She longed to chase the lohn birds through the moss,
To find the stars before the dawn's renewal,
To hear the sighing mists,
To see with mind and know with heart
The world beyond the school.

As he tended his small garden of rock dwellers, Ilean's sponsor Duregal felt the unusual pressure pattern of her senseless fall into the water. He heard the emergency ultrasonics of the school call him to the shallows. He pulled in his back-fin and leapt across the surface of the water, fearing the worst.

He took the fragile blue elll in his arms, and swam slowly along the ocean's sandy floor, imitating the soothing motion of the school. Ilean's limp blue-plumed figure sent him into grief as ellls know it— grief for the loss of awareness. "Come back, my Tad. You are missing too many moments."

Twenty-eight ellls gathered around the injured elll and her sponsor, covering them with pressure waves of sympathy. Until Ilean regained consciousness, they would not school normally. They shared Duregal's grief, while the physicians of the school examined her and applied herbs to the gills that lined her nose.

"She will live," the physicians told the school, "but we can do nothing more to reduce her loss of moments."

"The blame is Ilean's entirely." The judgment boomed out from Falll, a blue elll who often presumed to speak for the entire school. "She should not swim in such games. She is not . . . normal."

"The young ones pulled her into a leaping contest," an elder countered in precise ultrasonic language. "I agree that she is not normal, but she is not stupid. She remembers all the tales she hears from great-fish."

"Too often she gets lost from the school," the angry elll announced. "We can't go looking for loners all the time. There are difficult tides now. Our school is challenged by other schools."

"Please, listen to us." Two youths swam past the angry blue elll. "It was our fault. We thought we could guide Ilean over the rock."

"At high speed, reckless weedlings?" The elder stormed. "You gave her no choice."

"We didn't know. She can't do echo."

"I should have realized . . . ." Ba-ohl admitted. "She can't read. Ultrasonic pictures don't work for her."

Like a bird in flight, Falll snapped a roll in the water, disrupting the pressure patterns of the school. "I've made my point. Ilean must not play such games until she learns to read ultrasonic echoes and schools properly. We cannot afford to be continually herding lost strays."

"Please! Please," Ba-ohl cried out in youthful frustration as he joined Duregal in guiding Ilean through the water. "You are ruining Duregal's life–moments with your temper. You are piling grief on grief. Ilean's loss of life-moments is my fault alone. I insisted she swim the game. I didn't know how blind to ultrasonics she is. From now on I will keep watch on her. The school will not lose her again. I promise."

Anger faded and the ellls looked at young Ba-ohl, questioning his generous offer.

"The school has heard your promise, Ba-ohl." The elder Navell swam to him and clasped the youth's broad shoulders. "It was a foolish promise, impossible to keep."

– Δ –

For a tortuous hour, the school cruised the shallows, keeping in their midst Duregal, the generous youth Ba-ohl, and Ilean. All grieved for her lost moments.

When she awoke at last, Ilean felt a profound sense of failure. She had been unable to see the rock in time to miss it. She didn't understand how the others could.

Duregal's joy at seeing her conscious did not comfort her. "Come now, Ilean. Rest here in the rocks until the school is ready to swim on." Her loving sponsor spoke softly in the sonic code Ilean could hear. "That game of Ba-ohl's would make great-fish angry. That is no game for disabled loners."

Ilean shuddered. She had never before heard the dreaded word "loner" from Duregal.

"Loner. Loner, too? Along with buzzing sounds I don't understand?" She darted off before the old elll could stop her.

He had sense enough to leave her alone. She needed to recover from his loving truth. He hovered above, feeling helpless as he watched her swim off to hide in a circle of tall boulders.

Ilean's thoughts wouldn't leave her in peace. *I have always felt incomplete, an imperfect elll. I'm poor at schooling. I'm too eager to be alone. I'm always getting lost. I'm unable to follow the simplest instructions or conversation.*

She thought of her beloved sponsor. Duregal had tended her as a fertile egg, protected her as a budding tad, and taught her as a tailless youngster. Now he had confirmed her deepest fears. She was not just frustrated by the school's irritating buzzing; it was critical. She was a loner—yet crippled, absolutely dependent on Duregal and the school, unable to wander or live alone.

– Δ –

At the Varokian study center, the young varok Korad had settled into a routine that included physical conditioning as well as extensive orientation to the alien planet, its perceived needs, and its challenges. He disliked being confined to the varoks' stark buildings. He longed to go to the Northern Shallows, the most prominent feature on the planet's surface. Fields of moss and rock trimmed its southeast promontory of Nea, framing its changing blues with delicate abstract patterns of dull red and pale rusty brown. There, he believed, many ellls dwelt amidst the luxurious expanse of luminescent water.

It was some comfort for him to know that Tera had also absorbed that view with passion equal to his.

Now, as they shared one of their meals, they talked more seriously. "Surely, you don't call yourself an alien on this planet, Tehr Adkarian," Korad said. "You have spent more of your lifetime here than on Varok. I wish I was used to this gravity. I am not as strong as you." His mood-revealing eyes wandered over the massive muscles beneath the soft-woven slacks covering her legs.

Tera met Korad's eyes, and her face spoke caution. "Don't ever assume that you belong on this planet," she said. "We varoks are not built for endless water and gravity greater than Varok's. However much you appreciate the beauty and genius of Ellason's bioluminescence, its constant dimness can be depressing. Your body expects Varok's bright Jovian days."

She smiled and latched onto Korad's awareness, then she opened her mind to the young varok. *My patches see envy in your mind, Korad, envy for my durability, right? So, help yourself to my muscle-building course. Use your patches. The course is right here in my memory. It lies behind the pain I suffered when I tried to strengthen myself to Ellason too fast. Relax and let the pain do its work, like we females do giving birth. You will emerge with more physical tolerance much faster if you don't fight it.*

"Is tolerance all we can expect?"

"You will learn more than tolerance," Tera said. "A few varoks have learned to love Ellason, in spite of its uncomfortable gravity and growth issues."

"I have heard that Director Tekram believes that overpopulation stress will soon overwhelm the ellls' good nature and result in some nasty territorial struggles. What do the great-fish think?"

"According to their theory, the ellls love to raise tads too well. Life-experience means everything to them, so they will suffer from over-population stress, but not terrorital battles. Some ellls believe there is safety in greater numbers, safety from being eaten by predatory *eefl*. The most prevalent argument is that more tads are needed to tend larger gardens."

Korad remembered his studies at the Concentrate. "No species can survive a major population overload and collapse without suffering.

Our varokian history tells the tale too well, right? The ellls must learn to limit the eggs they choose to raise. Perhaps we have been too shy in our approach to them."

"I'm afraid that is exactly what Director Tekram has decided." A challenge was clear in Tera's tone, as well as in her mind. "He plans to broadcast underwater messages in the ellls' sonic code—or Tekram's immitation of their sonic code. I believe that's very intrusive."

To his credit, Korad thought carefully before he responded. "I would guess, from what I have studied, that any intrusion of noise into the ellls' sonic culture would not only drive them crazy, it would anger them."

Korad tuned his patches to hers. With all the finesse he could muster, he read Tera's mood. Beneath her amusement at his rude patch reading, he saw mental approval of his answer, and he smiled. Then he saw a note of grief in her thoughts, and the smile faded.

"The great-fish no longer tell us anything," Tera said.

– Δ –

The question of how to live as a loner, tied to the school as a cripple, sat painful and real in Ilean's elllonian mind. She poked a webbed finger into a crevice of a tall, mossy boulder at the bottom of the Northern Shallows and let a crawler attach itself to her webbed fingers. Her self-pity dissolved into fascination with this tiny delicious creature, but her question remained.

She swam back to Duregal and offered him the crawler still hanging on her finger. Other ellls in the school continued their garden work near the western shallows.

With a long flick of his tongue, the older elll took the crawler and swallowed it. "Thanks, Ilean," he said in sonics.

"I realize I'm a loner, Duregal, but what else are you not telling me? Why did I hit the rock? I thought I was told to jump soon enough to clear it."

Duregal avoided meeting her eyes.

"But it does matter. I like to go off by myself, but now I'm stuck with the school and their horrible buzzing sounds. My disability means I can't ever leave the school, doesn't it?"

Duregal took her head in his broad hands and looked at the swelling over her right eye. "Listen carefully to me, Ilean. You have done nothing wrong."

"I hate the buzzing. I don't understand it. Is that why I am a loner?"

"Perhaps you are not a loner, Ilean. You just have limited ultrasonics. Without them, you can't navigate or communicate quite like other ellls."

Ilean latched onto her sponsor's sturdy frame as they glided away to join the school at their sea-floor garden.

"When you come and go without stopping for a moment of adjustment, you disrupt the school," Falll shouted as she whipped past Ilean.

"There is no need for your rude instruction, Falll." In his anger, Duregal shouted in ultrasonics. "Ilean will make adjustment when she can. Can't you see her grief?"

"There is it, Duregal," Ilean screamed, "that horrible buzz."

ATTACK

The school, the throbbing lifeblood of her kind,
Was wracked with pain, and not for her alone.
Oh Ilean, speak truth
To crowding, an illness shared by all.
Are ancient ways o'er thrown?

The surprise in Duregal's narrowed eyes worried Ilean. She put a hand on his shoulder, and for the first time it felt bony, suddenly older. "It's okay, Duregal. I can stand the buzzing, but I would like to know what it means. Falll is right. I am always disrupting the school. Perhaps I am still like a tad, and I will never understand what I'm missing. I cannot school as I should. This adjustment we're supposed to do when we come and go means nothing to me. Perhaps I should swim alone."

"No." Duregal spun around and grasped her hands. "Never say that." Confusion and a kind of terror destroyed the life-joy that usually danced in his eyes. "You will learn, Ilean. We will work together and find a way for you."

Duregal relaxed with the flicker of Ilean's smile, but a vague sense of uneasiness stayed with them. Many things about the incident felt wrong. The playing ellls had never before insisted that Ilean join their tricky rock-jumping game. Never before had Falll spoken so cruelly. A new tension lingered in the school, like a trap ready to spring.

To avoid that tension, Ilean stayed close to Duregal, even when he went on dry watch. She didn't mind being out of water. She found herself enjoying deep breaths and clear vision in air.

In Ellason's sky above the sea rode a dim line of churning black clouds stretched to the broad horizon. It was as though they had thrown a palpable silence over the water. Far away, tiny creatures of the air took cover in the rocks that crowned the beaches of Nea. Brawny, stunted land dwellers retreated to their shallow burrows.

Ilean saw Duregal freeze, his eyes focused on a bright blue star, until it was no longer visible behind the mists.

"Another metal airboat has come in from above," he told Ilean. Then he slipped into the water to report to the school.

Soon he returned to where Ilean waited, on a small island in the Viortahk. He wore a wet-sweater of moss for his vigil and kept his digital fins coated with mud. From their rocky outpost, the elder elll and the tad he sponsored looked out to the sea. It stretched to the south like a vast puddle of mercury. No waves etched the dark granite of the tiny islands.

Duregal imagined walking off onto the water's surface, no stones to tear his toe-fins, no school to drive his cares. With a start, he realized that his thoughts were like those of loners, the ellls who lived apart from their schools. If only the loner genes had not come to fruition in Ilean, what a happier tad she would be.

He filled his lungs with air, finding it delicious. Then he steeled himself for the arguments to come. Falll was in the shallows, still breathing the thin mist, probably waiting to pounce with verbiage as stinging as sand bees. There would be no escape from her. She had seen him.

"Return to the school, Ilean," he said, and she did not argue.

Falll approached, already railing at Duregal, out here in the mist when she should have been reporting to the school. "The aliens must be bringing in reinforcements," she said, dabbing mud on her knees. "We can't tolerate more of them. They will try to capture an entire school this time."

"I think not." Duregal slipped into the water and opened his gills. It was all he could do to stay two lengths ahead of the blathering Falll. Summoning all his patience, he spoke with a well-tempered sonic code as he and Falll followed the school's pressure pattern in the water. "We have watched the aliens very carefully, Falll. Whenever a flyer comes out of the clouds with new aliens, an equal number leave. They have done nothing malicious. They are callous, and no respecters of life-time, but they are not deliberately aggressive."

"The pattern has changed," Falll insisted, and to dramatize her statement she tossed her webbed hands about in the water, sending a mix of pressure signals to the listening school. "The schools of the western shallows say that the aliens are now dropping metal objects beneath the surface. They are disrupting inter-school communications and long-distance safety checks with a jumble of sonic noise. We must make them stop."

"We agree on that, Falll. How do you propose to stop them? We can't let them disrupt our schools. We already argue too much. It is ruining too many of our life-moments." He rolled back in frustration and glided away from her, to the far edge of the school.

The ellls vibrated uncomfortably for many moon-light changes after such arguments. Duregal remembered Allran, a tall, unusual lad who had disappeared from the school after an argument over a choice *oeln*-fish catch. He had not been seen since, though tales of his lonely wandering had reached the school.

Duregal sometimes tried to imagine what it would be like to be alone. How could one swim without the comforting hum of other ellls warming one's skin tiles? How could one get up an appetite without an enticing consensus of hunger, moving one's juices into dining mode? Could one alone recognize the dangerous *eefl* in time? Or find salt-this-tle for tools and beam-fish for light?

One echo location signal meant very little by itself. Didn't it need to bounce off a rock to join the simultaneous echoes from the other ellls of the school? All the echoes together painted a picture of the entire rocky shore.

Duregal decided one alone could not survive without the school. Yet, more and more often, in these later years of his long life, he was hearing stories of loners: ellls who had left their schools—or were left behind. His own tad, Ilean, had been left behind far too often. The thought sent a shudder across his mid-tiles.

With some effort, he threw off the gloomy reflections. The school had moved back into the shallows, and he glided easily along behind it, threading his way beneath thick moss. He enjoyed the flow of the clear water as it passed through his nasal gills. With long webbed fingers he selected succulent varieties of moss and stuffed them into his mouth.

Suddenly an alarm struck the pressure sensitive tiles that covered Duregal's body: "Where is Ilean? She is not at school center. Find Ilean."

"I should always stay with her." Duregal moved quickly into the school. The ellls were swimming slowly, sending probes in all directions as they retraced their path through the shallow waters.

They made way for him. He was Ilean's sponsor. Though technically his responsibility for her would soon end, he had vowed to help her maintain her part in the school. She had wandered away from the school too often, especially when they were in the shallows. One time they had gone through adjustment, believing her dead. The ellls had swarmed together in an intense pattern, adjusting their pressure signals and sonar memories to define Ilean's permanent absence, sure that *eefl* had destroyed her. Then, quite by accident, they had found her. She was sitting near the shallows, using well-practiced lungs to breathe the moist air.

The school had questioned her as one: "What are you doing out here, Ilean?"

"Come look. Come quickly," Ilean had begged when she saw the ellls. "Aren't *lohn* birds wonderful?" She was watching the plump land birds waddle along a sandy shore. They were scooping up shore-pool lightning bugs with stubby wings, then tossing them into the air and catching them with a sharp clack of wide beaks.

For a short time the school had watched, entranced. Their relief at finding Ilean had doused their irritation. Then their sense-saturated minds drove them on to new stimuli.

Now, where could she be? Ultrasonic scans told Duregal she was nowhere near.

"Taste the school's path, and retrace it," Navell commanded. "We have left Ilean behind at the deep garden. High swimmers, check the surface as we go along. We must all be sponsors to Ilean. Ba-ohl and Duregal alone cannot be responsible for a disabled adult."

Though he felt a pittance of gratitude for the elder's offer of school responsibility, Duregal flushed with guilt. He realized now that he had been too easy on her, too fascinated by the things that fascinated her. She had loved the feel of her elllonian feet walking on dry ground when she visited the experimentalists who studied air-land phenomena. Duregal decided he never should have taken her on those strange excursions away from the school. They had only enhanced her loner tendencies.

"There she is," someone shouted from behind a large outcropping of rock on the ocean floor. "She's with Ba-ohl, her protector."

The school bellowed out their relief. It enveloped the youngsters, even as Ba-ohl tried to complete their mating, audience or no. He realized Ilean had been ready for him. It was her first, and Ba-ohl wanted it to be the best fun possible, but Ilean pulled away from him with a decisive stroke of her finned hands.

He let her go, good lad that he was. He had promised. Their time would be their own when they mated. She did not want to share her first experience with the school—a notion strange to ellls, who usually mated with the offhand panache of Earth's dolphins. Because Ba-ohl found Ilean particularly desirable, he had agreed to her odd request for privacy. Now, like a good team player, he accepted the school's reprimand for keeping Ilean away from its protection.

Quickly the ellls moved on toward their northern garden, where they expected to find the moonlight tulip pastures in full bloom. Familiar patterns echoed from the ocean floor. Bioluminescent lichen covered the muddy bottom with a pleasant glow.

As they approached the pasture, a new sense of alarm spread like brush fire across the water-pressure patterns of the school. It drew the ellls into a pinched formation around a tall, broken rock that overlooked their large cultivated field. The ocean floor spreading beneath them was empty, barren where it had once flourished. Nothing showed in the current-smoothed mud but the broken stubble of hurriedly uprooted moonlight tulips.

"Most of our planting is gone!" Falll pushed away from the rock and swam over the pasture, her short, round legs thrashing furiously.

As she gathered samples of ruined plants, she found evidence that ellls had been there.

"Look at this." She thrust a ragged stem into Navell's hands. "The plants have been ripped out. Stolen."

A frown gathered on Navell's brow. "Could they be so hungry? Or are they demented? It is insane to destroy a living plant for one taste of its large blossom."

No one moved. Their grief for the plants filled the water as they hovered in the rocks above the field.

The school master Sa-el, his thick growth of head plumes shaking with tension, moved toward Navell and spoke quietly.

Navell then took school center and spoke. "Sa-el suggests that we go directly to the nearest school and ask them to return our moonlight plants."

Falll exploded, racing like a mad shark out to the pasture and back. "They are theives, not ellls," she shouted.

Her furious pattern stirred most ellls in the school to displays of temper, and Ba-ohl found himself caught up in the turmoil.

"Peace. Peace." Navell cried out in ultrasonic. "You are defining the school with hate. Our tempers must not control us."

Duregal found Ilean, terrified, crouched behind a huge rock at the edge of the garden. The ellls were not listening to Navell. Slashing furiously back and forth across the ruined garden, they vented their frustration.

A cascade of sounds broke over them, snuffing out their tantrum. Loud and abrasive, mechanical, as if from something dead, the sound grew until it filled all the water. It drove the ellls mad with sensory overload stoked by fear.

"Varoks." Falll cried. "Alien invaders, with their noisy machines!"

Only Navell resisted going with the school. He stayed near the garden with Ilean, who had panicked and stayed hidden, understanding little of what had happened.

Sa-el tried to stop the school before it attacked the noisy gadgets, "You have deserted your oldest and your weakest," he shouted to the school in far-range ultrasonic. "Stop! Ilean and Navell will be taken by *eefl* if we don't return to them." Duregal joined him.

"We are coming, Duregal," Ilean called.

The school swam on, homing in on the sonic intrusion. Soon they spotted the source of the hated noise—an alien device.

Ba-ohl and Ilean followed their most trusted elder, Navell, and joined the school in circling the small metal box.

"Stop," Sa-el said. "It's trying to talk." Realizing there was a pattern to the sound, the ellls began to listen more carefully.

"Time gone," it said.

The sound was crude and barely recognizable, but undoubtedly a mechanical attempt at reproducing the ellls' sonics. "You are too many. . . balance—" It didn't make sense. "Fewer tads. Not enough food, tension—"

Sa-el had to agree with the ideas the sound suggested. "We-roks can help. Fewer tads—zzzz—snap—eee."

Falll announced angrily. "Destroy this varokian device." She began probing the device, seeking the source of its sound.

"I don't agree yet," Sa-el said, then he appealed to the school. "The aliens say—I believe—that they want to help us. They say many schools are too large. Perhaps that is why our garden was raided."

"The adjoining school is a lazy bunch." Falll tore open the device as she spoke. "Varoks mean us no help. Such noise is an attack, perhaps a lure. Ellls who have listened to such imitated sonics are captured and taken from the sea." The device fell silent as Fall scattered its contents.

"How do you know that?" Sa-el protested, disoriented by references to events not seen or heard or felt.

"It is a clear vision, written by great-fish. Ellls were drugged by varoks. Their life moments were cruelly taken from them. Have you forgotten all these tales, Duregal?"

"We will answer only for what *we* have seen," Duregal said. "The aliens are correct when they say that the schools of ellls are too large. We have seen it. We know it. If our school had been normal size, no more than twenty ellls, we would not have left Ba-ohl and Ilean so far behind before we missed them. There is truth in the varoks' lure. Though it is a mechanical insult, its meaning is clear."

"The machine told us nothing new," Falll insisted. "We must stop the aliens before they steal more life-moments from us. Noise is the cruelest of tortures, for it disrupts the essence of the school. I will stop it, whatever the cost. Who is with me?"

A chorus of pressure signals and sonic code sounded agreement with the powerful female.

"You speak violence," Sa-el said. His voice had dropped to sonic levels as he grew more sickened by the renewed display of anger around him. "We will not do more violence. Are you with me, Duregal? Dalllin? Ellinon? Cantrall? Navell? Ba-ohl? Ilean?"

Those ellls moved toward him in agreement.

"Who else?" he said. "The school is split. Not all will follow you into violence, Falll."

Ilean listened to Sa-el's speech with growing admiration. She glided closer. She saw him as the best of the new breed of ellls honored by great-fish. Finding him powerful and wise, she would follow him into whatever new awareness the aliens suggested. Such an adventure was surely worth the price of a few life-moments.

Navell circled the school with authority. "The school cannot be split. We would not survive such an adjustment."

The elder's words echoed through the school like a healing balm, and, as quickly as it rose, the anger began to dissipate. The wound began to heal. "You will find some better solution to the varoks' noise. First we must rebuild this garden. I will go to the adjoining ellls and demand that they help find plants to replace those lost."

Falll said nothing, but her angry look made Navell pause.

THE LONER

Though ellls were born to swim the warmest deeps,
One sought the misted rocks and shallows rife
And valued solitude.
A mind apart, she longed to know
The deeps and mists of life.

When the moon-light change sent its first showers of glimmering spores into the deeps, the ellls' world began to glow. Mindful of the spores' light, Sa-el, Duregal, and Navell set off to find their neighbors, the suspected thieves. They had traveled only four hundred leaps (*pallons*) when they came upon the school they sought. Its ellls were circling as if in adjustment.

Sa-el called a greeting, but the schooling ellls either didn't hear him or chose to ignore the call. Duregal and Navell made an approach request. When it, too, was ignored, their tempers exploded with an ultrasonic blast that thoroughly disrupted the school.

Three females swam quickly to them and explained that the school was adjusting to the loss of four of its members.

One spoke in sonics, her blue plumes quivering. "When four of our school returned with fruit and whole plants from your garden, many of us lost our tempers. Two of the thieves were killed before our tempers cooled. The other two have been driven off."

"Were they loners?" Sa-el asked.

"No." The girl's blue headplumes gave a shake of conviction, and speech failed her.

"Then they will die," Duregal said, horrified.

"They will have to learn to live alone," another blue elll said. "They can no longer be a part of this school."

"Perhaps we can take them in," Duregal said, "We will put out a call for them."

The third female had been watching Navell during the entire exchange. Her wide black eyes centered on his. "I will go with you," she said, "as guarantor of our school's good faith."

Navell swam beside the girl until she was gliding pleasantly in his pressure pattern.

Duregal turned to the smallest female. "You must not miss the adjustment on our account."

"Thank you. I often mated with one who was killed."

"Then you are central to the adjustment. Please go to your school."

The small blue elll turned back, but the third elll hesitated a moment, questioning the fire in Sa-el's expression. When she looked at Duregal, he waved her away. Gratefully, she followed her companion.

Duregal and Sa-el watched for danger until the adjustment ended. During such an intense internal experience, the school was deaf to warning signals from the surrounding ocean. At last the guilt-racked ellls were aware enough to be safe from attack, so Duregal and Sa-el swam back to help their own school restore its garden.

– Δ –

True to their nature, the ellls of Ilean's school soon forgot their differences. Their play-riddled lives danced on as if nothing had happened. Today's game was racing.

Ilean found races difficult to watch. She didn't understand how everyone knew who won. Ba-ohl was part of the last race, so he was not around to explain what was happening. Ilean could see nothing but the ellls' leaps over the weeds that decorated the surface of the shallows. Though she knew that the racers' leaps counted toward the final score, she could never guess who had won. The ellls who watched with her, however, were never wrong. They knew, all at once, though the finish happened far down the waves.

As the last racer dove out of sight, Ilean noticed a heavy feeling in her loins. The feeling was different from anything she had ever felt before. Without signaling her intentions to anyone, she left the young ellls watching the races and moved into shallower water.

Something began to emerge from her body, as if it already had a life of its own. Ilean smiled broadly to herself and quietly moved farther down the beach where the shallows were warm and gentle. Here she could be alone, unseen and undisturbed, to lay her first egg.

"I am Ilean. I am myself—alone." she whispered. "I am no more a tad."

As suddenly as it began, it ended. The egg came. She stared at the large leathery blue sphere hardening in the green moss. "I am the woman, Ilean; I am no longer a tad who clings to a sponsor—or to a school." She enclosed the egg in the webs of her long fingers, and she laughed at the urgency she had felt when she knew it was coming.

Ilean carried the egg beyond the weeds and beached herself comfortably in the thick arms of sea-moss that drifted lazily in the warm, shallow water near the shore. She felt light and free, like a lost plume floating on an endless breeze. She would chase the stars. She would catch an alien spaceship and ride it to a far-off sea. That would tell the school who she was.

She turned over and shook the drops from her head plumes. Her back-fin retracted, and she slid completely out of the water onto her stomach, pulling herself onto a carpet of shore-moss. How strange and interesting it felt to press firmly into solid ground, to leave behind the warm cloak of deep water. Still clutching her egg, she pulled into a sitting position and looked out over the horizon.

The surface of the ocean frightened her. There was nothing to see, nothing of the warmth of the red deeps or the richness of the elll-gardens. It seemed empty and dead compared to the life potential that lay within the egg in her hands.

"Ellason's ocean hides its secrets well," she said to the egg. She lay down in the moss, feeling very much in command of her existence. Now, here, by herself, she could focus on her first egg. It was still safe in her grasp. She fondled it, turned it over in her broad hands, and gazed at it with large black eyes, bright with the wonder of the miracle her body had performed.

"When the moonlight flowers begin their next cycle, I will lay another egg," she thought as she picked up a long *al*-shell that lay in the moss. With its sharp edge she tore open her egg and poured its contents down her throat. "I am the only elll, ever, to have properly celebrated her first *el* egg—on land," she told herself.

When she stood up to walk back into the shallow water, the tug of Ellason's gravity pressed her weight uncomfortably onto her webbed feet. All around her the thick moss of the shallows glowed with the warm red-orange of energy-efficient carotenyls that covered the beach. The moss clambered onto rough stone and disappeared in the low-riding mist. Here and there a sparkle of moving bioluminescence lit the dimness. Ilean drank in the rich aroma of the salt air as she watched the tiny marsh creatures.

Rough faces of tumbled rock stared at her from far up the shore. Peering at her through the drifting mist, they invited her to come to them. She knew they had a strange texture, a dry feeling without life-giving water to cover them with slippery algae. She wondered if they held predators, lying in wait to trick their prey with flashes of light that imitated the tiny edible creatures of the sea. What would it be like to live in a place so dry? She could not imagine it.

Her eye caught on a tall rock clothed in moss, rising above the water. It was standing alone on an island of fine red mud, its head above the mists. Ilean decided she must climb it. From its top she would see above the mists to the stars.

To save strength for the ascent, as Duregal had taught her, she moved slowly through the mud to the mossy ledges. The trick of dry-land navigation was to move carefully, continuously, rhythmically.

She pulled one leg up, then she let it fall slowly back to the ground and lifted the other. "Establish a smooth rhythm from the very first step," Duregal had said. "Effort on land must never be wasted." She believed she could walk the length of ten leaps without tiring, provided the walking surface was soft enough to protect her toe-fins from injury.

The moss sank pleasantly beneath her delicate feet. One step, then another. That must be right, she told herself. Keep the muscles rolling smoothly. Don't strain the thigh by lifting the legs too high or too quickly. Roll from one leg to the other, slowly, five counts per step.

When she reached the edge of the moss, halfway up the rock, she was panting heavily. Her gills ached from so much exposure to air. She struggled to draw breath into lungs seldom used for anything but hunting or lounging in the shallows. When at last she came to the head of the rock, she felt the harsh pressure of sharp cracks on the tissue-thin webs of her feet. She paused, knowing she shouldn't stop, but the feel of dry rock was harsher than she remembered from her childhood lessons.

Once, perhaps twice, Duregal had taken her onto muddy shores to hunt *brilln* and collect *challall* weeds with the harvester ellls. There he had taught her about the dangers of overexertion on land. He had shown her stones that could grind an unwary foot-fin to a painful pulp in a few careless steps.

How different the land was from the deeps, Ilean mused as she eased her feet upward on the rock. The mists here were dark, lit only by the mist-hoppers, who were stingy with their light.

In contrast, the garden waters of the deeps were ablaze with spots and sheets and flashes of bioluminescent flyers and creepers. Deep rock mosses glowed warmly, and dawn-fish eagerly tempted their prey with bright flashes imitating the shore-pool lightning bugs. Market shell dwellers signaled for mates, and beam-fish shone broadly, eager to see where they were going. The sea was a blinking, glowing, on-again off-again flowing world of light. Its patterns were as unpredictable as they were beautiful.

Ilean looked back to the ocean. She could no longer see the shoreline or the water. All was silent, lost behind the dense mist. Only dry rock existed, tearing at her feet. The rock glowed faintly, covered with a tiny mist-drinking plant that signaled its presence with light so mist-hoppers would chew its petals and spread its spores.

She thought she was alone and she loved how it felt.

The Eefl

Where Ellason's long tides creep into dark,
She crossed dry land alone to fill her mind,
But failed among the rocks
Without the gentle throbbing press
Of signals from her kind.

Ilean's eyes must have filled nearly half her face as she strained to drink in all available light. Too faintly did the mist-drinkers outline the rock all around her. She pulled herself up onto a grassy ledge.

The mists closed in even tighter. Ilean crawled through tiny islands of light on the dark roughness of solid granite. Suddenly the mist dissolved above her, and the faint glow of starlight filled her eyes. She moved a little higher onto the rock and looked up. Far overhead, in the blackness of space, there shone a star.

It must be the Bright Star. Yes. And there. Another star, very dim by comparison, but beautiful — a sparkling clear blue. l'Ran it is called. And another? There. But gone already. The mists have taken it. The mists will soon take them all.

Once again Bright Star shone over Ilean's delicate face, so filled with wonder. She remembered the tales that elder ellls told. They said that Ellason flew round and round in an ocean of nothing, along with blue l'Ran and its neighbors, Warm Star and Little Jewel. Ilean loved best the colorful little stars that danced around Bright Star.

Though she couldn't see them now, she remembered other stars from songs Duregal had sung to her as a tad. The stars were a swarm of salt-bees, far away in the black depths of the Ocean Canopy. The swarm of salt-bees never swam alone, Duregal sang. Other swarms, some warm and red, some blue-white, some yellow, joined the salt-bees as they danced in the deathless depths of the dark sea overhead.

At last the mists closed over Ilean, and she lost sight of the Bright Star. It was time to return to the school. She moved down the rock using her heels, holding her feet up at a tiring angle to save her webbing for the mud crossing.

The trip down the rock took a very long time, and the walking across dry mud went on forever. Finally, with a sigh of exasperation, she went down on her knees and crawled.

When she reached the mud beyond rock and sea moss, she was crying with pain. The frustration of the interminable, slow movement on land tore at her life–joy. Why had the return trip taken so long? Ilean lay exhausted in the damp moss for a while before she roused herself enough to crawl into the shallows. There, soothed by the gentle lapping of the warm water, she closed her lungs, sucked the ocean's soothing wetness across her gills, and slept.

Ellason moved a short way on its slow course around the sun. Spinning its way around a full day, Earth, the tiny bright blue star l'Ran, wandered across Ellason's sky somewhere near the sun, Bright Star. Only recently had the varoks learned that its clever inhabitants were gathering in villages along great rivers.

On Ellason the thin clouds rarely opened. To have a good view of the stars was a delightful piece of luck. Hence, for most ellls, the stars meant very little—a few lights scattered in the dark mists—uninteresting compared to their glittering sea world.

Ellason's large size and troublesome gravity had discouraged many evolutionary experiments on dry land. All major sources of life arose in the ocean. Most light came from the abundant bioluminescent salt species, and Ellason's steady source of heat came from its molten core and the natural reactors buried throughout the planet's crust.

Long ago the ellls had taken different paths of evolution from their cousins, the *ll-leyoolianl*, called great-fish. The ellls became optional air breathers and surface dwellers, but they found the atmosphere too dry for prolonged exposure. They gathered blue moss from the shallows for wet-sweaters and salad. They farmed the mist drinkers for lamps, the *lohn* birds for eggs, the *brilln* for meat and plumage, the *challall* weeds for pure gourmet delight. That was what dry land meant to them.

Elllonian adventurers and librarians were the embarrassing exceptions. Apparently, their thirst for knowledge was greater than their schooling sense.

When Ilean awoke, she found herself drifting in cool deep water. Unfamiliar currents had carried her away from the shallows. She remembered Bright Star and savored the memory of its light. The star was a gift to celebrate her first egg—a gift from whom or what she didn't care to ask—simply a gift, like the gift of life.

With a start, she noticed primitive steel gray eyes fixed on her. Ilean turned onto her stomach, ready to swim back to the shallows. Then she saw it—the dreaded arrow-shaped body and whip-like tail of an *eefl* slicing toward her through the gloom.

Ilean darted away toward deeper water. The tail lashed out, catching her arm near the upper joint, sliding around it, grating over her tender velvet flesh. She screamed out with horror.

An intense ache spread quickly over her arm. Ilean thrashed desperately, broke loose, and gained some precious distance from the *eefl's* jaws. It came toward her again, enraged at losing its prey. Her arms felt like leaden weights as she tried to propel herself faster, fearing that the poison would spread farther the more she moved. She concentrated on her leg thrust and gained on the *eefl*, but still it came, tireless and quick. In the unfamiliar cold water Ilean's legs began to ache with the effort. She dove, knowing that her best hope lay in depth, for *eefl* were surface dwellers.

The bottom was not as far down as she hoped. Still the *eefl* came on.

Searching all about, cursing the dark and the limited range of her eyes—wishing she had her fellow ellls' magical knowledge of the underwater world—Ilean skimmed the ocean bottom. Her legs refused to move faster. Her injured arm began to swell, useless now.

Ilean's anger fueled a burst of determination, and she dodged behind a massive rock that rose from the ocean floor. Beyond it lay another rock, then several more. She searched for one she could climb. Breaking the surface, she gulped in cold air, hoping her lungs would help her gills stoke her muscles with oxygen for the strength she needed. The *eefl's* tail slashed at her from below with deadly intent.

Ilean leapt onto a rock that sloped gently to the surface. She scrambled out of the water to a higher point. Then, safely out of the *eefl's* grasp, she lay back on the rock and fought for breath.

The *eefl* paced in the water, its pale eyes staring, its tail probing the edge of the rock.

She was alone and hunted. Alone! She could not survive alone. Duregal had said that. She was an incomplete elll, cut off from the school that sustained her. She had been ripped from her school by desire, by curiosity, by her need to be alone, to create, to know herself, to learn.

Ilean steeled herself to the increasing cold and the threat of being out of water. She tried not to think of Duregal and Ba-ohl and the school. Huddled against herself, aching in every part of her body, she waited nearly half a moon-light change for the *eefl* to forget her.

At last it did. With a lashing probe of its tail, the beast turned and moved on to look for a more promising dinner.

When it was gone, Ilean slipped back into the water and drifted slowly around her small island. Everything would be all right now. The school would find her soon. They always had before.

An icy current struck her from the north. She thought she could see the shore lying in the mists. To the west, tall rocks were outlined against a dense storm cloud. With a chill that went deeper than the cold of the water, Ilean realized that the rocks were not familiar. She swam against the current, hoping to retrace her drift from the shallows, but the current veered away from the shore at every sharp outcropping of rock. She lost all sense of direction. Another current joined hers and confused her even more. Soon she was surrounded by towering cliffs, faced with a bewildering choice of narrow channels.

How could other ellls always find the school, no matter how long they were gone or how far they went? How did the others navigate, with nothing but muted sound and dim light patterns to follow?

The rocks took an odd turn, then another, and then they came around on themselves. She was circling a large island.

She swam slowly now, hypothermic, unable to use her poisoned arm. She would try all four directions from the island. Surely one would take her to deeper water, below *eefl* ranges. There was some simple trick to measuring the depth of the sea, but Ilean had never learned that trick, and no one was able to teach her.

Long ago some ellls of her school had tried to explain depth sounding, but too soon their talk stopped. She would be left with nothing but the painful buzzing in her ears and half a puzzle to solve. Since she could never solve the puzzles, she soon quit asking for lessons. It was more pleasant to drift alone with her thoughts. Now she wished she had made the school explain the puzzles, had made them stop the awful buzzing.

She failed to find deep water in two directions, and the ocean bottom did not descend in the third direction. She retraced her wake and tried the fourth. As she grew more and more exhausted, her arm ballooned alarmingly. She swam toward the lifeless black rocks that rose straight out of the sea, carefully noting prominent landmarks that penetrated the mists. She hadn't gone more than a hundred *pallons*, leaps of an elll, before she recognized the first landmark coming by again. Another island.

There was only one answer to the puzzle. She was lost in the Viortahk. This terrible place was dotted with hundreds of small islands. Its waters, teeming with untold numbers of *eefl*, was dark, devoid of bright, tasty plants and crawlers. It was also very cold—too cold for an elll.

II. The Legend of the First Loner

At the beginning of each chapter of this history you will find excerpts from "The Legend of the First Loner," an epic poem discovered in 3634 *ir* Varokian calendar (4962 BCE Earth). The collected verses are my translation of a summary of events focused on the early interactions between visiting varoks and native ellls on Ellason. They were originally composed in symbolic mud and rock sculptures by the deep-sea intellectuals called great-fish, probably in 3631 *ir* (5000 BCE Earth), soon after the events of this story ended—not long after we Varoks discovered the remote planet Ellason.

—Aman Telariahn (Amantel), Varok, 2072 CE Earth

Assumptions

When strangers come to worlds they do not know,
They act upon raw guesses made in haste—
Though all intent be good,
The world perceives naught but the wound
And good intent's laid waste.

"Amanok. Good to see you." Tera sent her greeting down the laboratory hallway as if some loving river had broken its dam. Amanok (Aman Okrahlan), varokian Director of the Elll-Watch, stopped in his tracks. He was so delighted to hear her booming voice, he turned and greeted her as an elll would, with a grin that split his face.

He had not aged much, Tera decided. True, the silver of his hair nearly covered his forehead, and his patches protruded beyond his ears (a sure sign of superior mind-frippery, not age, as some suppose), but the flash of brilliance in his gray-blue eyes was as clear as ever.

"What? Shame on you, reading my first impressions, after all we've meant to each other." Tera covered her patches as if to block the rude exploration of her mood.

"The privilege of shared intimacy," he said. "How soon they forget." He extended his forearms to Tera in an unfettered varokian gesture of intimacy. "Welcome back, Tehr Adkarian."

She placed her palms on his arms and opened her patches so the mind flow between them sloshed freely back and forth. *I sense more than greeting in your mind, Amanok. I see relief. Can you be so glad to see me?*

In answer to her probe, she saw his mind leap to its central worry. *Indeed, I will be very relieved to have your help.*

"I have lost control of the elll-watch, Tera," he said aloud. "The Division of Species Welfare has preempted my plans for achieving contact with the ellls." The words set loose the anger he had been painfully squelching for nearly a Callisto Cycle. "Come into my space, Tera. I need to find release in a friendly mind."

He led her down the hall to his small suite of rooms. They were furnished sparsely with a g-brace and desk, but decorated abundantly with Ellasonian plants and a large aquarium.

Tera gave an audible gasp of delight when she saw the small globes of scintillating light bobbing up and down in the large sea tank. The tank was framed by tall moss-covered rocks arranged to shade it from the room's dim artificial light.

"What a beautiful arrangement, Amanok." Tera's auburn hair parted in bright sheets on the back of her neck as she bent over to examine the shimmering globes.

He noticed the beginning of silvering in her hair. *How much time would be left to us,* he wondered. *How much time before we will be too old to tolerate this indifferent planet?*

We'll never be that old, she answered him in mind, then she turned her attention back to the globes. *Amanok, these are nothing but beam-fish. Beam-fish trapped in the shells of mud turtles.* As Specialist in Elllonian Communication at the laboratory, she guessed without probing that the globes were imitations of a newly discovered elllonian device.

"The globes are lights to mark the way for ellls who would prefer not to rely entirely on ultrasonic echo patterns."

"A very romantic notion, Amanok," Tera laughed. "How can you be sure? The ellls would not need such lights."

"I believe the ellls would appreciate their decorative value. We have recently found such an arrangement of globes in the elllonian gardens of the Northern Shallows. Tekram discredits my small experiment here, but I am convinced that ellls do have an esthetic sense—and the manipulative ability to make living lamps such as these."

He lifted from the water one of the open mesh spheres. It was made of two mud turtle shells laced together. The beam-fish within fluttered as some of the water inside drained away from them. "See here, Tera. We have found knots just like these on the elllonian lamps hung from *ahl* trees in the deeps."

"That is an intricate knot." Tera looked closely at the contraption. "It is cleverly designed. It should pull free easily."

"The string itself is an ingenious invention. The ellls make it from the tough root of a sea weed that grows near ocean bedrock. They lubricate it with the oil of scar-fish so it won't become rotten or brittle. It took me some time to discover the trick."

"I don't see how the ellls keep beam-fish alive in captivity. Put the poor things back, Amanok, or they will choke in the air."

"Keeping the beam-fish alive has been a time-consuming

experiment, I must say." He lowered the delicate ball filled with living pen-lights back into the aquarium. "I tried everything before I realized that placement was critical to the ellls' underwater lighting schemes. The beam-fish survive very well in the shells if they are fed a certain phototropic algae. The ellls must have a good understanding of fish culture to make such a device."

"And I see in your mind that Tekram has formally declared that these lamps have no significance." Tera let her anger flare into her tone of voice.

"He believes that elllonian intelligence is restricted by their language. And he believes their language is nothing more than the infrequent percussive barking sounds they make between the back of the tongue and the base of the gills."

"Nonsense. He forgets their sonar and their echo-location."

With Tera's show of emotion, he warmed to his subject. "Tekram will not give credit to the ellls' manual talent or their large brain size. He believes they are locked into their tangled sensory inputs, into an underwater mentality that limits them to a simple struggle for survival. He also ignores their ability to invent games."

Tera sank onto her g-brace and leaned against the wall. "Underwater mentality indeed. Tekram has a short memory for the genius of great-fish. Why can't he believe in underwater intelligence? Great-fish perceive reality clearer than most of us. Does Tekram still refuse to work with them, too?"

"I'm afraid the refusal has become mutual." Amanok let their mental contact dilute his temper. "The great-fish are showing a distinct reluctance to aid us in our elllonian studies. I'm sure they could help us break the communication impasse, but they refuse to arrange any more meetings between ellls and varoks."

"Perhaps they think we varoks should find our own common ground with the ellls."

"The great-fish are trying to push us in that direction, but they are being too subtle about it. I am quite sure that they don't like our attempts to communicate with ellls. Tekram believes they have given up. He's going ahead with his so-called 'overpopulation emergency plan.' Already his damnable underwater speakers are blasting sonar messages of doom into the shallows."

"Oh no! Tekram will disrupt the ellls' schooling network." For a moment Tera's anger nearly robbed them both of reason.

"The Laboratory Directorate agreed that the noise might be disruptive. Then Species Welfare convinced them that the ellls will suffer even worse social trauma if their rampant population growth does not stop."

"Has it really gone that far, Amanok? Are the ellls doing themselves in by over-breeding?"

"The ellls are far more flexible than the Division of Species Welfare will admit."

"You don't think they could go into catastrophic population cycles?"

"Not for a long time, Tera. Ellls have too much sense and too many senses to outgrow their gardens. What really matters is that we agree on the more important point."

"Yes. Forced interference will never work. Underwater speakers will enrage the ellls."

A frown crawled over Amanok's face. "How many years have we set ourselves back with this intrusion into the ellls' water? Ten? One hundred? Will the ellls ever forgive such disruption?"

"They will love us when they realize the truth in our messages." Tekram interrupted from the doorway.

A group of newcomers to Ellason trailed wearily behind him in the hallway. Tera recognized one as the young relief scientist she had met on the flight to Ellason. "Nice to see you again, Korad," she said, and silently invited him to remain behind to meet Amanok.

Tekram and his group moved on as Tera got up from the g-brace and ushered Korad into the room.

"Typical argument-avoidance reaction," Tera laughed. "Too often Tekram throws a comment at an unsuspecting victim then moves on before an answer can reach his patches. He won't miss you. Come join better company, Korad. This is Amanok, former Director of the Elll-watch.

"Former?" Korad could not hide a startled gasp.

"Tekram and his Species Welfare Committee have persuaded the Directorate to ignore my better judgments." Amanok offered the youth a supporting arm. "Come in and lie down, son. This g-brace has seen six exhausted newcomers at one time, snoring off their gravity in one mighty chorus. Tera, help the lad off with his head brace. Its weight barely justifies the help it gives the neck muscles."

Korad tried to relax, but he was so overcome by respect for the renowned Amanok that he had to be persuaded to lie down.

"Don't fight it," Tera said. "Let the gravity have you."

Korad finally did as he was told, but his eyes stayed riveted to the ceiling.

"Can you understand why I disagree that a policy of amplified preaching will convince ellls they should love varoks, Korad?"

Korad swallowed hard. Tera saw that he was trying not to read the answer from the elders' obviously open minds. "From my studies, sir, I believe ellls would resent amplified sound in their waters. I was surprised to hear Tekram report its immediate success."

"By Harrahn! Immediate success?" Amanok hadn't heard that bit of puffery. "What exactly did Tekram say?"

Korad flinched. Tera could see that he had nerve, but the tension between the officials of the lab had caught him as unprepared as a mud hen on a sandy beach. Frank, emotion-tinged disagreements, which fired the neurons and kept the lab scientists honest, were uncommon in the formal, normally repressed society of varoks.

The youth chose his words with care, afraid he would choke on a wrong one. "Tekram told us that the new experiment—sending electronic messages in elllonian sonar code through the ellls' waters—has met with immediate success. At three of the ten broadcast stations ellls have shown interest in the amplified sounds. At first their talk peaked, then it subsided to below normal levels. This observation is taken as evidence that the electronic message was understood by the ellls and debated. A sobering conclusion was then reached."

"Nonsense." Tera noted Korad's discomfort at speaking from the g-brace, so she leaned back to face him. "Pardon my rudeness, Korad, but some of us who have studied ellls longer than Tekram would not put such a glib interpretation on the behavior of only a few schools. Every elllonian school has a personality unlike every other. Generalizations about sonar patterns should be made with great caution."

"Exactly how did the ellls react to the amplifiers?" Amanok doubted that unbiased observations had been reported. Apparently, Tekram felt the laboratory could not afford the luxury of accuracy.

Korad continued to stare at the ceiling, unaware that his patches radiated pride in feeling his mind's accord with Tera and Amanok. "I asked that very question of Tekram, but I could learn very little. The school raced toward the speakers. In their 'eagerness' to explore the devices, the ellls damaged three of them." Korad let his voice surge dramatically, and he dared to risk a quick glance in Amanok's direction.

The elders couldn't help smiling at the youth. "Did the entire school gather around the speakers?" Tera looked at Amanok as they both leapt to the same conclusion. If ellls were curious, they would explore new objects with care, gently, so as not to disturb their intended or natural state. Korad's report showed that ellls had not been gentle with the varoks' noisy devices.

"The school hung back while a few ellls made clumsy attempts at investigating the devices." Korad spoke with relish. "At least three of the ten devices infuriated the schools so much they ripped apart the speakers."

Tera sat up and looked kindly at the handsome youth. "Temper your enthusiasm, Korad. Arguments at so crucial a time are rarely helpful."

"Yes—but this is important. I couldn't help seeing the worry in Tekram's mind. He too fears that the speakers were attacked."

"If you probe your superiors too often, Korad, they will soon avoid all your questions." Tera laughed. "Then you will learn nothing here—and be given no responsibility."

Amanok frowned. "Ellls respect the limits of their senses. They limit the effects of their schooling and their gardening so they won't intrude on the senses of other schools. That means they have to watch the effects of their sound and smell, as well as their pressure sensitivity and ultrasonics. Ellls are empathic, and their empathy is the basis of their territorial definitions."

"Empathy? Tekram told us that food and living space define elllonian schooling limits. He talks simplistic nonsense."

Amanok stared at Korad soberly. This boy was a bit too sure of himself. "Can you tell me what defines your living space, Korad? Are you aware of your impact wherever you go?"

"Yes, Aman Okrahlan."

The unexpected answer nearly shocked Amanok speechless. "Call me Amanok," he said. "Henceforth I am your tutor. Request a transfer to my division, Korad. I need your help. We will be doing long and arduous battle with the mechanists and the survivalists." He directed a sly glance at Tera. "Now leave us, Korad, and continue your orientation. Tera and I will take some time alone."

The Search

> *"Come, Ilean, the school throbs hollow now*
> *"Without you here, where all our hearts reside.*
> *"Your place cannot be filled."*
> *She knew their pain and grieved for them,*
> *But rode the loner's tide.*

The hexagonal tiles on Ba-ohl's left side registered the rippling nudge of the awakening school. The ripple flowed down the ell's leg then moved laterally over tiles exposed to open water. Loving sleep as he did, like a mudwort in hibernation, he closed his eyes tighter and nestled deeper into the sandy mud of the ocean floor. The annoying wake-up call caressing his exposed tiles grew more and more insistent, until it resonated over his entire body and compelled him to respond. Thus, he awoke as a small part of the larger body of ells.

With a rake of salt thistles, he groomed the mud and sand from his crown and hip plumes. When all the ells of the school were ready to feed, the water pressure that enclosed Ba-ohl danced with anticipation, then caressed him with the flowing signal to swim. His dark green body sprung from its resting place on the ocean floor and followed the guiding stream of pressure signals from the school.

He turned and looked briefly behind him. Ilean was not in the hollow where she usually slept. Probably, she was being held in the center of the school so she would not disappear again. Surely she had been found after she laid her egg.

The school followed a line of bright globes that hung from cultivated *ahl* trees. The tall marine trees were pruned at various levels to provide stubby hangers for the globular lamps. As the varoks had discovered, the globes were made of the calcareous mesh work of the mud turtle.

The lamps were the work of ell tads. The children loved to hunt for discarded shells and tie them together with tough *ahl* fibers, so they could fill the lacy spheres with bright beam-fish. The tiny fish were enticed into each lamp through a narrow gap in the shell's seam, a challenging task that delighted the young ells' puzzle-solving nature. Once trapped in the shells, the beam-fish threw into the deeps a pleasant light, prized by the ellls for its softly changing hues.

Ba-ohl always felt a little uneasy while swimming past the living lamps. What if the beam-fish had enough sense to know they were trapped? Were their life-moments being cruelly destroyed by their captivity? It didn't seem likely, for they were protected and fed plenty of their favorite algae, but how could one be sure?

He swam quickly past the lamps and followed the school through a broad range of hills that rose from the ocean floor. The hills enclosed a wide valley laid out with precise squares of cultivated plants and domesticated sea-life. This was the school's largest garden.

"There lies the finest example of the gardening art." Falll swam near Ba-ohl, as the school entered the garden and began to forage for their favorite breakfast. "Come to me before you start eating, Ba-ohl. I have decided that you should father my next tad."

"You have only just seen the tail off your last tad. Why do you choose another egg so soon?"

He was pleased with the honor, but her direct invitation struck him with all the romantic impact of spawning egg-droppers. Ellls selected eggs for the long hatching and nurturing process with great care.

"Sa-el has decided to sponsor a tad," Falll said as she dove for a large tuber beneath a square of brown flat leaves. "He wants to raise a tad with my characteristics, 'for the good of all ellls,' he says."

"A strange notion," Ba-ohl said, pulling a weed from the row of rooted clams he had chosen for his meal.

With a sudden scooping motion they both tumbled over the rocks that edged the garden, and Falll offered herself to the young male.

Before they mated, an ultrasonic code and a wave of alarm pressure tore through the school. It was a search order: "Ilean. Locate Ilean. All must join the search. Navell did not find her."

With single thrusts of their powerful legs and a chorus of sonic calls, the school came together as one giant organism and began the search for their missing elll.

They received no answer to their persistent ultrasonic locator signals and pressure calls for the girl. The school spread to the limits of their coordinated ultrasonic echo-location capabilities, swimming back and forth, covering the entire area between the garden and the shallows they frequented.

Once in the shallows, they called again in simple sonar barks, knowing that Ilean responded more often to low pitched code. When the shallows did not reveal the lost girl, the school rode the currents toward the Viortahk, the maze of channels and islands that separated their gardens from the Bay of Varoks.

The varoks were more feared than the *eefl* that dwelt in those waters. Ellls did not frequent the bay, for at its cusp varoks had built an immense structure totally alien to them.

"Ilean could not be in these cold channels." Ba-ohl spoke the common thought while the school circled, uncertain whether or not to take its search further into the dangerous waters.

"You saw her before the races?" Duregal asked.

"And during the races." Ba-ohl was terrified for Ilean. It wasn't just the danger she faced alone; she was losing life–time when she was away from the school. As a tad, her lonely trips of exploration might have been of some value. Now, as an adult, her place was with the school. Her fellows were incomplete without her, and she was nothing without them. How could an elll go off alone? Ba-ohl's imagination soon dissipated along the channels of logic that crocheted his sensory input into ingenious patterns of comprehension.

"Ilean was with me until after the second race. I can still remember her shudder when Elanall took a hard dive." Ba-ohl's eyes narrowed with anger at himself. "I should have stayed with her. I will never again let her swim out of my pressure range."

The school answered as if reciting a catechism. "Such a promise is impossible to keep. You tried. It couldn't be done." In a variety of high cracking barks the ellls flooded Ba-ohl with reassurance. "The entire school is responsible for Ilean."

It didn't help. Ba-ohl wished they would stop.

"You are no loner, Ba-ohl, nor am I." Duregal interrupted the school's failed message by circling Ba-ohl closely. "No elll can expect to stay tuned to just one other. It is she who must stay attuned to all of us. I was her sponsor; I have not saved her from these wanderings. We must say it: she is a loner."

"Ilean is no loner!" Ba-ohl shouted. He tore away from Duregal and circled the school at high speed.

"There is nothing we can do to make her cling to us." Duregal spoke in ultrasonic so Ba-ohl could not ignore the message. "Wandering alone is an aberration seen in many ellls now: loners cling to one or two in the school or to none at all. Sometimes they prefer not to school."

"Not Ilean. She can't swim alone. Something is wrong with her ultrasonics. She can't be a loner. We must find her." Ba-ohl let loose with the piercing sound of elllonian grief, and launched himself into the cold waters of the Viortahk. The school followed as if they had no choice. The youth would find relief only if they continued the search with him.

For nearly a full moonlight change Ilean's school scanned the cold waters of the Viortahk. Sending continuous echo locator signals into the rocky cliffs of the thousand small islands, calling in sonar code as they swam methodically back and forth, they finally came to the varoks' observation posts. Smoothed rocks and wide beaches marked the entrance to the bay where the alien laboratory buildings stood on dry land.

The search ended. The school dared not stay any longer in the cold currents favored by *eefl*. In despair, they gave up and returned to the deeps to adjust to their loss.

THE ALIEN

Where wave and terror mix too well with stone,
She saw her life–joy gone and welcomed death,
Until a stranger came
To seek the heart of Ellason
And breathe an elll's sea-breath.

Kor Adtalorian was confident. He would contact ellls before his watch ended. Twice in the last moonlight cycle he had seen them, swimming back and forth between the islands of the Viortahk as if they were searching for something. Surely, they would not be in such cold waters without a definite purpose. They were not as simple-minded as most varoks liked to think. Korad believed them wise beyond imagination, their head plumes covering brains as clever as any varok's.

Korad pulled his lifters onto his feet and peered out into the mist that shrouded his rocky outpost. How could he attract the ellls' attention if they were to swim by again? The deep water far below gently nudged the dark granite. Clear and restless, it broke once over a low boulder, then settled back to its lazy rocking.

He wondered why the great-fish had not introduced the ellls to varoks—at least to Amanok, before this. Now, instead, the great-fish let ellls flounder around in the *eefl*-infected cold water. Without the great-fish, they would never gather enough nerve to approach the laboratory. Of course, the varoks could not approach ellls without an invitation. The great-fish made that quite clear.

It had been some time since the great-fish of Ellason first established their working relationship with varoks. Why were their descendants, the ellls, so difficult? The first great-fish had consented to accompany varoks to their home near Jupiter in 2203.3 *ir*. Now it was 3631. For more than thirteen hundred Varokian years varoks had known the great-fish.

For eager, young varoks like Korad, such time was difficult to appreciate. The enormity of thirteen hundred Varokian years could be seen more clearly on Earth. During that time, as varoks watched from Earth's moon, cave-dwelling Neanderthals disappeared and Cromagnons, or hybrids of both, became farmers and copper technicians. The rigidly planned Varokian society had changed little over that time.

During one of the orientation sessions, Amanok had asked Korad to recite what he knew about great-fish.

"We varoks have known the great-fish for a very long time," Korad recalled from his studies, "not as aliens, but as tutors and political guides. We have trusted their intuition in the councils of Varok since they agreed to join the Concentrate during the First Conference on Ellason in 3215 *ir*."

Why did ellls fear varoks now? The answer was not obvious. The history of varokian exploration on Ellason was innocent of violence. The varoks took the utmost care to leave Ellason's oceans undisturbed. Captured ellls were treated kindly. They were immediately released when their distress became obvious. Very few died as a result of varokian carelessness. Most of the deaths were accidental. At least, the great-fish understood that the deaths could not have been avoided, but could those few deaths be the source of a universal elllonian hatred of varoks? Not likely, Korad decided. Ellason was too big, and its communication networks were limited by their biology.

From his lookout in the Viortahk, Korad saw no further sign of the ellls. The waves of the channels gave him a feeling of emptiness, as if the few glow-fish that lit the deeps were asleep. Apparently, the ellls he had seen go by had finished their mission or given up their search.

The latter thought would not leave Korad's mind. The ellls behavior had been peculiar. They had been swimming very slowly, in an unusual snaking pattern. He could think of no reason for that, except searching. Yet, with their ultrasonic echo capability, ellls could scan the entire space between islands without such a pattern. Even their pressure sensitivity would give them a useful internal map. Either sense could detect the shape or movement of whatever they sought in the narrow channels. If it were a young elll who was lost, the child would immediately answer the ultrasonic calls and find its school by echo location or by zeroing in on its pressure signals.

Korad dismissed the idea of the search and decided that the ellls had been performing some sort of ritual. Perhaps they thought they could purge the islands of the alien varoks or dispatch the *eefl* by swimming their incantations. He was not convinced, as some varoks were, that ellls were a superstitious species, but it was a possibility he could not dismiss.

According to the great-fish, the ellls were not much more advanced than their dry-land counterparts, the human beings of Earth. In comparing the two societies, Korad decided that elllonian schools were very similar to the human villages that had recently appeared near sources of water on Earth. Also, the ellls' careful herding of large gray *oeln* fish and their planting of moss were similar to human farming. Both ellls and human beings had developed to a high primitive state the art of using and making tools. The only real difference was that humans were making lethal axes of copper. The ellls preferred toys, underwater gardening tools and musical instruments fashioned from sea plants and rocks, materials used in their natural state.

Neither species had learned to systematize knowledge and record it. Yet how different they were: abstract human thought was still frighteningly underdeveloped compared to their technical skill. The ellls, however, exhibited only simple technical skills, while the great-fish

insisted that their abstract logic was highly developed. At the time
Korad was trained, many varoks disagreed.

Now the ellls' technological development had reached a plateau,
though everything else about the ellls was growing and changing rapidly. The structure of the schools was larger and more varied, for their
population growth curve had become very steep. Gardens had recently
appeared in wild, irrational patterns, as if a Great Sea Land Grab had
begun. Also, more and more loners were leaving schools without suffering any distress, an evolutionary complication of another sort.

So, here I am, Korad mused, *sure that some ellls have entered the Viortahk
in order to honor me with their trust and their secrets. What a fool I am.* He
got up carefully and walked slowly toward the other side of the stony
island that overlooked the major channels of the Viortahk. "Why don't
you ellls come swimming back now," he said aloud. "Call up to me.
Ask me to accompany you back to the lab so we can become acquaint-
ed. The great-fish say we are perfect complements to one another. We
should be partners."

He laughed at himself—a quality in varoks as rare as teeth in a mud-
turtle. *Such a dreamer.* In spite of himself, he walked on, consciously
willing the ellls to reappear in the waters below, before the threatening
low mists filled the channels.

He disliked the noise of the lifting devices strapped to his feet, but
he turned them on now, for they made walking tolerable. Forcing a
cushion of air downward like small hovercrafts, they helped his leg
muscles move his feet one at a time against Ellason's grasp.

Soon he was on the far side of the island, near the edge of a cliff that
rose one hundred meters out of the sea. He looked down and stared at
the waves undulating against the rocks. The water looked like molten
black glass.

The mists had filled the larger channels to the south. For one last
time he activated the search light he carried on his belt. Its beam swept
across the channel to the tiny islands nearby. The light glanced over
sharp rocks, caught rolls of mist, then drew a line over the water to the
few islands still visible—where it caused something to stir.

The motion caught Korad's eye, and he swung the light back over
the rocks. *Where? Which island?* The mist was closing in. *There.* The
light grazed a small greenish blue animal huddled in a basin of mud
just out of reach of the cold ocean waves.

"An elll." Korad gasped.

With no further thought, he turned his lifters to flight power and skated off the edge of the cliff. With a swooping motion he righted himself onto the surface of the water and crossed the channel. He was within three meters of the small island when the mist closed in. He could make out a landing spot on the shore some distance from the elll. He slowed and sank toward the water, then prepared to shut down the lifters, when an unseen rock near the surface tipped him over. Korad's right arm smacked the rock, and he yelped.

The yelp thoroughly terrified the elll, who was already frightened by the lifters' noise. She did not move.

Korad floated toward her, just off the rocks, until he was close enough to scan the elll's mood. Surprised at the ease of reading her alien mind, he saw that she was too dry and cold. Something had drained her of hope.

Korad reached for her hands but missed, fearing he might injure their delicate webbed structure. She panicked and pulled away.

"Please." He spoke in Varokian, softening the tones of his voice. "Please help me."

Weighted down with the water-logged lifters, his one good arm tiring with the effort of swimming against Ellasonian gravity, he knew he could not stay on the surface much longer. Perhaps it no longer mattered; he had looked into the eyes of an elll.

Korad saw that his pleading tones rang true in the elll's mind—generous soul that she was. How simple it was for his patches to tune in to her mood.

She thought he, too, was lost. He would understand the sadness of the life-moments she had lost in this cold place. This alien—obviously newly matured—did not want to die, not any more than she did.

Slowly the elll reached out over the water, this time with her legs. As her feet approached Korad's brown hands, she winced and closed her eyes. The varok's patch-organs told him that she feared his touch.

Korad took a precious moment to reassure her. He slowly laid the palm of his hand over her webbed foot and waited until she opened her eyes. It was worth the risk. She thanked him with a tired grin.

She could not pull him out of the water, but Korad slowly worked his way up by bracing against the rocks as she grasped his good arm. His hair-trigger nerves exploded with the stimulation of the contact, but he saw that the elll was reassured by the touch. She moved with him in concert as he worked his way out of the water.

When he was safely aground, Korad pulled away from the elll's touch, but quickly checked himself when he realized that she welcomed his life-giving warmth. Slowly, he moved around her, until she was protected from exposure, then he tried to relax.

The intensity of the elll's touch made the pain from his broken arm seem like nothing. He assumed that he would soon get used to the contact, as he would in a sexual embrace, but it was no use. His nerves fired relentlessly. Since no sexually enabling hormones were released by the embrace of the elll, nothing eased the effects of the nerve-bending contact. He bore it to save her, but he could not control the occasional spasms that shook his body. Still she clung to him, and Korad understood that she would die if he left her. He was amazed when the elll fell asleep.

When at last Ilean awoke, nearly recovered from the cold, she sat up and examined Korad's arm. She knew it was broken. Without apology or warning, she yanked its bones back into place. Then, with a gesture that warned the varok not to move, she slipped into the sea.

Soon she returned with a dead *ahl* branch and a length of sea-vine. In spite of the ache where the *eefl*'s tail had cut her, she fashioned a splint on the varok's arm, then sat back, and a grin danced across her face.

Korad saw that she expected to be captured, and she welcomed it. She was tired, every limb ached, and she was still too cold. If the varok took her to the aliens' square building above the beach, she might survive a while longer. She had heard that varoks kept warm pools for ellls there. She had no hope of returning to her school.

Korad silently promised that she would have everything she desired and more—if he could only get her back to the lab safely.

FIRST LESSONS

"Come, hear my voice. Come know my every thought,
"And through your mind your heart will be my guide.
"Our lives must soon be joined.
"We cannot let this chance go by
"And fail, while worlds collide."

Korad reached for his locator. The laboratory would respond to his signal and send out a skimmer to take them back to safety.

He turned it on, then off again. He adjusted the range. He tried everything he could imagine, but the signaling device was dead. It had not survived his fall into the water.

For a moment he thought he would go irrational with frustration. Then he looked again into the elll's hopeful eyes and regained control at once. Perhaps he could repair the damaged lifters.

He took his survival tool from his jump suit pocket, unstrapped his disabled lifters, and started taking them apart, laying the pieces out to dry on the rocks.

For a moment the elll looked puzzled, then she pushed a flat rock toward the varok.

"Thank you," he said in Varokian.

When he had finished refurbishing the lifters, he glanced up at the elll. The green moss of her face shimmered with mixed emotions. The tiny blue plumes framing her eyes were pulled high, as if she were half frightened, half curious, tense with expectation. Korad's patches automatically locked into her thoughts, and he found there a very specific curiosity about the words he had just spoken.

What a mind she had! Even in this strange situation, it was like a ten-armed sponge, grasping at every juicy drop that rolled by.

"Thank you," he repeated. "It means—" How could he tell her? Ellls had no patch organs. They could not read minds as varoks did. "Thank you means something like . . . this symbol."

He found a rock with a sharp edge and scratched on the flat rock the great-fish symbol for pleasure and appreciation. "Tk tk," Korad pronounced, imitating the great-fish sonar code for the symbol.

Ilean nodded, recognizing the symbol he had drawn.

"Thank you." Korad pointed to the symbol again.

The elll laughed weakly and shook her head, saying "Tk tk."

"No, no," Korad said, amused. "'Thank you' is my word, the Varokian word for 'tk tk.' He tried writing great-fish symbols in the sand in an order that would convey his lesson. First he wrote *kahla*, the great-fish symbol for stranger, alien, or varok. He pointed to himself and said, "Thank you," then he pointed to Ilean, said "Tk tk," and wrote its symbol.

Ilean thought for a moment then tentatively pointed to the last symbol and repeated, "Tk tk."

Korad could see her mind stretch toward the connection. Before she could grasp the meaning of language, she had to see that the written symbols meant the same as the sounds. "Yes. Yes. *An. An,*" he said, nodding vigorously, scratching the pleasure symbol again. "Tk tk." He jabbed at the symbol as if to push the meaning into it.

"*An an,*" Ilean corrected his poor approximation of the sonic code.

"*Vi. Vi.* No. No," Korad cried, frustrated at the confusion he had caused. He saw the connection between sound and symbol slip from Ilean's mind. "*An* is this." He scratched the great-fish symbol for yes, anything positive. "*Tk* is this," and he pointed to the pleasure symbol. He repeated the sounds and their symbols, until Ilean, thankful for the distraction, repeated him accurately in sound and motion.

Then, in spite of her pain, she sat back on her feet and laughed and shook her head.

She had seen the connection between symbol and sound, Korad realized, as he watched the thoughts race through her mind, but she believed that the varok had the connection all wrong. The written language of great-fish had nothing to do with the sounds of ellls. Ellls used sonar signals to talk to other ellls, but there were no great-fish symbols associated with them.

"Do we have it wrong?" Korad reviewed the great-fish language. It translated to Varokian easily, and the great-fish had made the connection to elll speech—to elllonian ultrasonics, not sonics. So that was it.

Her mind was open, as if she knew enough to welcome the intrusion of his patch sense. Korad could see that ultrasonics had never meant much to Ilean. Words meant a form of status seeking, she believed, status through the use of puzzles, sentences left half finished, ending with a peculiar buzzing irritation.

Korad stared at the little blue elll, as she carefully rubbed out the symbol for pleasure and said, "*Vi tk tk.*" Could she not sense the ultrasonic code? It was the ellls' principal means of navigation and communication. What had she meant by *puzzles left half-finished*?

He watched her watching him, then he drew the great-fish symbols for "new ideas, try them."

She nodded, and he saw that she understood what he wanted. He pointed to the symbol for pleasure and pronounced, "*Tk tk,*" then he pointed to the symbol for "yes" and pronounced "*An.*"

"*An,*" Ilean repeated, rolling the delicate sound from her throat with exaggerated relish.

"*An, an,*" Korad replied with enthusiasm.

"*An an an,*" Ilean laughed, and she shrugged her shoulders and turned away to watch a tiny *brilln* hopping on the rocks below.

It means nothing to her, Korad realized. *She's made the connection, but she doesn't care.* He felt a little desperate. He didn't understand. Something was peculiar about the elll's thought patterns; they didn't fit the text-book description. Surely, he could make her understand the importance of spoken language as a key to abstract thought. "Varoks can't hear in the ultrasonic either. We must translate great-fish symbols into sonar so we can speak together." As he spoke he tried to display the idea symbolically.

She gave him some polite attention, but as Korad probed deeper, he saw that she was no longer curious about his varokian ideas.

Quietly, she watched the *brilln*, aware that Korad was watching her. She was no longer interested in his lessons.

Had she forgotten him? She was moving slowly toward the *brilln*, as if driven by hunger. She was on the hunt. Would she eat such a beautiful creature?

Too curious for his own good, Korad rudely probed deeper so he could watch her thoughts. He saw that she could not—indeed, would not—destroy the bird-like being. She only wanted to see it better. She had already decided that her life-time was at an end. Pain clouded her existence. Any peaceful moments left to her now were pure gifts.

Korad's foot slipped and set loose a rock. Ilean startled. As she stepped backward, her delicate right foot came down too hard. With a cry of pain, she rolled down the steep incline and hit her head on a large boulder at the water's edge.

Korad could not move fast enough to catch her. Fighting off his anguish, barely able to stay rational, he climbed down to her and searched for a sign of consciousness.

Quickly her huge black eyes filled with awareness, and one long green webbed finger reached out to pull the corner of his mouth upward.

He smiled to please her, realizing his varokian face bewildered her.

Instinctively, Korad's patches probed deep. "What is wrong? What is wrong? You mustn't die," he commanded.

The ell opened her eyes and tried to smile at him. The *eefl's* poison had spread up her leg. The smile pasted her long tongue to her throat. She choked, and her cough sounded painful and dry.

"Yes. yes. *An, an,*" Korad said. "We'll go to the lab immediately. The varoks there can help you."

He climbed back up the slope and reassembled the lifters, then set them for underwater propulsion. Carefully he made his way back down the rocks and helped Ilean into water.

When he tried to coax her into a life-saving hold with her head above water, she struggled free. Again, and she fought him off. The third time made her laugh, and she found enough strength to sink beneath him and grab his waist belt.

At last he understood. He secured her grasp and rode on her buoyant form. Of course she preferred to be under water. He turned the lifters to full power and pulled her through the maze of channels toward the laboratory.

They traveled past several islands. Korad felt his grasp weaken. They were moving along too slowly, sinking lower and lower. Though the ell tried to kick, she was too weak to be of much help.

With a sudden, desperate effort, Ilean pulled her full length underneath the varok and grasped him about the waist. Now she could use her back-fin as a rudder. She placed his arms and legs against his body, urged him to relax against her, and at last the lifters pulled them both more easily through the water.

The warmth of his body and the restoring moisture of the sea revived Ilean's hope. For the first time since Korad found her, she longed to be fully alive again.

Shamelessly intruding, Korad read her mood at every accessible level and came to realize that contact meant everything to her. At some deep level, she missed being with other ellls, to be surrounded by them, to be a part of her school. How could she tolerate being away from them? Most ellls could not stand such separation.

When he put aside the unanswered question, Korad heard a name in the elll's mind.

"Ilean." He had heard her name ring clearly several times now. With a surge of joy, he pulled back to find the elll grinning at him. Their clasp tightened, and they moved on through the water.

At last the varokian observation laboratory came into view. Broad clay beaches reached out like welcoming arms to greet Korad and Ilean and guide them into the currents that fed the lower levels of the laboratory's sea aquarium.

Before they reached the narrowest part of the varokian-made channels, Korad lost hold of the elll. Something had pried them apart. A heavy wall of water threw Korad to one side. As he recovered his balance and coughed water from his throat, he saw the long, forked tail-fin of a great-fish disappear beneath the waves.

"Ilean!"

Frantically, Korad searched the water until his damaged lifters gave out.

"Ilean. Ilean!" he screamed and went irrational with horror. There was no answer. She was gone.

In the City of Great-fish

The great-fish found her in the varok's grasp
And took her from that lethal devotee
To safer, healing arms —
To ancient hollows drawn with moss
Beneath the warm-red sea.

The ellls of the Great Basin referred to their distant cousins, the great-fish, as the masters of Ellason. To ellls, great-fish were the ancient fathers of wisdom—those who saw more than the ellls' seven senses could describe, imperturbable, all-knowing and unknowable—a generous piece of nonsense, given the fact that ellls were multi-talented compared to great-fish.

Varoks regarded the great-fish with less awe. Being bipedal mind-readers, however, they did have a deep appreciation for the great-fish's ability to see the whole, in spite of its confusing parts. No one could be sure, and the great-fish wouldn't say, but many varoks believed that the great-fish were, at one time, if not mind-readers, at the very least excellent mood-readers.

Twice as long as the average elll, great-fish measured some four to six meters from the tip of their narrow, forked tails to the blunt smiling end of their broad triangular bodies. They exhibited no ultrasonic sense, seemed to experience poor sight and pressure sensitivity, and had no ear plaques with which to hear. It was a mystery most ellls preferred not to explore: how could such senseless denizens of Ellason's deeps know what was happening so well? How could they communicate with most of the sentient beings of Ellason, predict disasters, and advise their contemporaries so wisely?

Some ellls whispered answers most did not like to hear: The great-fish could penetrate the black eyes of ellls and grasp the living essence of the mind within. They could easily strip away the veneer of any elll's driving emotion and travel the logical maze of elllonian thought.

As she lay helplessly wrapped in great-fish fins, Ilean felt no fear. She had heard that great-fish were fine nurses, and the great-fish fin wrapped around her felt warm and secure. It carried her at great speed through the water away from her varok and his square land-dwelling. She didn't like that, but at least she might learn something of the great-fish mystery. She would have them all to herself—apart from the school. She wondered if her mind were being read. Maybe, if she lived long enough, she would learn something from them. No bothersome elder would be there to stop her asking questions.

Her poor varok with the broken arm would have liked to meet the great-fish, Ilean decided. No doubt he is very angry at them right now. She and the varok had been about to enter the varok's bay, when three great-fish had surrounded Korad, and a fourth had pushed the varok aside and carried her away.

She had liked the warmth of the varok's strong, smooth body and the kindness she had seen in his eyes. *I should not have left him*, she told herself, forgetting that she had no choice in the matter.

The dark cold waters of the Viortahk lay far behind as the great-fish carried her past the scattered islands and into the larger ocean. Clutching the herbs the great-fish had given her to eat, she dozed on and off, feeling tired—too tired.

When she awoke, the water was clear and light and warm. On the sea bottom far below, the red glow of a hot chasm was visible. It must be the Engine of Ellason, part of the great tree of cracks that exposed the very heart of the planet.

As the sea bottom rose to meet them, Ilean realized that the continental shelf was reaching out from an unseen shore nearby. The water danced with the wavering glow of long-haired sea moss that covered great rocks on the sea bottom and provided drifting curtains over the dark entrances to great-fish caves.

Ilean thought this must be the City of Great-fish, the labyrinth of underwater dwellings that encircled the Southern Shallows across the Great Chasm.

Why had they stolen her from her kind rescuer? He wanted to be her teacher. "So, the great-fish had better teach me plenty," she whispered to herself.

In answer, the great-fish who carried her made a low warbling sound, then turned sharply into a dark crevice. The clear light of the ocean moss went out, and a warmer glow appeared from beyond the bottomless dark of the entryway. They swam through a narrow channel in the rocks. Ilean bumped her head twice trying to get a view of their destination.

The first time she bumped her head, the great-fish grinned, shook with another warbling laugh, and pulled her closer; but the second bump startled him. He didn't smile again. He clasped Ilean to him more securely and moved slowly through the last hundred meters of the gorge.

The walls of the sea suddenly opened into an enormous cavern lit by the most beautiful moss Ilean had ever seen. It hung over the rocks in bright exploding bundles of iridescent blue and yellow. Floating from the ceiling and walls of the cave, it covered hidden corners and shelves, hammocks and sleeping rooms on every rocky surface. On the far side of the cavern the moss had been woven into a dense net that enclosed the living stock of the great-fish's garden. Mud turtles, nightfish, and market shell dwellers, a plump fish Ilean had never seen before, and crawlers of every description moved about in their massive pens with the dull calm of domesticated beasts. Beside the stockyard was a thick growth of cultivated sea plants. The familiar scent of moonlight tulip blossoms stirred Ilean's appetite, and the small stand of *ahl* trees growing along the cavern's rear wall made Ilean feel at home. Then she noticed the many openings in the rock.

The question in her mind was immediately answered in sonic code by the great-fish who carried her. "The City of Great-fish is made of many rooms like this, and smaller ones," he said. "They are connected by tunnels carved into the rock by the elllonian chemists from the Great Bay of Shallows."

"Chemists make explosives?" Ilean laughed, delighted that the great-fish had finally chosen to talk in sonar code. "I have learned of such things. Duregal told me."

"Your elllonian experimentalists stir up some dangerous chemicals," the great-fish said with a smile, "dangerous, but useful, at times. Come now, we had better join the others."

The great-fish glided to the center of the cavern, and his three companions gathered around.

They spoke to her in sonic code, but with obvious difficulty. They could mimic the hollow sound of ellls only by vibrating the back of their tongue against their deep gills.

"Ilean." Her rescuer finally released her from his fin's embrace. "We do not normally communicate with ellls using Elllonian sonics. We can't maintain the sound for long. Please listen carefully. Call me Harrahn. I am named for a legendary beast of Varok's Misted Ocean."

He turned toward a magnificent great-fish with an enormous tail. "This elder you may call Ahlkahn, after Varok's central transport mechanism. This small gray person call Vior, after the great city of Varok's inhabited land. And this great-fish call Orlegh, after the hot acid winds that have killed too many ellls taken to Varok."

"Varokian names?" Ilean turned to find an identifying characteristic on the last great-fish. With a toss of his head, Orlegh grinned at her with such obvious delight that she knew she would never miss him in a crowd. "Why do you use alien names?" she asked.

"Because we will be your guides when it comes time for you to go to the varoks, if that time should ever come."

"Why did you snatch me away from that young varok? He was very kind to me."

"He did not understand your trouble," Harrahn said. "Varoks might not have been able to prevent your death. You are very ill, Ilean, and not just from *eefl* poison. Why did you leave the school?"

"Because I'd just laid my first egg. I wanted to enjoy it for a moment."

"By yourself?"

"Yes." She stared at the great-fishes' thick frowns. Their gazes moved searchingly over her eyes, and she realized that they were only puzzled, not reproving. "Why not?" she asked. "The other ellls were laughing at me. They don't appreciate eggs—not even a first egg."

"Where did you get such a wonderful idea?"

"From the *lohn* birds. I often go to the shallows near the cliffs, where I see their nests. I love to watch them working their wings as they go up the cliffs. They are so powerful and so ridiculous in their pink moss. They make a great noise and have a wonderful celebration whenever they lay an egg."

"You go to watch the *lohn* birds alone?" Vior smiled, as if it were a great joke.

"No one else will go with me, but I usually make the school promise to wait for me—because I have trouble finding them when I go back to the deeps. This time I didn't care if they found me or not. I am no longer a tad."

"Tad or no, you need the school, Ilean," Ahlkahn said. "You are not well enough to live the life of a loner."

"I still hurt all over."

"No, no. You don't understand. The *eefl* poison will soon be gone. We are worried about something else. We know why you have trouble finding the school, Ilean." Harrahn was still frowning. "You should not have bumped your head as we came through the passageway. Do you often bump into things?"

"The ellls call me simple because I bump into things when I try to play their games. I also get lost and can't guess their riddles or learn their terrible long history of echo pictures. They make me swim in the center of the school like a tad because I'm so stupid." Ilean pushed off the mud and settled back again, impatient to know what the great-fishes' questions meant, but still feeling sick from the *eefl* poison.

"It is time for you to learn about your unnatural condition, Ilean," Orlegh said. "You are not simple, my dear, you are quite intelligent, but you are blind."

Ilean giggled at the wonderful grinning face trying to look so sober. "You are kind to say such a thing, but I can see quite well. You needn't try to be tactful."

"I'm not being tactful at all. When you are blind, you can't know what you don't see. But we will deal with that later. You and your school must have been very confused by all your odd ways. Have any ellls suddenly left the school, Ilean? Do you know any others who like to go off alone?"

"I've seen Sa-el start to go off alone, but he's got better control than I do. Then there's Allran. He left the school. It was terrible. He just disappeared, and no one knew whether or not to adjust to his absence. It left a terrible open wound in the school. They were off balance for a long time. If Allran had been killed, the school would have gone through a simple adjustment to his absence, but not knowing—"

"'They?' Dear Ilean, you are indeed a loner," Orlegh declared. "You called the school 'they.'"

"*Aeyull*. No." The sudden accusation was a confirmation of her deepest fears, a condemnation for being an adventuress, a terrible person, unfaithful to her school. She curled into the mud, grasping her head with her hands. "I didn't mean it the way it sounded. I didn't mean it."

Orlegh scooped the elll into his huge lateral fins and rocked her gently as his prehensile tail-fin came around and wiped the mud from her plumes. "You have done nothing wrong, Ilean," he said. "It is no sin to be a loner. You must follow your nature. Ellls are changing, becoming more adaptable as a species. It is your privilege to be one of the first."

"We ellls are changing? How can that be?"

"Being a loner is a gift from the Source of Life itself. Look what the gift has meant to you. You have celebrated your first egg. You have known the *lohn* birds and seen the stars. You could be an experimenter, working tools on dry land, or a librarian, one that records the knowledge of ellls."

With the end of his tail Orlegh pulled her chin up until her black eyes focused on the mild, faceted gaze of his sensors. "You could become the link between ellls and varoks, the interpreter of minds, the harmonic bridge between two discordant songs. You have won the care of a great varok."

Ilean laughed. "You mean my poor, broken young varok?" She smiled at the thought of him, and she let Orlegh's kind lecture sink in. "Does 'link' mean that if I am careful to be very considerate of the school's need to adjust, I can come and go as I will?"

"We hope to make that possible for you, Ilean. That is why we took you away from the young varok, Korad. Somehow we must teach you what you cannot learn. You have a blindness that has nothing to do with your being a loner. Because of that blindness, you crashed when you tried the rock-jumping game. You could not sense the rock, or the other elll coming toward you, could you?"

"No. No. But I am not blind," Ilean insisted. "No one could see anyone coming so fast that way. It's a crazy game. And I couldn't have avoided bumping my head as we came into the cavern. How could you expect me to see? With my plumes? I have only two eyes in my face."

She must have known, even as she spoke, that Harrahn was probing her thoughts, rooting out the core of her being. It was not a pleasant sensation, and she resisted the intrusion.

"You must learn something that is very painful to know, Ilean. I must tell you the truth so you can survive."

With the tip of his tail-fin, he traced the hexagonal pattern of light green that outlined the mossy tiles of her skin. "Most ellls," he began with emphasis, "continually put out very high sound waves that bounce off everything that surrounds them. The sonic melons you wear above your eyes should also receive sound waves and talk to the lines around your tiles, helping you interpret the echo of those sound waves. They should tell you exactly where you are in relation to everything around you."

Ilean looked at the great-fish as if he were talking nonsense.

"It is true, Ilean. It is the answer to the riddles ellls tell you—the unfinished sentences. They are not riddles. The ellls extend their speech into the ultrasonic, into sound waves you cannot sense. You are expected to understand the patterns of echoes that reach your hexagonal mesh work."

"Is that why I get lost, when no one else does?"

"Not entirely. There is more. The echoes of very high sound waves travel some distance and are useful for finding the school and recognizing the topography of the ocean floor, but ultrasonic sound waves are also read in conjunction with pressure signals. The patterns of pressure define the school."

The great-fish ran a gentle fin over the surface of her body. "The hexagonal tiles all over your body, Ilean. Why are they there?"

"They are soft, and they protect my innards, I suppose."

"Your tiles should be very sensitive to any change in pressure in the water surrounding you. Close your eyes and stop your ears for a moment and tell me if you know where I am. I will move away and then signal to you. All the other great-fish here will remain still."

Ilean did as Harrahn asked, and she waited for a long while. Nothing happened. With her eyes closed and her hands pressed against her ear plaques, she felt as if she were suspended in empty silence.

"I can't tell where you are, Harrahn." she cried, opening her eyes. She saw him suspended in the water directly behind her, beating his tail in opposition to his fins so that he made a turbulence in the water.

"You could feel nothing?"

"Only a tickle on the bottom of my feet."

"There are no tiles on the bottom of your feet, Ilean."

"No wonder I am an outcast." For a moment she was overwhelmed. "I have never understood why the school made such a fuss over adjustment. It's all done with pressure signals, isn't it? No wonder I could never get it right. I was flapping about, messing up their patterns." Curling in the mud to escape the shame she felt, she said, "I disrupted those patterns whenever I went off by myself, didn't I?"

Quietly, the great-fish waited. They were kind but never indulgent. They knew the attack of sorrow would soon pass. The emotions of ellls were as mobile as their thoughts. Grief would go, but it would come again, soon, often.

"We believe, Ilean, that you will recover, because between the times of grief and anger, you will be eager to learn."

"What am I going to do? I can't return to the school. I would like to stay here with you."

"We know you mean that, Ilean, but an elll with no ultrasonics and no pressure sense cannot live apart from the school."

"I don't see why not. Others do. I have always lived by myself—even in the middle of the school. I have no reason to go back where I am half deaf and blind."

"Your feelings will pass when you learn to speak in ultrasonic."

"Why should I speak a language I can't hear?"

"Because then you will never be lost again," Ahlkahn explained. "We can teach you to call out a message in ultrasonics. We will teach you to say 'Ilean is here, please come.' The school will hear and know where you are."

"Then they will have to come way out of their way to find me. It's humiliating."

Harrahn scooped her up in his fin to keep her from curling back into the mud. When her eyes met his sensors, he spoke. "Can you imagine the grief the school suffered when you were lost? They searched everywhere for you—even into the coldest channels. They put themselves in danger from *eefl* and from varoks. When we heard the young varok's lifters go to high power we knew he had found you and was taking you captive. We could not allow that, for the varoks could not have healed the poison in your body. We found you by the noise of the varok's lifters. Then we sent a message to your school, telling them that you would be our guest, our patient, for a long time. They know that you are here in the City of Great-fish and that we will bring you home when you are ready to go."

"I will never be ready to leave you. I have too much to learn."

"Good." Harrahn laughed, a sound between hot lava hitting sea water and the mating call of a sick *lohn* bird, Ilean decided.

"You still have *eefl* poison in you, and I am very tired from carrying you so far and talking so much."

Ilean smiled and playfully sent a rush of bubbles to the cave's ceiling from the back of her nasal gills. "No wonder you get along with the aliens. You are good diplomats. First you tell me how weak I am, then how weak you are, so I will do as you say."

"Right. You disobey us at your own great peril," Harrahn said. "Now, come over to this shelf and you will find soft mud."

The other great-fish, Ahlkahn, grinned, and they all sighed with relief, making Ilean smile again. "Vior will go for something to eat. The beamers are swarming now. It won't take him long to trap some."

"When you have eaten you must sleep," Harrahn said.

Ilean noticed that Harrahn's throat was now barely able to make the sound of her language. "There will be little need for speech, Ilean. Trust us. You will learn quickly."

She nodded and let Harrahn carry her to one side of the cave, where a blanket of thick moss hung over a comfortable alcove. She curled into the soft bed of mud behind the moss and fell asleep before Vior returned with her meal of beam-fish.

A Rebel Loosed

"I see myself," the varok told the youth.
"In you my rage is harnessed once again.
"For Ellason, go forth.
"Go find your elll, and wisdom too,
"Within the great-fish den."

For one dangerous moment Korad succumbed to pure varokian rage. He struck out blindly at the great-fish that had taken Ilean away. His reason gone, he tried to follow.

The water was as cold as Varok's deepest lakes. Korad kicked free of the now useless lifters and tried to swim upward. The water grew colder and colder. He thought he must be swimming deeper, so he reversed his direction and swam toward warmer water. He needed to breathe, but the surface was not in sight. He had forgotten that Ellason's surface was often cooler than the deeps, which were warmed by the huge planet's volcanic fissures and pockets of nuclear fission.

Panic drove him back to a rational state, and he felt a massive fin lift him to the surface. There he coughed and choked and finally gulped Ellason's misted air into his lungs.

After that, he remembered long, endless gliding through cold water, the lights of the observation laboratory, the jumbled sound of varoks worrying over him, the firm warmth of a g-brace, and welcome, heavy sleep.

The lab was long into its work-period when Korad received a signal directing him to report to his supervisor, Amanok. He believed his career would be ended. At least he would have a good length of time on Ellason before the next ship would return to Varok.

The youth moved slowly off the g-brace toward the closet where he kept the back brace and head cup prescribed for constant use. Though the artificial environment of the lab provided varoks with many comforts of their home planet, permanent devices to counteract Ellason's gravity were considered too expensive. Precautionary conditioning for varoks required three Varokian light-periods spent out of the braces every moon-light cycle.

Korad realized he should not have spent his watch-duty without the braces. His ordeal in the cold water had almost ended his life. By the time the great-fish had taken Ilean from him, much of his strength had already been wasted in the effort to hold his head upright on his shoulders.

He sighed with relief as his weight sank onto the head cup and back brace. He strapped on a small pair of lifters and made his way down the hallways, past the crystal precision of the laboratories to the starker offices beyond.

When Korad appeared in Amanok's space, the elder greeted the youth with enthusiasm. "Come in. Come in. Quite a brush with death you had out there, Korad. Glad to see the light and take your punishment, I trust?" Amanok sounded like a hunter loading a laser pistol. "You wouldn't want to tell me why you ignored regulations and tried to travel across the channel with lifters, would you?"

"I found an elll, a wounded female. The great-fish must have taken her. They nearly killed me doing it. Please read me, Aman Okrahlan. My throat is too raw to talk."

Korad spoke no more, but ran the entire story through his mind. He tried not to leave out anything, so Amanok could see hope painting everything he thought. Maybe he would understand, perhaps forgive, both the taking of the elll and her loss.

When the story was told, Amanok leaned back in his reading couch and probed deeper into Korad's mind.

You believe that the elll was not afraid of you?

She showed surprisingly little fear—but that is understandable. She was very near death. I could see the defeat in her mind. She didn't care what happened to her.

That makes sense, I suppose. But you must know that this incident brings us no closer to understanding the ellls or to reducing their fear of us. Amanok toyed with the laser pencil in the pocket of his jump suit. "You say that the great-fish tore the elll away from you? Left you to drown? I can't believe that, Lok Antalorian. The great-fish called us; one was seen carrying you up to shallow water. He almost beached himself trying to get you onto the shore before we got there."

"I remember some of that." Korad was having difficulty controlling his anger, but he found his voice. "Did the great-fish leave any message, any indication of why the elll was taken from me? I thought they were trying to help us establish contact with ellls."

"Calm yourself, Korad." An understanding smile painted Amanok's face. "We don't want you going irrational with some fool emotion like anger. We don't want to make contact with ellls at the price of trust, do we? Legends die hard among the elllonian schools, Korad. The ellls fear us because of the forebear's mistakes. When our ancestors first discovered this planet, they took a large group of ellls back to Varok for observation. The mistake was repeated six hundred years ago when we varoks rediscovered Ellason. We sent a colony of ellls to Varok under the care of the immigrant great-fish there. Despite all efforts, the ellls didn't survive long on Varok. Over the years, stories about those transplanted ellls have kindled the imagination of the ellls here.

"Most ellls here hate us, and all ellls fear us—for our machines and for our curiosity. Our approach to the study of Ellason has been harsh and impersonal. We have much to learn from the great-fish, but we can't seem to learn what we most need to know. We can't seem to learn how to travel beyond ourselves, so we can approach the ellls on their emotional and ethical plane."

"I was making real progress with the blue elll," Korad protested. "She was beginning to understand the connection between my words and the great-fish's written language. I'm sure she did. She said *an* several times when presented with its symbol."

"She *what*?" Amanok rose from his chair as if he'd been stung by a nettle flea. "You tried to teach throat sounds to a dying elll? Have you no sensitivity, Korad? No wonder the great-fish took her from you. In addition to repeating our ancient mistakes, you have disregarded what the final moments of life would mean to an elll."

"She and I—we were becoming friends."

"The point is that we still don't know the ellls well enough—not even enough to succeed in keeping one alive in our care."

Reaching for the electronic scribe, Amanok sank back into his support chair. "I wish I didn't have to do this, Korad, but your arrogance leaves me no choice. You are assigned to reprimand duty for the remainder of your stay on Ellason." Slowly he dictated the order into the laboratory records: "Lok Antorian will return to Varok on the next transport, due to arrive 3 Callisto 2. Contact with ellls is hereby denied him, either on Ellason or Varok, until he has attained sufficient patience and maturity to deal with them on their own terms. Aman Okrahlan."

Korad scanned Amanok's mind for understanding and a hint of mercy.

"Strip my mind, Korad, so you can understand what you have done," Amanok said. "You have broken our trust with the great-fish. They have asked that we approach the ellls on an elllonian level—that we forsake our own curiosity, that we deny our untamable desire to communicate on our own terms, that we listen and watch and wait and build trust. How many years have you cost us? We may never regain the ground you have lost. The tale of your attempt to capture a wounded elll will ride the waves of this planet for an age. If it hadn't been for the great-fish's message on the beach, we would have to abandon this station as a symbol of good will and agree to leave the ellls at peace from now until the sun balloons into a red giant."

"I did nothing wrong," the boy said. "The elll agreed to come here with me."

Amanok rose to his feet. A wave of emotion he didn't recognize knocked him off reason. He slammed a hand on the desk to drive home his point. "You were taking advantage of her weakened condition."

"She wanted to come. I'm sure of it," the boy cried, startled by his mentor's sudden show of uncontrolled emotion. "We were already good friends. She liked me. I could see it in her mind."

"Ellls aren't so easy to read. I see an unhealthy ego in your mind, Korad." It took some effort for Amanok to regain control. He was still largely dominated by emotion, mixed emotion. In spite of his outrage, he admired the youth's conviction. At some level, he wanted Korad to be right.

Korad felt a surge of terror at seeing Amanok so dangerously exposed.

Words did not come easily to either of them. "In your short time here, Korad, I have come to love you like a son. But your mind is clogged with desire for success with the ellls. I want you to succeed in your work, but you must learn from this mistake."

Amanok tried to burn a hole in Korad's pride by staring him down, but the effort was a total failure. The elder loved the boy's zeal and faith in himself. Korad was too much like Amanok's younger self had been. Rational thought left the elder, and he consciously let his emotions rule his actions. He stretched out his forearms to the youth.

Korad stared at the time-worn leather of Amanok's skin, confused and shaken by the intimate gesture, hardly able to maintain a hold on rationality. His voice crumbled. He desperately wanted to accept Amanok's protection.

"I can't," he stammered, refusing Amanok's patronage by holding his own forearms to his sides. "I can't take your protection, as much as I need—and want it. I believe you are wrong. The great-fish are wrong. Our whole approach to the ellls has been wrong. I have violated nothing but varokian rules that don't work."

"The elll's name was Ilean," Korad continued. "She whispered it to me, before she was taken by the great-fish. She and I were becoming friends. I made her laugh. We embraced—like brother and sister. If I take your offer, Aman Okrahlan, absorb your mind, bow to your absolution, I will never see her again, and varoks will never know ellls. Together, she and I can reach an understanding that would enrich the lives of both our worlds for all the ages to come. I must try to find her."

He turned and left the room, knowing that Amanok had to let him go.

As he moved quickly down the hallway to his room, he resolved to leave the station, to find Ilean, to forge the link between elll and varok.

Then the gravity of Ellason slowed him to a painful crawl. With sudden dread he realized that he could not carry enough supplies to live alone on this alien planet.

His resolve wavered as he stuffed a few packages of survival rations and an extra tunic into a small pack. His search for Ilean would end in fatigue and starvation, but he had to try.

Korad's Bane

The varok trusted none,
Although he knew that great-fish see the whole,
The parts for what they mean in fine relief.
How could they understand an elll
Whose life was edged with grief?

Korad added extra lifters and a full set of braces to his pack, then he walked through the laboratory complex to the central land entrance, expecting—and half hoping—to be stopped.

No one spoke to him or questioned the heavy pack.

Once outside, he set off on foot across the wide beach of flat clay, past the launch pad, toward the black rocks that covered the southern shore of Ellason's major continent Nea.

The clay-streaked mud was hard. Walking was easy at first. Korad turned the lifters to low power and breathed in the cool mist with relish, daring himself to believe in his quest.

Time passed with no marking but the ever more insistent pain in his legs and back. The planet was pulling him down already. The lifters, now on full power, were no longer enough—and the rocks seemed no closer than when he set out.

He was not surprised when he heard the hum of a land rover behind him; he had expected to be arrested before this. He did not look up as the vehicle stopped beside him. There was no escape. He would be held in security at the lab and sent back to Varok on the next ship.

Amanok broke the silence with a gentle tone, though he looked stern and sober. Staying totally rational was no small feat. "You will never find your elll on foot, my dear son. Be somewhat less an idiot than you appear and take this rover for your search. You may have it until 3 Callisto 2, when the cruiser arrives from Varok. I trust you will not disgrace your species or compromise the trust of great-fish."

Korad dared not look into Amanok's eyes. He could see, with his patch mood vision, the cloud of fear in the elder's mind, but he didn't trespass further to discover why Amanok was helping him. Neither of them could afford the luxury of released emotion now.

"Certainly I don't deserve this from you, Master Amanok."

"Good. I like to see a spark of humility in my students."

Korad saw a glint of humor in the deep blue glance. "I do this be-cause I believe some great-fish have more faith in you than they should."

"Great-fish?"

"It was they, the ones who took her, who must have told you her name. We get the transliteration of elllonian sounds from the great-fish. They wanted to encourage you. Ilean would not have told you her name. Elllonian names are used only within the school. You must go cautiously, Korad, for the sake of a very foolish and sentimental old gambler. Climb in. I don't want to walk back to the lab."

Amanok turned the rover toward the lab like a racer going for the finish line. Within minutes they were hovering beneath the cold exte-rior of the varokian building. The elder descended to the beach and spiraled a hand upward in farewell.

Korad's mind was too full to speak. He invited Amanok's probe with a patch signal, but Amanok shook his head and pointed to the driver's seat. Then he waved the youth away.

– Δ –

For a long while Korad took the rover over endless clay beaches decorated with gently weathered black rock. His mind held a welcome, meditative blank. Except for the lack of ruins along the shore, he might have been on Varok.

The rocky wastes were a welcome relief. On his path to the great-fish cities, he slowed in order to navigate massive, sharp boulders and miniature cliffs that teased the sea inland. Tiny shore creatures and shallow burrowers stayed well hidden as he passed.

Only when he reached the end of the rocks did he feel the full im-pact of the alien planet. The moss flats engulfed him. The rover was a tiny gnat swallowed by a dense, glowing greenness that stretched over the land in all directions. The wind breathed heavily with the soundless talk of the mists, and the electric scent of Ellason's biolumi-nescent life forms crackled in Korad's nose. He missed Varok's quiet sounds: the mewing of migrating ilara flocks and the soft whistling of huge daramonts grazing in lush fields. In contrast, Ellason reeked with silent indifference.

He slept frequently during the long trip, ate when his body insisted, and exercised on waking. Only dimly aware of the changes in moonlight patterns, too often obscured by mist, he tuned his moments to the needs of his body. Gradually his strength increased and the braces became less critical.

He traveled over the moss flats as fast as he dared, then headed straight across the Bay of Shallows to the underwater caves where great-fish lived.

As he approached the eastern side of the Bay of Shallows, huge rocks emerged like monsters from the deep crystal blue of its clear water—the color of Amanok's eyes, he thought, though not nearly as dark.

He realized that he was intruding into the city of Great-fish, rudely flooding their homes with the noise of his rover. Embarrassment and fear nearly took over, and he shut down the power. "Go cautiously," Amanok had said, and meant it. Korad remembered in time. The rover settled onto the water's surface, and he pushed on with the emergency oars.

The vehicle made a clumsy rowboat, but soon the water grew shallower, lighter and blue-green. He could see rocks lying on the ocean floor. Great black crevices broke their symmetry, as if part of the rocks had been blasted away, as if they had been engineered to be entrances to dwellings.

The great-fish had built three cities for themselves. To approach them, undefended, underwater, with the rover's minimal scuba gear, would be to put his life in the hands of that enigmatic species.

"They never make sense." Korad calmed himself with the familiar sound of his own voice, hoping someone was nearby to hear him. "Great-fish are forever predicting and surmising and contradicting themselves. Why did they translate Ilean's name for me when they forced her away? I would never allow anything to harm her. So why did they take her from me? They forbade me to take Ilean to a lab where she would have had the best of care. What medical technology do great-fish have? None. And the ellls have little more than that. Ilean is probably dead by now."

She didn't deserve her fate. A beautiful creature, abandoned by her school for no apparent reason, blameless and desperate for companionship and security.

With that vision in mind, Korad decided to ignore Amanok's

advice. He would not consult with them. He would find Ilean and steal her back.

Korad flipped on the rover's power pack and drove further east, over the cliffs, beyond the eastern side of the Bay of Shallows.

When he found Ilean, he would take her in the land rover to warm shallows, far from interfering great-fish and lab officials. They would live on *challall* weeds and scar-fish, until they had worked out a language suitable to both species. After presenting their new language to the varoks at the laboratory, they would travel together over all the seas of Ellason, teaching the language to the ellls and arranging for meetings between their species.

The mists had rolled back to the lowlands, revealing a broad expanse of jumbled granite defining a tortuous shoreline. He cruised on low power through the moss-filled shallows embracing the southernmost peninsula of Nea, until his scanner picked up the sounds of elllonian life. Then he adjusted his cruising height to twelve meters and sped at full power over the rocks toward the sounds.

The warning light of an overworked hydrogen packet failed to attract his attention. Now only mud flats stood between the rover and the warm shallows. Perhaps Ilean's school frequented this area.

The shoreline was undisturbed. No trees marred the smoothness of the skyline. Only a tough, flat, mist-drinking shrub decorated the gentle rises set far back from the water's edge. In the distance, the moss shallows appeared as a green smudge on the yellow-gray horizon. Korad's eyes pulled at the vision, as if to make the moss come to him more quickly. Instead, he saw that it was sinking out of view. The rover was dying beneath him.

He felt the vehicle scrape to a stop on the beach and watched helplessly as the right hydrogen pack winked off and sealed itself into safety mode.

Korad unpacked the tools from the emergency hatch and tore into the faulty hydrogen pack, sure he could repair it. He worked on the power drive until he could no longer lift his arms to work the tools. Then he collapsed into the rover, re-secured his back brace and head cup, and promptly fell asleep.

– Δ –

Not long before the moon-light change began its subtle display of dancing colors in the deeps offshore, a tall figure emerged from the water and strode toward Korad's disabled land rover. The figure was followed by two more thin, dripping bipeds. They walked with the slow-motion roll of ellls on land. Silently, they paused, then came on again, until they stood around the machine, touching it cautiously, as if it would suddenly come alive.

They looked to each other for shared confidence, then, with deft finned hands, one of them disconnected a small cylindrical fitting from the outer circuitry of the hydrogen drive Korad had left partially repaired. The three laughed silently at their good luck and walked off with their treasure, while Korad slept, still believing in his assured destiny and trusting to good luck.

III. Difficult Beginnings

The errant ninth planet in our solar system, Ellason is very difficult to see from Earth. It could have been a normal planet, if it hadn't been clobbered. In the formative stages of the solar system, Ellason was already larger than Earth and still growing, busy scooping up icy planetesimals. While our young sun was fusing hydrogen into helium, Jupiter was kicking nearby icy planetesimals out to the young Oort Cloud. Some, kicked too hard, went sailing off into interstellar space. When Ellason came under Jupiter's influence, however, the giant merely sent the smaller planet off course. No longer in the orbital plane of its fellows, Ellason careened like a billiard ball through the embryonic solar system, until, after a history of near misses, one large ice ball gave it a glancing blow, shattering part of Ellason and slinging the planet into an eccentric 12,000-year orbit, in Earth years. Ellason sped away from the outer planets, and, just beyond the Kuiper Belt at 1100 astronomical units, it reached aphelion and looped back toward the sun, while its broken pieces continued to orbit. Slowly they gathered into thirty moons circling their mother planet, Ellason.

—Aman Telariahn (Amantel), Varok, 2072 CE Earth

SYMBOLS

The great-fish taught her more than senses five
Convey to varoks viewing waves with dread,
Confined to live on land.
They showed her paths that few ellls know
And few would choose to tread.

"This is the path to the hidden library of the ellls," the great-fish Orlegh said, thrusting his powerful lateral fins toward a narrow spit of sand on the ocean bottom.

Ilean's gaze wandered over a jumble of giant boulders crowding the ocean floor. The sand laid a clear path between them, into shallow water on its way to dry beach and cliffs beyond.

"Follow the sand as it widens. As you leave the water, look for a cave in the cliffs to your right. The librarians will meet you and guide you to their cache. Select one instruction leaf and bring it back to me here, so we can begin your lessons."

Ilean swam off eagerly, following the narrow stretch of sand. The water around her was curiously clear. There seemed to be few crawlers and dim-weeds here in the Bay of Cold Deeps. Soon, the shallows met the shore and she was forced to stand. The difficulty of walking meant very little to her, however. Her mind was focused on the exciting task the great-fish had defined: she was to learn the code of written symbols. If she succeeded, she might be apprenticed to the school of librarians. She might become one of the mysterious elite that preserved the history and knowledge of all the ellls of Ellason.

Just ahead, Ilean could see sand piled up in miniature dunes against the cliffs. She carefully placed one leg after the other, following the sand upward. When she stopped to rest, she scanned the cliff for evidence of the library cave. Finally she saw it, a dark shadow high on the face of the cliff.

"Come this way," a gentle barking voice instructed. It sounded strangely muted in air.

A long blue elll wearing a wet-sweater of moss stood at the foot of the cliff. She was a proud female with long plumes and oversized legs made powerful by frequent walking on dry land.

"Ilean, your great-fish friends have forgotten to give you protection from the sand." The tall elll was obviously annoyed. "Take my walkers. There are more in the library." She bent down, slipped thick moccasins of moss from her feet, and watched while Ilean pushed her webbed toes into them. "The library is directly above us in the rocks. It is not far."

Ilean hoped that the librarian meant what she said. Already her legs ached from walking. How could she climb straight up a steep cliff?

She followed the blue elll up a narrow path as it wound through the rocks along the cliff's edge. Giddiness nearly overcame her. In a moment it passed, and she dared to look out over the ocean below. The small cove where Orlegh waited was no longer visible.

"Come."

Ilean followed the librarian as fast as she could, hugging the cliff side as she went. Near the top the path turned and Ilean could look back over the vast ocean. Though she knew its depths were vibrant with life, it looked impersonal and lifeless, giant blobs of angry water bumping endlessly against the stubborn rocks.

As the path broadened, she felt more balanced. Soon she saw the entrance to the ellls' library, a gaping wound in the mountain's side. A few more steps, and it was invisible again, hidden by boulders and scraggly bush twigs. She made her way through the scrub until she was within the cave, a huge open place nearly as large as Harrahn's great-fish cavern.

The library was lined with hand-worked rocks, stacked to make broad steps. A thick growth of tough silver moss warmed and softened them. On the back of each step were racks filled with strips of preserved *ahl* bark.

Two ellls stood high on one wall of steps. They turned to greet Ilean with broad smiles, and a third elll offered her a wet-sweater.

"No thank you," Ilean said. "The great-fish Orlegh has told me to select an instruction leaf and return to him immediately." Her sounds echoed strangely in the great cavern.

"Very well," said a long blue elll. "We would much prefer to teach you ourselves, but we won't argue with the great-fish—at least not yet. When your tutor proves inadequate, do come to our school for help. Our gardens are below the rocks; we will adjust most happily to a new student."

"I'm sure Orlegh is a very adequate teacher. I really have no choice."

"He is not an elll, Ilean. Remember that. Great-fish have one view, a broad view no doubt, but they have fewer eyes than ellls. Their minds are not fed by as many precise senses as ours." The long elll motioned to a stack of *ahl* sheets lying between two rocks on a large central platform of rock. "These are the instruction sheets. You may start wherever you like." She quickly spread them out. "Which leaf do you choose?"

Ilean gingerly reached out to touch the sheets. "May I have this one, please?" Her fingers pointed to a sheet of symbolic characters representing the natural life of Ellason's shores.

The librarian did not hide her surprise. "All right. You may take that sheet," she said, "if you will also take this one." She handed Ilean another. "An elll must know things of the school, as well as things apart. Can you find your way back to Orlegh now?"

"Yes, thank you." Ilean was eager to be off. "But the foot covers . . ."

"Leave them on the shore for your next trip," the tall elll said, "and next time, wear a wet-sweater so you may stay longer."

"Thank you." Ilean backed out of the cavern. *What a beautiful place,* she thought. *How I would like to have it all to myself—to read whatever I pleased—to write my own history. But what a bother these ellls are, inviting me into their school. Now I am bound to them.*

She was right. The invitation was an unkind remark to one so obviously a loner.

Grateful that she was allowed to find the beach alone, Ilean made her way down the path through the rocks, moved clumsily across the sand, and slid into deep water.

"Now where is that great-fish?" She was annoyed at the maze of rocks that surrounded her. She swam between them for some time before she realized that she had wandered into unfamiliar waters. "I'm always lost." Then she remembered. As the great-fish had taught her, she pressed her double soft palate tight against the roof of her mouth and tried to bellow until she felt the awful buzzing in her head.

Apparently, the great-fish Orlegh heard her ultrasonic distress call, for he was soon by her side, reaching for her instruction leaves.

"You have selected two very interesting sheets." He scanned them quickly with the tip of his dorsal fin.

"The tallest elll of the library made me take this one," Ilean said, pointing to the schooling dictionary.

Orlegh looked it over by touch and opened his great jaw with delight. "Yes, I'm not surprised. It is a very good place to begin, I must admit, though, it's hardly a comfortable place for you. Rub your finger from top to bottom here, Ilean, and look carefully. This first symbol represents the idea of an elll who spends time away from the school—a loner."

"But that's me." She was pleased at being represented by the symbols.

"And next to that symbol is one very similar," Orlegh said, watching Ilean closely for her reaction. "It is the symbol for traitor—a false elll."

"I am not a false elll." Ilean touched the symbol with certainty. She would never forget it. "Dumb and deaf and imperfect, but not false."

"Good. You are a loner, not a traitor. You needn't be ashamed of wanting time alone, away from the school. It is sad what is implied by the similarity of these symbols. More and more ellls are becoming loners. It is a gradual change occurring in your species. Soon the schools will have to recognize the loners for what they are, a mutation that will benefit the entire species by broadening its experience."

Orlegh's left fin-tip suddenly whipped around and snatched a crawler from beneath the sand. "Food is scarce here. Eat this, Ilean."

"You must share it with me."

The great-fish hesitated, but accepted the morsel when Ilean bit the crawler in half. "Come and learn more symbols. Then we will go hunting. Later we will see how the symbols can be put together to run smoothly through the logic-clogged channels of your mind."

An Unseen Murder

When fate gave anger's vent its awful chance,
The broken ellls let vengeance fire their zeal;
Thus violence split the school—
For gentle hearts, once torn by hate,
Are rarely known to heal.

Korad woke with a start. The young varok was moving. His rover was far down the beach, and he was being carried away in the firm grasp of six ellls.

The ellls tightened their grasp when they realized that the varok was awake. Korad watched them, fascinated. How similar to varokian faces they were, yet how different their expressions. The ellls' huge black eyes never stared blankly or rested calmly within their faces. They narrowed with every shift of focus, their gaze dancing this way and that beneath delicate laugh lines and brow plumes. Their facial creases flowed with a thousand sensations along gill-lined noses and over high cheekbones.

The blue elll supporting Korad's right leg opened her mouth and turned to the others. He saw her throat contract in sharp pulses, but he heard nothing. Another elll answered her with the same motion, and a high tone penetrated the varok's brain somewhere beyond hearing.

Shamelessly, he probed their minds uninvited. They were taking him into the ocean to leave him tied to one of the varokian sonar transmitters as a warning to all varoks.

"I will die under water!" Korad screamed, suddenly kicking and twisting against the ellls' firm hold.

The ellls grasped him even more securely.

Korad dared to read the ellls' mood again. They were determined to use him to convince the varoks that ellls would tolerate no more noise in their schooling waters.

He moaned and turned his face away. Then he cried out in helpless frustration.

The ellls stopped and looked at him in dismay. They couldn't stand the thought of causing such anguish. Indecision was clear in all minds but one. The blue elll's anger was so full of hate, it allowed no room for pity. To her, the varoks were unfeeling torturers; they deserved no consideration of their life-time. They must be driven from Ellason.

Korad tried to catch the eye of the blue elll, but she would not look at him. She snarled a command to move on and stared fixedly out to sea as they walked into the quiet water nudging the beach.

When his body touched water, Korad struggled in earnest, lurching and rolling and thrashing. It was no good. His back brace and head support were secure in the grip of two ellls, his lifters and clothed legs were held securely by two more.

With a cold surge, water covered him. The ellls were swimming. He cried out again, but the ellls' grips tightened. Their back-fins and broad pedal fins carried him along easily, his head high in the water.

"Why don't you drown me outright?" he shouted angrily in Varokian.

Some of the ellls startled at the sound of his voice, but the blue elll turned in her stroke and clicked off another angry command. Korad's head went under water and was held there while the ellls swam on.

When at last they pulled his head out of the water, he gasped and sputtered and tried to read the blue elll's mind. Her snarling lips sat strangely on a countenance designed by nature for quick smiles and easy laughter. He struggled to trace her mood through a tangle of convoluted channels and interconected senses, so different from Ilean's clear depths. Korad saw no compromise in her. The peace of the ellls had been stolen. As a varok, he would pay for the crimes of his fellows.

On they moved into deeper water. Encased in his braces, exhausted by his efforts, Korad was powerless. How could he tell them who he was—how much he cared for them?

The ellls dropped him and dove out of sight. When they returned laden with *ahl* vines, they pushed him to the surface and tied him to a large varokian buoy floating at anchor nearby. His body slumped painfully against the vines, but at least he could breathe.

A new elll circled behind him, worry knitting his brow plumes. Korad called out for help, and the elll paused in his path, then followed the others into the deeps.

Slowly, the dark sea took on a cap of dense mist. Occasionally a swarm of salt-bees flew by. Korad realized that he was just beyond the shallows, near the deeps where the ellls tended their richest gardens. The upsurging water was pleasantly warm, and a faint red glow far below suggested that he was above one of the great hot chasms that laced the oceans of Ellason.

His only hope lay in what he understood to be the kindly nature of ellls. If another school heard his cries, he would surely be saved. He began to moan, not too loud, but with as much honest anguish as he could muster.

Soon a strange elll appeared. The elll had enormous eyes that dwarfed a face topped with coarse green plumes sprinkled with red and yellow. Korad shrank from him, terrified, for he carried a razor-sharp shell in one hand.

The elll circled the buoy that held the varok captive, then motioned with the shell toward the vines that bound him.

Eagerly, Korad nodded assent and watched the elll begin to cut the vines. Soon another elll joined the first. He was an elder, his plumes touched with gold.

Korad motioned wildly for help. His gravity braces made swimming impossible. He couldn't tell if the message got through or not. The first elll sank out of sight and soon reappeared with several others, among them a handsome large elll, a nervous youth, and a young blue-plumed girl. They swam around the varok, still hanging precariously from the buoy, all the time producing in their throats the barking sound of the sonic code.

Korad saw the angry blue elll who had directed his capture. She came leaping at them in a fury and attacked the large elll with a lethal grip to the gill tissue of his nose. The elder grabbed her from behind. Other ellls converged on those circling Korad.

He looked for the ellls' weapons, but he saw none, only straining arms and thrashing back-fins and kicking feet with web-claws unsheathed.

The blue elll freed herself from the elder and lunged at Korad with her powerful feet. The force of her blow knocked the breath from him and snapped the remaining fibers of the vine that held him to the buoy.

He sank quickly, before he could gulp air or escape from his heavy braces. As he lost consciousness, his last thought was regret. His observations of mixed elllonian behavior would be lost to Amanok and Tera.

– Δ –

Duregal saw the attack and felt the force of Falll's feet on the varok's body as if it had been his own. He exploded with fury and dove for the blue elll, screaming, "Destroyer of schools! Murderer of helpless strangers!" He yanked from his hip plumes the sharp shell knife he had used to cut the varok's bindings. "Go to oblivion. You are no elll." Blind with tears of rage, he easily overtook Falll, rolled under her, and slashed viciously at her throat.

Mercifully, he did not see her startled eyes. His anger turned to anguish as he turned away and dove after the rapidly sinking varok. He called for help as he swam, knowing that he could not lift the unconscious alien to the surface by himself.

The ellls came to him with Melo, the new member of their school, followed by a very disturbed Sa-el and grim-faced Ba-ohl. Together they lifted the varok back to the surface, hauled him into the shallows and tried to clear his lungs, as they would an elll crippled with faulty gills.

The school was calling to them for the accounting. Fighting had stopped, but tempers were still high. The school was divided. There would be no reconciliation now, Duregal realized. He had killed one of their own. There could be no simple healing adjustment for ellls who wrote their anger in blood.

– Δ –

For twelve moon-light changes Ilean studied with the great-fish Orlegh, until the great-fish Harrahn joined them. He was wild with anger. Or was it grief? Or both?

With little rest, the two great-fish led Ilean to her school's eastern gardens. Great-fish don't mince ideas. "This is to be your last and your most terrible lesson," Harrahn told Ilean, and he towed her to the shredded remains of a large blue elll.

"That is nothing I care to see." Ilean said to the great-fish. A flock of scar-fish swarmed about the broken frame of an elll stripped of its flesh, the tips of its scattered bones still decorated grotesquely with blue plumes.

"That was the elll known as Falll," Harrahn said. "She was once a living elll of your school."

"Well, it's quite clear Falll no longer lives," Ilean said.

"Look here, Ilean." With the tip of his long tail, Harrahn pointed to one of the bones. "There is enough flesh left on Falll's neck to see how she died." The great-fish turned the body over with his back fin. Duregal's sharp-edged shell was still lodged between the vertebrae of her neck.

"What a strange accident," Ilean said. "At least she didn't lose a life-moment in pain. There is no reason to grieve, Harrahn."

"There is every reason to grieve, Ilean. Your sponsor, Duregal, killed Falll. He destroyed Falll's life with that shell."

"No." Ilean backed away. "It must have been an accident. Duregal could not be so angry." Her great eyes dwarfed her horror-stricken face. "Anger goes away in schooling." Pain-filled, her sonic staccato rose in protest. "Anger flows into the ocean and is gone. Duregal does not kill other ellls in anger. He is not like you others."

"Others? What others?" As he circled around her in the deep water, the smooth corners of Orlegh's great-fish body flashed by Ilean, his long tail slicing back and forth behind him. For a moment Ilean shuddered at the thought of *eefl*.

"So. You equate great-fish with *eefl*, Ilean? Why are you suddenly frightened by your teachers? Is it because you don't like this lesson? You cannot easily give one elll's death a name or a symbol, can you? But Falll's death does have a name, Ilean, a large name. Look beyond the moment. Transcend the five senses left to you. Look to the future. More than all other ellls, you can understand what might be, for you are not encased in the present by your senses. Your deafness to ultra-sonic signals and your lack of pressure sensitivity leave you free to consider the future as no other elll can. Let the logical channels of your mind understand Falll's death. What will her murder do to the school?"

"I don't know," Ilean cried. "I can't know what hasn't happened." She looked from Harrahn to Orlegh as they swam near her, refusing to let her swim away from the gruesome banquet still in progress.

"What might have happened after Duregal's anger was spent?" Orlegh asked. "Would he return to the school? Would he be driven off?"

"I didn't see him do anything. I wasn't here."

"You see what he did. Here is Falll. Was his the only anger? Who are the 'others,' Ilean, the others that get angry? Would they care whether or not Duregal slashed Falll's throat?"

"I don't believe Duregal killed her."

"Ellls cannot school when they carry such anger against each other."

"Duregal is with the school," Ilean said. "He would not be driven away for this. Falll was always angry. It was her fault." Ilean stared at the great-fish. Why had they turned on her so cruelly? She didn't want to look into their grievous future of split schools.

Orlegh caught her in an embrace that forced her eyes to his sensors. "Duregal has been driven away." The sorrow in his tone overwhelmed her. "He has taken refuge in the rocks of the eastern shores."

"No." Ilean beat against his massive fins. "Let me go. Duregal is safe with the school. He must be."

Orlegh unwrapped the elll, and she darted away, racing against the ideas they had planted in her mind. She would get away, far away from the great-fish, so their ideas would not take root.

She glanced back. Orlegh and Harrahn had made no move to follow. She swam on even faster, determined to leave them.

As she sliced through the bright water, she felt time flowing over her, time sewn with anger. She saw visions of schools at war, murder between ellls, rotting elllonian bones littering once-beautiful gardens. The seeds of the great-fish's broad vision had found fertile soil in the logical channels of a mind too long denied all its sensual input. The great-fish had lifted her away from her immediate senses to possibilities never before realized in an elllonian mind. The future was suddenly hers to ponder, and she was terrified by it.

More Assumptions

The varoks clung with fear to plans undone—
The patterns of their minds so etched in stone,
Entrapped in all by pride,
They could not credit ellls with this:
A vision not their own.

"For all that was ever sacred on Varok, open your mind to me, Tera," Amanok whispered as their forearms made contact. "I need to be released. If I could cut loose from this miserable temper, I could absorb this managerial attack of Tekram's and come away stronger."

His best friend, the elder Tera, the comforting woman he loved better than hot *challall* cakes, leaned into his body as touch became bearable. "If I could split my mind in two, half would be yours, Amanok. You know that."

"Yes, I do. And that would be more than enough, Tera."

"Thank you for that."

"I need your thoughts right now." Amanok was finding it difficult to stay rational. To be so close to this magnificent woman was to be undone if there was to be no mind-link with her. *I need your temperance, your judgment, your ability to reserve judgment,* he urged in mind. *As director of our effort to contact the ellls, Tekram has spared nothing in his attack. If the boy Korad fails, I will lose all credibility on Ellason. My work will come to an end. I should not have sent him off to seek out ellls.*

"You brought a rover to him right after you reprimanded him for his treatment of the injured elll," Tera continued in speech. "Your emotions took charge."

"It is no secret. I have treated him as a son."

The amused glint in Tera's eyes helped Amanok maintain control. "Tekram will use my indiscretion to his advantage, you may be sure." He gathered Tera in his arms as they stretched out on the g-brace. "I am too old for extended mental struggles like this, Tera."

"You have ignored the rule books, my half-released old fool. Be grateful and keep your insults for Tekram."

"I'm thankful that the members of the Directorate are not strict authoritarians."

"It's true the rules here are meant as guidelines, not rigid tracks. The Directorate gave Korad his chance because they saw that the boy had convictions. They agreed to let him round off his sharp corners on Ellason's rough beaches."

"A cruel decision, really. He could die out there alone."

"I believe that he might accomplish more with the ellls than we thought possible, Amanok."

"He is a genius I think, and an idealist. He could set back our mission here a thousand years."

"I think he won't."

Amanok felt the reserved corner of Tera's mind sticking like a thorn between them. "Why do you say that? How can you know him so well?"

"During the long flight from Varok, Korad and I bonded as mentor and student. He would not deny me the emotional release it provided."

"You are capable of such release, Tera."

She sat up on the g-brace. The light brown of her powerful body contrasted with the darker folds of Amanok's time-roughened skin. She brushed the silver-tinged hair from her eyes and straightened her tunic.

"You, too, Amanok, are perfectly able to return to reason at will, when you go on your emotional jaunts. You sink into pure devotion; quite deliberately you take the risk of not regaining rationality. Then you recapture your reason and start a good argument before I have time to defend myself." She laughed with the delight Amanok found so infectious. "I think you've had enough admiration for today. We had best get to work."

"Ah, but it would be such a pleasure to love you and be rational at the same time. What a varok I could be."

"Love was never meant to be rational."

She gave Amanok a playful nudge, and he jumped as if she had branded him. "Have pity, Tera. I am no longer in any state to tolerate touch." He started to get up, but returned the teasing by grasping at Tera's arms to pull himself up.

Their laughter was rudely interrupted by a loud knock on the entryway.

"Yes? Come." Tera undid the entry's closure.

"Conference area two. Now." Tekram looked angry, standing there as though he had been waiting for his opportunity to interrupt. "We are under attack by ellls."

"That cannot be." Amanok had no faith in Tekram's interpretation of elllonian behavior.

"On the contrary, it cannot be denied," Tekram insisted. "Come at once. We have an emergency."

"Who's emergency?" Amanok called after him down the hallway.

"Let him go," Tera pleaded. "Don't press him. We might still find a way around his faulty convictions."

"I doubt that, Tera. His mind is like knotted iron. Didn't your patches catch his mood? He is convinced that the ellls must be tamed—caught and trained like incognizant beasts—for their own good, Tera, for their own good. Can you imagine it?"

– Δ –

The Directorate always stood during conferences. It helped shorten the meetings and reduce the talk to essentials. Only those with a case to build wore braces.

While gathering in the conference room, they found displayed an intricate, delicately balanced array of joined shells and woven sea vines.

"This device is ingenious," Amanok said "Whoever made this understands the propagation of sound in water."

"Ingenious?" Tekram's annoyance was obvious. He did not like the focus of the meeting as it shifted away from the attack on the varoks' sound device. "Ellls could not have made such a thing alone. The great-fish have allied themselves with the ellls, against us. They have designed these sound-triggered traps, built them with the aid of elllonian hands. The ellls set them out where our divers were sure to be caught while working on the elll-varok communications network."

Amanok disagreed with everything Tekram said. "The ellls have systematically destroyed only those loudspeakers that adjoin their gardens. Is it surprising they have set traps? The attempt to communicate by broadcasting propaganda into the ellls' waters has failed."

"The ellls object to such sound intrusion for good reason." Tera chose her argument with care. "It disrupts their lives and well-being at every level."

"I must agree." Okarian Telrak, Chief Observer of Cognizant Life, could be trusted not to compromise. "Our team has reviewed the ellls' behavior. We have also studied the damage done to the recovered loudspeakers. The speakers were attacked." He nodded to Tera. "Ellls of all the schools we observe have bitterly resented the alien sound."

"We agree," Tekram snapped. "The ellls erupted violently to a modest intrusion. This experiment has demonstrated conclusively that the ellls are enduring severe psychological pressure from overcrowding."

"The sound you blasted into their gardens was not a 'modest intrusion,'" Tera said.

Trehn Okarian joined the argument with a thoughtful observation. "For many centuries intrusion of excessive noise has been a crime on Varok. I object to applying to alien species intrusions that are unacceptable to us."

"The transmission was not excessive." Tekram put an end to his pacing by standing stiffly beside the lab director, Mahar.

"There was an immediate migration of scar-fish from the affected areas," Trehnor said. "That is an excessive effect."

"According to great-fish." Tekram spoke with an immobile face. "The great-fish are taking belligerent action against us."

"We have no evidence for that." Mahar's tone had the force of the laboratory's integrity behind it.

"The intricacy of this trap—this great-fish trigger mechanism— proves that the great-fish are inciting the ellls to violence." Tekram countered. "The trigger is perfectly balanced to go off as soon as the loudspeakers begin transmitting. One diver, Teklor, was caught by the leg and nearly drowned as he attempted to service a damaged speaker."

"How was he caught?" Amanok asked.

"The sound of our broadcast sonic code triggered this mechanism, which released a large net. The net was propelled toward him with small explosive packets fixed to its circumference."

"Then why is Teklor still alive?" Amanok saw the omitted information in Tekram's mind. He looked to the other varoks of the Directorate to approve a mind probe of Tekram.

The approval came with the Directorate's silent meeting of minds. To avoid the embarrassment of a mind probe, Tekram spoke fully. "A large elll, an elder, I believe, released our trapped diver before there was brain damage from unconsciousness."

"So they meant no harm to anything but the devices." Tera was thoroughly relieved. "We have seen it proven over and over again, Tekram. Ellls want to be left alone. Our job is to convince them that they need our friendship."

Tekram began pacing again, controlling his rising frustration with visible effort. "We have failed—after centuries of trying."

Amanok saw that most of the varoks in the room agreed. "Failed only on our terms," he said.

"The traps were meant to kill," Tekram insisted. "The elll that released Teklor was a renegade, a rough old loner, half-starved, obviously not part of any school. His interference means nothing. The fact remains that we are being attacked by healthy ellls. Our intentions of goodwill are being ignored."

"It is not goodwill to disrupt the ellls' schooling with alien noise." Tera forced the issue. "I insist that all programs of sound intrusion and aggressive contact with ellls be stopped immediately."

"And I insist," Tekram said calmly, "that a large sampling of ellls be taken captive immediately, that they be educated in population control and released throughout the oceans of Ellason to re-train the major schools and disperse them into more remote areas."

The Director of Integrated Studies, Loktel, approved Tekram's counterproposal. "We have done all we can to induce the ellls to come to us of their own volition. On the large scale, the ellls are in more danger from their own rising tempers and food-competition than from us. We can't do more harm with an educational program than we have already done."

With a strong patch signal, Mahar agreed. "Extended contact will make the ellls see who we really are. Now, please, back to the more serious problem. If the great-fish are instigating violence against us, we had best go directly to them and find out why. Iktel, organize an expedition across the Great Chasm to the City of Great-fish."

"Now wait. Wait just a moment." Amanok didn't like the sudden turn in the argument. "You are assuming that ellls did not design this trigger mechanism. I don't agree. No great-fish ever devised such a thing. Great-fish are mental giants, philosophically and historically, but they couldn't fit two turtle shells together to make a lamp, as ellls do."

He continued, and the others began to listen. "We have always underestimated the ellls' intelligence, because it is exhibited in very subtle ways—in the location of the gardens to trap the most heat, in their use of natural fertilizers and intricate plantings to maximize fruiting and reduce disease. We haven't guessed half of what they can do. We have found tools that are used to facilitate underwater gardening, devices that seem to be ingenious musical instruments. And don't forget: The great majority of our finds were a mystery until we realized that they were toys: game pieces for mental gymnastics, selective shields for ultrasonic sculpture contests, sports equipment for echo dodging and water games of all sorts. A case can be made that the ellls have a finely developed, highly selective technology."

Tera agreed. "All the evidence, including this newly discovered sound-activated trap, supports my theory that the ellls have a huge memory and an intricate sense of logic located in their large forebrains."

"I thought the forebrain was linked to the echo locator organ behind the ultrasonic generator in the ellls' mid-ventral skull," Trehnor said.

"Their forebrain is as large as ours, and it does contain echo location sense." Tera grew more uncertain as she threw out untested theory. "Something more profound, like a special logic or memory capability, must also be located there. The ellls are not stupid just because they make toys out of natural materials."

"Be that as it may—the ellls' intelligence is limited. Their sonic code is not a pricise language." Oktel stated the ancient doctrine as a matter of fact. "Elllonian intelligence is also limited by the fact that they are locked into an aquatic environment by Ellason's huge size and intense gravity. We are seeing in ellls nothing more than the partial development of intelligence related to their excellent prehensile hands.

"However, for more intelligence to evolve, one needs speech, a written history, accumulated knowledge, the specialization and integration of huge amounts of information that only a written language makes possible. I don't know if ellls invented these traps you hold in your hands, Amanok, but to ascribe to them some purposeful, long-range plan is too much."

"Thank you, Oktel." Mahar looked to the Directorate as one by one they nodded their assent. It was finished. "We will follow Tekram's program of direct contact."

Amanok glanced at Tera. A hollow knot of helplessness spread through their minds. "You have not heard us," he said. "You are blind to the ellls' intelligence, because it is not varokian in nature."

Strange Homecoming

Her dullness to ellls' bounding sounds that see,
Her deafness to the high-pitched calls that rule
Had left her mind undone.
Thus blinded as no elll had been,
She saw beyond the school.

Ilean raced blindly away from the great-fish and the horror of Falll's corpse. She did not think of the dangers of being alone, of hunger and cold and attack by *eefl*.

A vision of terrible futures filled her mind, distorting everything she passed—rocks and sedentary plants, light sea moss and the dimly flashing patterns of mud-worm and dawn-fish. Time swam loose and wild.

If all newly hatched ellls were to become loners, schools would soon be obsolete. If too many ellls were hatched, schools would grow too large. If all ellls ate too much, gardens would have to be bigger; other schools would have to move over. When there was no more room for gardens, ellls would become angry.

Angry enough to kill? Ilean could not believe the great-fish. She would prove them wrong. Duregal would tell her what really happened to Falll.

Like a cat playing with an armed mouse, she toyed with the idea of looking beyond the present. *What might be—if?* A new concept, *if.* Change followed *if* and whole new futures blossomed. Even good ones. *Why not? Good things could be made to happen.*

The thought of Duregal gave her purpose, and she began to accept the concept of a knowable future. Some futures were good. It would be good to be home in the unchanging, ever-changing shallows where the life of sea and land joined.

Instinctively, she followed warm waters and worked north, then westward across the Currents of Altoon. Quickly she by-passed the great-fish caves bordering the Northern Shallows. Finally she arrived at the familiar rocky shallows frequented by her school. She realized that time had been her friend. She had fed well and gained strength. Distance was no longer daunting; fear had become a stranger.

Smooth water, glide across my moments,
Warm depths of the sea, hold me safe.
Deep tangle of worm and fuel leaf, grow to feed me.
Warm bubbles sailing upward, carry my comfort.
Great Heart of All, breathe deep into my mind.
Don't let me sleep too far from time unseen.
Don't let me dream when I should wake,
And when I wake, don't let me hate the dream.

She sang alound and laughed at herself, loving the singing more than the song. "Such wonderful nonsense, these words. Fun and non-sense for an elll trained by librarians and great-fish. But not all of it is nonsense. Words carry more than definitions, don't they, Orlegh? I miss you. You would love Duregal."

She decided to find her school as soon as she could, to tell Duregal of her adventures, to teach the school what the varoks' sound intrusion really meant—what the great-fish believed it meant—to help them re-adjust to the new Ilean. She was a loner who could come and go without disturbing their patterns, without forcing an adjustment every visit.

As she approached the moss-framed shore of the Rocky Shallows, Ilean began to call out her presence, using the high ultrasonic locator signal the great-fish had taught her. She could feel the signal she made, but she could not see the echo it generated in most elllonian brains. She would never experience a three-dimensional picture of the ocean and its restless inhabitants—but she knew it would bring the school to her, if they were within three or four hundred *pallons*—her *pallon*, surely now as long as Duregal's.

As she came over a familiar rise in the ocean floor, she saw, spread out before her, the school's moonlight tulip pasture. It was lush and orderly once again. The moonlight plants waved to her with broad leaves on long slender branches, their blossoms hanging like miniature lanterns, nearly ready for eating, their overlapping petals plump and white with tasty sap.

Ilean drifted down into the garden and moved through the waist-high rows. Around and under, over and down again, she swam like a tad, oblivious to everything but the mystery of the circles of tall green leaves hovering over their white treasure.

"Who is there?" An ultrasonic demand sent a faint buzz through

Ilean's skull. Now Ilean knew what the buzz meant. She answered with the ultrasonic cry of welcome. It echoed off the rock-studded hills that surrounded the moonlight pasture.

Immediately her call was followed by a stronger vibration. Someone had answered her. She was ecstatic. She had heard—not understood, but at least recognized—an ultrasonic signal from another elll. The buzzing irritation was now a golden thread leading to full acceptance by her school.

She gave her cry again, then emerged from the rows of moonlight plants and drifted upward over the garden, waiting for the school to come to her.

Suddenly three ellls dove out from behind the rocks that bordered the western edge of the garden. "What are you doing here?" It was Sa-el. He swooped down on Ilean and clamped a lethal hand over her nasal gills.

"Don't you see? Let her go. It is Ilean." Navell's familiar sonic bark sounded like the most beautiful of songs.

Ilean tore away from Sa-el's grasp and embraced the elder, who rolled over the garden with her in a welcoming embrace that restored her to the life of the school. Here was the acceptance she had always wanted.

"This is Melo." Sa-el reluctantly met Ilean's questioning gaze. "She came to Navell from the school that raided our moonlight pasture just before you disappeared."

"I have been adjusted to this school for many moon-light changes, Ilean," Melo said, "and still this monster remembers the sad reason for my happy change of schools."

"I can't deny that you were a prize hostage," Navell teased.

"I have never been a hostage," Melo argued. "Come, Ilean, adjust with me. These others can do without us."

"I am blind to your patterns, Melo, but I will imitate you."

"That will do." Navell nodded approval, and the males drifted aside to watch the slow, pulsing dance of the two females. Soon the tempo of their adjustment began to accelerate. Navell and Sa-el tried to join in their swimming pattern, but Ilean and Melo dashed away. The chase was on. The four ellls sped back and forth over the garden, around the border rocks, through the sparse *ahl* grove, and over the surface of the ocean in close arcs that threw them together and set them to mating with complete abandon, until they sank exhausted to the ocean floor, thoroughly adjusted.

"The great-fish have taught you many things, Ilean," Navell said with a huge, tired smile.

"I can go through the motions of adjustment. The great-fish taught me what to do, but I can't really feel it, except for the mating. The great-fish are gloomy tutors who smile a lot. They take weird delight in teaching poor ellls what they can't ever learn."

"I am so glad to see you school . . . normally."

"As a 'real elll' is what you meant. I heard you, Navell." Ilean understood he was trying to be kind. "The great-fish also taught me to read minds." She got up with a laugh and dove quickly around her three fellows as they lay on the soft moss floor. "For instance, I know from your mind-body language that there are two loners here."

"Nonsense." Melo laughed "You know that from the adjustment."

"But don't you see, Melo? I wouldn't have known that before the great-fish taught me to see with more than eyes."

"You see too much then," Sa-el snorted angrily. "I am no loner."

"Did I say you were?" Ilean asked.

"You know Navell is no loner." Sa-el pushed off from the ocean floor and paced quickly to the nearby rocks and back.

"How did I know that?" Ilean asked. "You forget my disability, Sa-el."

The magnificent dark elll stopped his pacing. "I'm sorry, Ilean, forgive me. I don't like to admit my loner tendencies."

"You must all be loners to stay out here, apart from the school."

"Necessity makes loners of us all, my dear. I ache for the school and wish I had never agreed to this job as watchman. It's quite unnecessary."

"You're wrong, Navell," Melo's urgency was alarming. "We have chased many strange ellls from these borders. Navell really stayed here to be with me, Ilean." The lovely blue elll glanced uneasily at Sa-el. "I was the logical one to stay, being a loner, with Sa-el."

"Does Ba-ohl know you are alive and in your home shallows, Ilean?" Sa-el's discomfort rang clear.

"I haven't seen Ba-ohl." Ilean tried to remember everything that had happened to her since Ba-ohl left her in the shallows to join the races. "I wandered off and was attacked by an *eefl*. A varok saved my life. Then the great-fish took me to their city. Didn't the great-fish tell you I was with them? They know how it pains the school to have an elll leave."

"They told us only that you were alive, that you would be changed."
Navell spoke with a new tone. His sonic voice was measured, almost
respectful. "We didn't understand what they meant, so we assumed
you no longer existed."

"Well, now the school will always know where I am. I will be
no more trouble to you. And I have learned the most exciting thing,
Navell—"

"But you must wait to tell all of us." It was a request. "We are only
three here. We are watching this garden while the school checks between the eastern garden and the Viortahk."

Ilean's stomach turned. "Why did the school go there? That is an
awful place—cold, and full of *eefl*. I hope they are not still looking
for me. Why didn't the great-fish tell you where I was? They used to
tell us everything that happened in the Great Basin and across the
Great Chasm."

"No longer, I'm afraid, Ilean," Sa-el answered. "The great-fish will
tell us very little these days. They are concerned that we destroy the
varoks' noisemakers, but they will not tell us what else to do. The
varoks' sound makes mating and eating impossible, and it muddies
our echo pictures. The school can't navigate with that noise blasting
through the water. Even our gardens are suffering. The blossoms are
late. The school has gone toward the Viortahk to find and destroy all
the aliens' noise makers."

"The varoks will just make more. Will you destroy the source of all
their gadgets? Their stone cave is far beyond the beach. Only a narrow
channel flows to it. Will the school try to go in there?" Ilean felt nothing but disdain for the thought. "Ellls can't climb the straight cliffs of
stone. If we go too close, we will all be taken captive."

"You talk of things that are not happening here, like a great-fish.
Have they taught you to see more than the waters tell?"

"The great-fish taught me that sounds echo on, far beyond the rocks,
into time that has not yet passed."

"I don't understand how that can be, Ilean." Sa-el circled very close
to her and led her away from the others. He spoke in a confidential
sonic tone that puzzled her. "But I love you better for your strange talk.
You are no longer a loner tad who must hide in rocks to mate, and
you are more than a female who treasures her eggs. When the school

returns, do not ask questions or talk of things that have not been. The past is done, and the future does not go beyond the moonlight tulip harvest or the next egg laying."

As he spoke, Ilean's heart leapt to her throat. Sa-el was not only accepting her for herself, he was joining in her uniqueness, respecting her experience apart from the school and revealing to her the hidden channels of his mind. She loved Sa-el then with the full power of her loner qualities and vowed she would be the link he needed between his own desires and the school's demands.

He accepted the commitment, moving through the water with her. Their mating was like no experience either had ever had before. For long moments they knew only each other.

Finally, the water took substance around them, and they found their voices.

Sa-el was troubled. "I have just remembered that you don't know about Duregal."

"The great-fish told me what happened to Falll."

"Did they tell you about the school?"

"No," Ilean said. "I know nothing about what happened after Falll's death."

Sa-el's eyes grew strange and hard. "For Duregal's sake, try to learn how you might help him. He has been banished from the school. As his tad, and a loner returned from across the Great Chasm, reeking with the smell of great-fish, you will be watched closely. When you and Ba-ohl and I help Duregal, it must be with great caution."

Sa-el's words grew hesitant, as if it took all his courage to say them. "There are stories about you. And from what you have said, some may be true. Someday you must tell me how you came within mating distance of a varok. Meanwhile, you must not speak of him, or any varok."

Ilean was not focused on thoughts of varoks. She could not believe what Sa-el had said about Duregal. He couldn't be banished from the school. Such cruelty was impossible. To a schooling elll, separation meant torture and death.

The Tearing Away

Bright water moved the weeds in dances wild.
Waves filled with pain, tossed high, bedecked with grief,
Fell crashing round her soul.
The school was split; the tide was turned.
The sea cried disbelief.

"Ilean." Ba-ohl whispered low sonic code so that his sound would not alarm the sleeping school. "I have found him."

From her bed on the ocean floor beneath a large overhanging rock, Ilean awoke. Quickly, she moved behind the rock so they could talk.

"Is he well?" Ilean asked. "Can he find food alone? When can I go to Duregal?"

"Don't speak his name," Ba-ohl cautioned. "The school must not know where he is. He has your young varok with him."

"My varok?" Ilean paled, remembering Sa-el's warning. "Then it is true. The great-fish tried to tell me. Duregal releases trapped varoks. The school calls him traitor."

"I also release trapped varoks," Ba-ohl confided with huge, frightened eyes. "Sa-el, also. We believe you when you say the varoks mean well. And Duregal has seen varokian kindness in Korad, as you did. He has become Duregal's school. That is why your old sponsor is still alive. He lives because he must—to keep the varok alive."

"Then you know that the varoks' sound devices are not meant to harm us," Ilean said. "The great-fish told me what the noise means before they showed me Falll's bones. They said there would be more deaths when the gardens of ellls become too small."

"The great-fish are more to be believed than ellls who take life-moments away from varoks," Ba-ohl agreed. "Come with me now. I'll take you to them before the school awakens."

Ilean and the young male drifted slowly upward in the water, away from the garden where the ellls rested.

As they swam away, their pressure registered on the hexagonal plates of three ellls who kept watch. A ripple of alarm sped across the school. It roused itself from the garden as one large organism and followed in the wake of Ilean and Ba-ohl's scent.

– Δ –

Sa-el, Navell, and others who believed in Ilean followed along with the school. Sa-el grew more and more alarmed as their trail led toward the eastern rocks. Ba-ohl must have found Duregal. The fool was taking Ilean to the old renegade.

Sa-el believed the school would kill Duregal on sight; his name was evil. A primitive, cold logic had infected their minds, a logic far different from the clear reasoning of happier, freer times, when gardens were not raided and all ellls could sleep as a school, without constant guarding.

Suddenly the rocky shore became visible to ultrasonic search probes. With the crack of its whip-like temper, the school reprimanded the impatient elll who had sent it. "Keep silence. Ba-ohl will detect your signal," the lead elll whispered in sonar.

Sa-el apologized, hoping that the probe had warned Ba-ohl away.

– Δ –

Ba-ohl felt Sa-el's ultrasonic probe like the shocking sound of a burglar alarm. He turned and quickly scanned the water behind him. The school's flowing outline echoed in his ultrasonic sense. "We will change course, Ilean," he whispered to the frightened girl. "We'll head into the warm deeps and let them find us absorbed in a loner's retreat. They will remember how you preferred to mate in warm hidden places."

"It won't work, Ba-ohl. They know I was welcomed back to the school by common mating. It was quite normal. The great-fish taught me how to be a part of the school. Everyone knows I no longer insist on a lonely mating."

"Except with Sa-el."

"Yes."

Ba-ohl recognized Ilean's passion for Sa-el, but it meant little to one so closely knit to the school.

"What shall we do, Ilean?" Ba-ohl's mind worked sluggishly, as if his thoughts could not stir without the impetus and collective assurance of the school.

"Let's go to the bottom and pretend we are searching for mud turtles," Ilean said. "We'll say I've decided to make something beautiful from the shells. The school will believe that."

The two ellls dove for the ocean floor, but as they neared the warm currents of the deep, Ba-ohl felt the ultrasonic probe of a single elll, searching from the direction of the rocks.

"No, stay back," Ba-ohl cried in ultrasonic, knowing the signal could not reach the old elll in time. Already a flashing of echo locators told him the school had found Duregal. It was heading toward the rocky coast to intercept him.

"Make for the shore, Ilean," Ba-ohl shouted, sprinting ahead. "We've got to reach Duregal before the school takes him."

Ilean followed Ba-ohl's trace as best she could. Upward they swam. They could travel faster by leaping rhythmically across the surface. For a time Ilean kept pace with the larger male, until he drew near the rocks.

Ba-ohl swiftly threaded his way through the dangerous outer rim of the shore, where large boulders tore the deep water into unpredictable and treacherous three-dimensional patterns. Ilean, relying solely on her underwater vision, could not keep up. "Go ahead," she shouted to an unseen Ba-ohl in her limited ultrasonic vocabulary. "You can find me later."

A faint buzz in her skull told her that Ba-ohl had probably heard her. She swam to the rocks and pulled herself out of the water. Her varok should be somewhere nearby. She would warn him to stay on land.

With great effort she climbed a rock near the shore and looked back. In the center of the small bay, a circle of frothing ripples told her that the school was no longer moving through the water.

Ilean's first impulse was to join them, distract them, but the water boiled and seethed with the green arches of leaping ellls. Then the boiling patches of ocean parted, as if the school itself was dividing. A shiver of dread crept along Ilean's back-fin. The boiling patches came together, retreated, and came together again.

"No! No!" she screamed, terror-stricken, determined to stop her beloved school from tearing itself apart.

As she started down the rock to reenter the water, a strong brown hand caught her arm, and a familiar, soothing sound demanded that she stay. Ilean turned and stared into Korad's varokian face. He was panting heavily, holding on to her for support, exhausted from running to catch her. He shook his head, and she knew that she was as helpless as he. There was nothing they could do to help Duregal or the warring school.

For moments that seemed like the longest of moon-light changes, the elll and the varok sat together on the rock, watching the tragedy unfold on the ocean's restless face. Ellls clashed in eruptions of foam. Tangles of blue and green appeared and disappeared.

Then, as if the nightmare had suddenly ended, the water's surface fell quiet. The sea lay leaden and gray, undisturbed, as if nothing had changed. Dense warm mists rolled down from the inland hills, like a shroud covering Ilean's school.

ELLL AND VAROK

Upon the rocks she found a comfort strange,
A mind that knew hers well, yet could not say
What dwelt within its own.
As one, they sensed the edge of doom
And ran from danger's way.

Ilean found herself clutching the varok. When the battle ended they didn't move, and Korad read well what was in her mind.

She remembered his shuddering when she had clung to him for warmth on the tiny island in the Viortahk. She pulled away now so he wouldn't suffer.

"No, no, it's all right," Korad said in Varokian. He stroked her hand, and she drank in the comfort of his touch and the sound of his speech. "Duregal has helped me to accept the touch of ellls. Your skin is like moss. It has the feel of cloth."

Ilean heard the varok click off Duregal's name in an imitation of the ellls' sonic code, and her mind leapt with hope at the sound.

She looked out to the sea, praying that the rough old elll would soon emerge from the waves with Ba-ohl. And perhaps Sa-el would come with the others. They had all been good to her since her return from the great-fish. They must have been the ones who tried to stop the school from taking Duregal. They would come to her soon, if they could survive the splitting of the school.

She and Korad waited, until the moon-light change waned. Nothing moved but the shore pool lightning bugs. Ilean studied Korad. He was not beautiful now—not as she remembered him during their first meeting. His face was drawn with sad lines and angled planes even sharper than she remembered. Dark hollows beneath his eyes made his stare seem haunted and wild. His covering of woven thread hung loosely on bones she hadn't noticed before, and his hair lay in long, dull strands around the warty patches behind his ears. She realized he had been living away from his varokian school for a long time—at least since Duregal saved him from Falll's attack.

"Duregal has been keeping you alive," she said in a dry sonic bark, "and now I will do the same." She was startled to see the varok nod his agreement. "Perhaps I should take you back to the Viortahk, back to the place where varoks live."

"No," Korad said with a vigorous signal of head and hands.

"So, you are like great-fish," Ilean said. "You know me before I know myself. I don't like that, you know, not one bit. My mind is not for the school, not for great-fish, not for varoks. I am Ilean, a loner. I care for the lost and the sick. You may not read my mind without my permission."

Korad nodded agreement and covered his patches with his hands. Then he drew the outline of a great-fish in the sand, indicated smallness with fingers barely separated, and pointed to himself.

"Just a little like great-fish," Ilean said in sonic, and Korad nodded again, uncovering his patches with a questioning grin. "You have promised," Ilean said. "You will not read my mind unless I give you permission—like this," and her hand spiraled upward in an inviting gesture.

Korad allowed himself a laugh of delight. As her signal for permission, the elll had used the gesture varoks use for greeting. This elll was far more creative than the kindly Duregal, who had never caught on to varokian mood-reading as a simple method of communication.

Before long, a cool wind drove them to shelter on the shore, where they sat quietly, still waiting, until Ilean lost patience. "Why haven't they come?"

The desperate sounds of her sonic code beat like a bad whistle against Korad's ears. He took Ilean's hand and turned it into her spiraling gesture. She nodded. "Ba-ohl should have come to me by now," she said.

"I'm sure Duregal would come to me, also," Korad said in Varokian, "if he were still alive. Does Ba-ohl know you are on shore?"

He wished desperately Ilean could understand him. He pointed to the sea and to his own head then to Ilean and to the sea again, crossed out the sea, and finally pointed to the rock on which they stood. "Do they know you are not in the water, but on land, here?" he repeated in Varokian. Then he tried imitating the ellls' sonic code, but it was no use. His soft noises were too poor an imitation of their hollow sonar clicks. Finally, the varok managed to click off an approximation of Duregal's name, saw the recognition in Ilean's mind, and pushed her toward the water, motioning that she should come back quickly.

At last she understood. She would try the ultrasonic locator signal the great-fish had taught her. If Ba-ohl and Sa-el or Duregal were still alive, they would come to her immediately once they picked up her sound in water.

She slid into the water and welcomed the sea as a comforting blanket around her. The horror of the school's splitting was not a memory to cultivate. It was soon lost in the friendly lights of tiny creatures and glowing, moss-covered rocks, resting on rippled mud. The battle was a memory to be discarded, another mindless tragedy of marine life.

She swam beyond the field of rocks and sent her signal into the deeps. While she waited for Ba-ohl to find her, her mind fought to preserve her usual sense of the present. She wanted only to feel the sea around her, to forget that Ba-ohl might be dead. She couldn't believe that she would be in danger if the alienated part of her school found her.

Hanging on to thoughts of possible futures was too difficult, and not pleasant. Korad's warning had been clear enough, but it was a varokian sort of warning—not something an ell was likely to mind for long. The thought of real danger from her old school was too alien. The self doesn't turn against itself.

Then, memory of the school's battle rose like a new plant, growing in the soil the great-fish had cultivated. She could not ignore it. The great-fish had opened the flood gates of her thought beyond the present, and she was faced with a reality larger than the immediate warmth of friendly seas. The school had turned in on itself, destroyed itself. The unthinkable was done. It would not be undone by forgetting. If the sundered school found her before Ba-ohl did, they would instinctively kill her as the bitterest of enemies.

Like a sudden shaft of light at the end of a very long tunnel, she realized she could choose her own fate. She didn't have to wait to be found. Ba-ohl, if he were still alive, would know to look for her on shore with the varok.

She rushed for shore. More frightened than ever, she saw three alternative paths into her future. She was desperate to avoid the short, violent one. The school must not catch her.

She leapt through the water, frantic to gain more speed, heedless of the rocks hidden just beneath the surface. She slid past a giant boulder and skinned her shoulder before she slowed enough to see her way more safely. The mosses outlining the rocks glowed dimly with a deep purple color. She longed for the bright light of the moss of the Northern Shallows so she could move through the rocks at better speed.

At last she found the rock where she had left her varok. She pulled herself out of the water and lay out flat, expanding her lungs and closing off her gills, listening, waiting for the firm brown touch of the alien.

Nothing moved but a tiny crawler. It scurried on four legs beyond Ilean's long, fast tongue and dived on luminescent silk into a deep crack in the rocks. The mist covered the shore, obliterating all but the dim infrared outline of the cliffs beyond. Silent and gray, the sea became an invisible canopy of time, hiding the ominous future of ellls.

Ilean shuddered with cold. The varok could not have gone far, she thought; he had little strength for walking.

She tore two broad sheets of moss from the rock and tied them to her feet with a length of sea vine. Cautiously she inched away from the sea. Rocks of every size and shape lay scattered in shallow water. She tired before she had crossed half of them. The varok was not to be seen.

Could he have found a better path across the rocks? She rejected the idea. Where was he?

"Three more big rocks," she told herself, and she pushed on. Though somewhat hardened by her treks to the library, her feet, designed more for speed in water than support on land, still barked loudly after just a little abuse.

From the base of the third rock she could see a length of flat mud leading onto a sheltered beach. Surely Korad had found this beach. He must be resting in a warm corner protected from the mist.

Ilean worked her way toward the beach until the rocks ended. Expecting at any moment to see the brown figure of the alien waiting to greet her, she stared into the mists, willing him to appear.

Instead, twenty ellls appeared before her—ghosts out of a past she already mourned. Ellls of the alienated school were rolling on moss-covered feet toward the open water.

Ilean stood still, as if frozen, fascinated by the sight of so many ellls out of water. She watched as their green legs strained against the ground and their necks bent under the weight of their plumed heads. Long painful scratches broke the symmetry of their hexagonal lines, and dark bruises marred the smooth moss of their skin tiles.

Far worse than their injuries was the smoldering anger that filled their eyes and the clouds of grief that distorted their faces. The splitting of the school had left scars far deeper than moss. Even now, long moments after the battle was done, it was still eroding away joy in the ellls' life-moments.

Ilean wondered if they, too, had seen beyond the present. *The bitterness of the battle will not fade quickly from their echo location memory*, she thought, *because their tile moss will not grow where they have been scratched and hit and scraped with sharp shells. The anger will come back every time they look at the scars, every time they see the ellls who attacked them. The school will swim together very closely now. Surely they must fear a future of closed seas and ugly suspicions.*

They passed her by, too engrossed in their own pain and effort to notice her dim shape in the shadow of the rocks. Ilean did not move until she had heard all of them enter the water. Then she followed their tracks back from the beach, into the rocks tumbled together at the base of a jagged cliff. Had they taken Korad?

"Please, my varok," she screamed, "be alive!"

Her cry was answered by the rasping throat noise of the varok.

"Call again," Ilean cried in sonic code. "The school's tracks go every which way. Where are you?"

The sound came again, hollow but muffled. Ilean turned to follow it, working slowly up the rocks until she came upon a deep cleft in the side of the jumbled cliff.

Korad called again. "Here, Ilean. I'm in here."

The elll squeezed through the cleft and found the varok huddled behind two huge boulders. His hands and feet were tightly bound with sea vines.

"Thank goodness your friends didn't know enough to gag me," Korad said. "Get something to cut the vines, Ilean. We must hurry."

His sounds had a nice rhythm, Ilean thought, wishing she could understand more of them.

"The ellls will be back in less than a thousand leaps. They want to use me as a decoy, then attack the varoks who come to help me."

Korad motioned as he spoke, hoping body language would fill the gaps.

Ilean heard no mirth in his voice. She guessed that he wanted the vines cut so he could walk. She tried to bite through them, but they were too unpleasant and tough, so she backed through the cleft and started down the rocks to find an *ahl*-shell in the shallows.

"Hurry." Korad called. "Hurry, for the sake of Harrahn."

With the desperate noise from the varok, Ilean stopped. Slowly, more painfully now, she made her way back up to the cleft to see what he wanted and to reassure the poor alien. She looked in, hoping he could read her eyes, as he had before. "Rest now," she scolded. "I will help you. The other ellls have not meant to be so cruel in their anger. Rest now. I will help you,"

Korad nodded in agreement. He struggled urgently at the vines, trying to impress Ilean with the need for speed.

"I will help you, I said." Her temper flared with the lack of trust the varok displayed. "I am like Duregal."

Still the varok fought his bonds, nodding toward the sea.

It did not occur to Ilean that the ellls might return, that they were capable of planning to use him in a scheme against the varoks. In the old way of ellls, they had simply vented their anger on him. Now they would forget him.

"I will take care of you," Ilean said once again, and, still frustrated with the varok, hurried as best she could down the rocks to the beach to find a cutting shell.

The effort cost her a ripped toe fin and many aching muscles. By the time she had reached the beach she was dried out. Her moss skin tiles were tender from being out of water so long.

Instinctively, she moved toward a warm deep pool formed by rocks and mud at the seaward edge of the beach. There she stretched out beneath the water to rest, took some time to catch an extra large and elusive scar-fish for the varok to eat, and returned to find him near panic.

Korad refused the scar-fish and concentrated all his addled attention on getting the vines cut. When Ilean had cut through the last of the vines, he moved as quickly as he could out of the rock cleft, upward over the piles of boulders, away from the beach.

At first Ilean did not follow him. She felt rejected, sensed the varok's impatience with her, and decided he no longer needed or wanted her care. She would return to the sea and let her call bring whom it would — or she would return to the great-fish and tolerate more of their lessons.

Korad's hoarse call interrupted her musings and made her aware of her foolishness. He motioned for her to follow him, then pointed toward the beach. Far below, several ellls had made their way across the shore rocks and were already crossing the beach.

DOUBLE MINDS

There is no helping one who paints his face
With lies, and robs the truth of all its worth —
Or heedless, mocks it sore.
There is no friend in those who cheat,
Denying faith's rebirth.

"Tera, I don't want you to go." The words popped out before Amanok's brain engaged. He looked helpless standing beside the land glider watching Tera load her gear.

"A selfish, beautiful thought," she said, "but someone has to go with Tekram to the ellls' gardens — someone who can admit that we don't know elll plumes from *lohn* feathers."

"We have already set a tragedy in motion with the loudspeakers. The ellls will not welcome you to their gardens."

"Tekram will make it clear to the ellls that we will leave their gardens, as soon as some ellls agree to go with us and memorize our words of wisdom." Tera couldn't help blaring out the sarcasm, so her young crew mates could drink it in.

"Help him make it very, very clear, for my sake." Amanok extended his forearms in farewell. "Watch him, Tera. Tekram could do great damage."

– Δ –

The Viortahk held no terror for varoks. Tera and her companions enjoyed the ride through the cold passages. Its small islands and tortuous channels of cold water resembled many such stony places in the inland seas of her own planet, Varok. The glider passed close to Ilean's Rock before it veered away from the Rocky Shallows and headed for deeper water.

As they crossed the endless flat beaches of moss and mud stretching into the northern horizon, Tera thought of Korad. Where was he? How could the boy survive out here, where the harsh treeless land met an ocean too vast to comprehend? Would the great-fish watch out for him? Would they help him, or would they insist that ellls and varoks find their own way to coexist?

If she accomplished nothing else on this misconceived expedition, Tera decided, she must contact the great-fish.

Before the first moon-light change etched the water with the living green of microscopic plants, the glider crossed the Bay of Shallows and entered the waters near the great-fish caves. There, along one arm of the Great Chasm, flourished the underwater gardens of twenty-six large schools of ellls.

"An awesome sight, isn't it?" Tekram joined Tera on the instrument-packed foredeck of the glider. "Not a tree worth the noun on this planet. Nothing but mist and mud."

"You forget that the planet of Ellason lies beneath the sea," Tera replied.

"True. True. It makes me wonder what will eventually evolve out of the moss."

"Why should anything evolve on land here?" Tekram's narrow varokian view often goaded Tera into exaggerating and over-simplifying. "It is within the sea that the planet will continue to experiment and bloom. The ellls embody Ellason's greatest promise."

"Not if they continue as they are, Tera. The ellls are taking a self-destructive turn. Their emerging intelligence will soon be wasted on territorial defense. It is silly to expect any linguistic or intellectual development from them."

"Is it? What makes you so sure the ellls are illiterate, Tekram? The oceans of Ellason are very large. Who knows what lies beneath the surface?"

"We have evidence. There is nothing hidden. The ellls have hands to manipulate their environment as well as we do. So where are their foundries, their telescopes, their space explorers? There are none—because the ellls have failed to develop their sonic code as a useful language. They have no written history, no accumulated knowledge—and no potential until we give it to them."

"The ellls must develop on their own—science, language, whatever they need. The great-fish have realized that. Why haven't we?" She was too polite to say "you."

"I disagree, as you know. The great-fish have devised a scheme to rid Ellason of us varoks. They will use the ellls' hands to do their work."

"For what purpose, Tekram? Great-fish are our mentors here, as well as on Varok. They have hands enough in the tips of their fins. Your theory makes no sense at all."

"I have no theory. I merely observe that the great-fish are our adversaries here. They no longer consult or advise us. They obviously want Ellason left to themselves."

"I think not." Tera wisely put down her anger. "You see my mind, Tekram. We cannot agree. I believe in the integrity of great-fish. It is no use discussing it further. I want you to leave me here, in the waters over the underwater caves, so I can consult with the great-fish alone."

"I'm afraid that is impossible, Tera. We go directly to the elllonian gardens, at high speed, so as not to be discovered."

"By whose orders? I was not consulted." Tera abandoned herself to rage. "I am representing the elll-watch on this trip, Tekram. I will be informed." She moved quickly toward the control center to make a formal protest to the lab.

When they reached the elllonian gardens, their glider circled slowly while three divers descended to the ocean floor and waited for the arrival of ellls. Tekram could not stop Tera from joining the dive.

The divers moved cautiously, slowly lowering themselves through the top branches of a forest of spreading *ahl*. The smooth branches grew thick. The varoks feared getting tangled in the flowing lengths of the flat leaves.

Toward the shallows the forest gave way to rows of cultured vegetation and thickets of fruiting bushes. Hanging baskets of succulent sea foliage hung from *ahl* branches. Beneath the baskets lay vine-mesh pens enclosing choice cultivated fish.

Without warning, Tera's foot slipped off a low place in the ocean floor. A cloud of tiny snapping furies engulfed the varoks. Every movement brought on a new attack, and in the midst of the chaos Tera heard the unmistakable, musical gurgling of elllonian laughter. She looked up and wiped the crawlers from her oxygen mask as six elllonian figures darted by and settled in the rocks bordering the garden.

Tera cautioned her companions to stand still, then she opened her arms and nodded, signaling appreciation for the beauty of the garden.

With sonic shouts of welcome and pressure signals meant to enclose them in the school, the ellls rose from the rocks and converged on the three aliens.

Though Tera's nerves throbbed with the intense vibration of the unexpected greeting, her diving suit protected her from the tactile assault. She was able to concentrate on the ellls' minds as they swam by.

She discovered curiosity in their mood and real pleasure at seeing the varoks swimming free of their noisy surface vehicles. They seemed to understand and accept the varoks' oxygen tanks. They knew that varoks did not have gills.

Tera made no attempt to suppress her joy. This greeting was more than she had dreamed possible. When she tried to approach individual ellls, however, they quickly swam away. Trying to convey safety, she got close enough to an ell to sense his thoughts for an instant. In his mood was a disturbing flavor of cynicism. It was well hidden behind the minute-to-minute processing of his senses, but distinct enough to give her warning.

"We had better return to the glider," she said quietly into her communicator. "These ellls are not quite what they seem."

"I'm sorry, Tera. We have our orders," one of the divers answered. "We are to bring three ellls to the glider. They are not violent."

"You're right. There is no violence in their minds. But there is something else—some hidden purpose behind their friendliness."

"Ellls don't have hidden purposes." The young diver was very sure of himself. "Their minds are simple, channeled in logic and locked to the moments' sensations."

"Forget what you have memorized," Tera said sternly. "This is not a study center at the Concentrate. You are in the heart of Ellason. Listen to its beat."

As the varoks talked, the ellls had closed in. Thoroughly frightened, Tera increased the ballast of her diving suit and pushed off for the surface.

A wall of green figures moved swiftly over her. Most of them carried unhealed injuries. Others were missing large areas of plumes. *Eefl*, or something worse, had taken its toll. Their angry determination washed over her with a flavor of sorrow.

Tera saw that they grieved for the loss of something they called life-moments. Anything less than joy was defined as such a loss. "Come with us," she begged, motioning to the surface. "We must learn to talk with you."

She saw that the ellls understood very well what she wanted. It was an old request—the persistent quest of the aliens: "Come with us and talk with us and we will give you a better life."

This school did not believe it. These ellls hated the surface, hated the noise of the varoks' machines. The varoks' invitation meant certain death.

One belligerent thought dominated them all. If the varoks wanted to talk with ellls, they would have to talk with the entire school at once.

"Yes, of course," Tera signaled jubilantly. "You may all come together."

Was that their hidden agenda? It was obvious to Tera that the school was calling her bluff. No wonder varoks were hated. Whenever they had taken an elll alone, they had stolen its life-moments—there was no joy apart from the school. Alone, life was no longer worth living. The torture was too great.

The ellls seemed to understand Tera's idea. They swarmed around her, strangely eager to follow her back to the glider.

"Wait. Wait," she tried to restrain them. "After so many ages—why do you reveal a secret so well kept for so long? I see now why the great-fish insisted that we discover it ourselves. If we could not see such a truth, and you ellls would not tell us voluntarily . . ."

There was no way to ask them. Tera decided not to analyze it. Since this school was eager to come with her, all to the good. She would worry about their motives later. The lab facilities could be quickly expanded to house twenty ellls.

Tekram was adamant. "No. We cannot house and feed an entire school, even a small one. We can properly work with no more than three ellls."

"Three ellls mean nothing, Tekram," Tera argued. "The school is an organic unit. It can communicate only as a unit. We have ignored that. We have always taken individual ellls. We have read them; we can no longer deny it was torture to take them alone. They cannot live apart from their school."

"Read my mind well, Tera." Tekram stood tense and implacable on the deck, watching the ellls circle the glider. "They wait too eagerly for an invitation to come aboard. In some minds I see a desire for revenge. I see too much hatred of varoks."

"You can't read such detail at this distance," Tera said. Something in his voice was wrong. "In any case, their attitudes will change once they are given the full hospitality of the laboratory."

"The ellls' minds were read by the divers who accompanied you to the garden. These ellls are treacherous."

"Yes. I saw a flavor of treachery in them," Tera admitted. "But they can do nothing against us, and once at the lab we will easily win them over. You must let them come on board voluntarily, Tekram."

She saw it then, the truth in his mind: the nets had already been deployed. "No, Tekram!"

IV. The Library

As Ellason's moons congealed, they churned with volcanic fury, and the planet's surface glowed with their reflected light. Meanwhile, the ice of captured planetesimals melted to cover Ellason with deep oceans.

As on Earth's sea floor, sulfur compounds in deep cracks powered life in the warmer waters of Ellason. Tiny living things fed larger creatures, until the oceans teemed with life. Soon the more venturesome organisms tested the shore lands. In places, a symbiotic compromise was made with the persistent sea life, and oxygen began to accumulate in the atmosphere.

For photosynthesis to occur on Ellason's sparse land, a polyene (a biochemical with alternating double and single bonds) was needed to capture both incident and internal light. Such a molecule was selected in the natural jostling for reaction under Ellason's warm moons and beside her veins of molten volcanic and tectonic rock.

— Aman Telariahn (Amantel), Varok, 2072 CE Earth

A New School

The young companions saw how life was good.
They knew the joy that caring love compels.
As one, they nurtured hope
And dared to probe the secrets held
Within the hearts of ellls.

Cautiously, as though trying unknown waters, Ilean caught Korad's smooth, brown arm in her webbed hand. He stopped, grateful for the excuse to rest, and turned to look where she was pointing. Fourteen ellls had crossed the beach at the foot of the cliff. They were moving in various directions, weaving in and out of the rocks as if they were looking for something.

"Aeo-o-o." Ilean sent an ear-splitting call out over the rocks.

Korad panicked and crouched behind a large boulder. "Quiet. Ilean, quiet. We'll be found." He had never heard such a sound from an elll. How did she do it? And why? Why reveal themselves now, when they were about to escape?

The searching ellls looked up and spotted Ilean standing high on the cliff. "A-leel." One answered her with what one could call a laugh, and the joyful sound told Korad all he needed to know. These were Ilean's friends. He recognized the rough figure of Duregal among the ellls.

"Aeyoo," Korad called. He couldn't mimic the toneless, lapping quality of Ilean's sound, but Duregal answered with a recognizable laugh.

Ilean rushed down to the beach, and Korad watched her greet Duregal, Sa-el, and the remnants of her school.

When the varok reached the beach, Duregal welcomed him into the celebration with open fins, and the gentle touch of the old elll released all the terror and fatigue Korad had repressed since he left the lab. Rivers of emotion ran deep beneath his expressionless face, and he sank to the ground, shuddering.

The ellls had never seen a varok express such emotion. They drew back in alarm. Most of them believed the aliens were not capable of such intensity. Duregal, however, knew that Korad was a complex soul. He had saved Korad from drowning, had breathed life back into his limp body, had fed the varok the best food the sea rocks could offer. He had kept him warm in beds of moss, had learned to recognize some of his strange throat sounds as requests for cover or food or drink. In those efforts to keep the varok alive, the elll had also found strength, enough to survive without the school.

Before long the old elll had realized that Korad could read his thoughts as they flashed through his mind. Together they had faced the terrible questions: Why had Duregal wielded the shell and split the school? Regret was dulling Duregal's life-joy, slowly killing him. With a spontaneous show of emotion and sign language, Korad had adopted the elll's anguish, forcing him to call up the memory of the tragedy and wash the ugly stain from his mind.

Ba-ohl, with Navell and others who didn't believe in vengeance, had confirmed his redemption. Duregal had a school of his own again.

Slowly Korad gained control. He barely had the strength to pull himself out of his irrational state. When the ellls took him into the water to clear his head, he was too exhausted to protest. At least the water was warm. He hoped the ellls remembered that he had no gills.

Indeed, they remembered well. They swam on their backs, very close together to form a living raft. Their back-fins undulated rapidly to keep them on the surface, so the varok could lay across them.

He rested well, but sensed something was happening in the school. At close range, pressure signals and ultrasonic echoes were reflected and concentrated, as the school's concept of itself came together.

He was startled to see a reflection of himself in their collective consciousness. In their adjustment as a new schooling entity, they were pledging themselves to his life, to friendship between ellls and varoks, to stopping belligerent ellls from attacking varoks or their lab.

The latter thought brought Korad fully awake. He looked around the raft of ellls and found Ilean. Then he eased his body across the living raft until he faced her happy gaze and found her thought: *Now you are a part of our school.*

He tried asking a question in the ellls' sonics, but Ilean caught only the concern in his eyes, so Korad used his patch organs to explore her thoughts. Followers of the dead Falll were planning an attack on the varoks and their machines, perhaps even their laboratory.

Ilean looked at him as if he were a great-fish, to see if he understood what she had said to herself. When he nodded, she went on, pleased with this silent means of communication. *Falll's school wants all varoks to leave Ellason forever. It is too bad, my dear varok, that they cannot know varoks, as we do.*

"But they can, Ilean. If they can think that far ahead, if they can plan such an attack, we can talk to them about any kind of future." He signaled his meaning frantically with his hands. Finally he made Ilean understand that what was in his head could be hers, as her thoughts had become his. "Ellls will soon be able to understand varoks," he cried in Varokian. "They must."

"We will go to the library." Ilean tried speaking in sonics, remembering the symbols Korad had drawn for her when he found her in the Viortahk. "Maybe, if you saw the lib—"

Ilean's sonic code was cut off with a severe reprimand. Sa-el's sharp command echoed through the school. "Aliens must never know."

Korad checked and double-checked the agitated minds around him, but the meaning 'library' was clear in all of them. What library? What kind of library could illiterate sea-dwellers accumulate?

"The aliens will not learn about the library," Ilean argued. "Korad is no longer alien. He is tad to us, a ward of this school. If you don't want him to tell other varoks about the library, he won't."

"How can you be so sure, Ilean?"

"Because I will tell him to keep it secret."

Duregal moved to the edge of the raft. "I agree that this varok can be trusted."

"How are you going to tell him about such a thing as secrecy," Sa-el demanded. "He knows very little sonics."

"He already knows what we are asking, don't you, Korad?" Ilean said, laughing. "He is like a great-fish, don't you realize that, Sa-el? He probably knows your mind better than you do."

Korad nodded and forced a smile across his face. Then he motioned to his patches and to Ilean's head, where a small ear disk defined the pattern of her plumes.

"You see?" Ilean's eagerness spread through the school, and the raft became a little less than stable. "He understands us. Now he wants us to know what is in *his* head. I think the library will help us find a way to understand varoks. We must be able to explain them to the schools of the Great Basin, if we are to convince them to stop their stupid attacks and start listening instead."

"This varok will be killed outright if the librarians find him near their precious *ahl* leaves," Ba-ohl observed.

"Then I will have to take some leaves to him in the shallows so he can see them."

"That would be very dangerous, Ilean." Duregal's golden-edged plumes were trembling. "The librarians will call you traitor. They are a stern school."

"Is it really necessary to take this varok to the library?" Navell's question echoed Duregal's concern.

Ilean looked carefully at the old elll. *All right*, she thought, *he has asked a real question, not a test for a tad or a loner; I will give him a good answer, and Korad too.* "The great-fish taught me that only in ultrasonics are the fine shadings of our thought expressed. The varoks don't know this. They think the sonic code is the only language of ellls, as I once did. Now I know that my lack of ultrasonic echo detection and pressure sensitivity make me a functional illiterate. I couldn't know, and the varoks still don't know, that ultrasonic echo patterns are a vast 3-D language, stored like moving pictures in the enormous memory banks of ellls' brains. In the library, the ellls' ultrasonic echoes are preserved on embossed *ahl* sheets for those who wish to learn to read by touch. The varok can help me find a way to translate the symbolic echoes. Then they can talk to us. If ellls understand varoks, they won't attack them."

"I still don't understand why the library is so important?" Sa-el said.

Ilean wondered if she were missing something. Or perhaps Sa-el was not able to see so large a picture of the future.

"There are symbols there . . . for elllonian thought." Ilean was treading new water. "We must listen to varoks; but first, they must learn how to talk to us."

Sa-el looked hard into Ilean's eyes, until she looked away, frightened by their intensity. "Sonic code that comes from cold metal endangers our schooling. It is not good, for anything," he said.

"Our varok knows that. And he knows more that we need to know. Help me get him to the library, Sa-el. I won't ask you to stay there if the librarians are difficult."

"I do not fear librarians. I won't go with you Ilean, because we must go at once to gather a large school. The attacks on the varoks must be stopped."

Korad looked more closely into the strange elll's mind. Sa-el had a yearning in his eyes that extended beyond the small world of the Great Basin. He would not be satisfied with anything less than the joining of ellls into one mighty school. All ellls together could pull out the roots of violence once and for all. All ellls together could meet the varoks on equal terms.

"You had better leave at once, Sa-el, if you and Duregal are to gather the ellls of the Far Deeps," Ba-ohl said. "I will go to the cave of records with you, Ilean. "You cannot take this varok to the library alone."

"Melo and I will complete your school, Ba-ohl," Navell said.

"Should we split this school again?" Duregal was not sure he approved of Ilean's venture, and he didn't like Sa-el's plan. "Ba-ohl, you are poorly defended against the *eefl*, with only five together. Sa-el, you will not convince ellls of the Far Deeps to come into the Basin and talk with varoks."

"We must try." Ba-ohl now spoke with conviction. "All other choices allow violence and hate to determine the fate of ellls."

Treachery

> *What end so fair is worth a trick so foul —*
> *To take a free-born soul and close it in*
> *For purposes ill-found?*
> *What good can come from trust betrayed?*
> *Why now can't love begin?*

At first the frightened ells—the varok-haters, Falll's loyalists—could not believe they were trapped. They were pressed together in confusion by the drag of the net that enclosed them. In a constant state of adjustment beneath the varokian glider, they slammed repeatedly into the steel net, expecting it to give way.

When the glider's engines whined to full power, their worst suspicions froze them into one determined unit. Against the drag current, each elll took his turn at surveying every possible route of escape. The knife shells that a few carried in *ahl* belts could not scratch the tough links of the net.

"The net is made of metal," one huge elll told the school. "We can't cut it."

"The net may be harder than tooth or shell," another elll remarked, "but it can be undone. Look at the loose edge. There are simple hooks fitted there. If we can unhook enough of the net, we can go over the top."

"Help me climb up there." A small elll clung to the net and struggled upward, but the force of the water tore open his grip, and he was thrown back into the school.

"We will never move those hooks while the net is pulled through the water," an elder grumbled. But still the ellls tried, by ones and twos, crawling upward on the straining net and falling back, pushing desperately at the hooks as the vessel lurched and dipped. Too soon their finger webs were torn and their muscles were spent with the effort.

– Δ –

"We are in the warm shallows," the varok Tekram said as he looked out from the glider's deck. "We will move along the shore now so the ellls will be more comfortable."

Tera turned away from the ellls' desperate struggle within the net as she edged closer to the net hooks.

"You don't have the strength to unhook the net," Tekram said, his disdain for her thoughts evident in his tone.

"You dared to read my mind?" Tera flared. "Have we varoks abandoned integrity as well as pity, Tekram? We will 'save' this planet to suit ourselves—at all costs—is that it? Ellason will be safe and secure, locked into a varokian-dictated society in spite of itself, in spite of the mental anguish of ellls, the betrayal of great-fish, the privacy of varokian minds."

"Those who ignore the orders of their superiors are no less than traitors, Tera. We risked our lives, at least our good health, in coming to this planet. It is mutinous to frustrate the stated goals of the laboratory."

"You are the one in mutiny, Tekram." Tera yanked defiantly at a net hook. "By forcibly taking these ellls back to the lab, you assure our failure to establish friendly contact with them."

Suddenly the hook gave way beneath her angry hands. Before the net sagged fully onto the adjoining hook, Tera leapt to undo it, too, but it pulled sharply out of her grasp.

Tekram pushed her away from the railing. "You are charged with subversion."

His voice was cut off by the ship's scanning officer: "Large metal object detected on the beach, west of the line of rocks protruding into the sea from the eastern shore."

"Identify," Tera demanded into the nearest intercom. She turned away from Tekram, choosing to ignore him and put down her anger.

"Shape and density indicate a small varokian land rover."

"Korad must be on the shore. We'll go to him. He may have valuable information for us."

"Countermand. He will have no information that can convince me to release this school of ellls." Tekram spoke with admirable control. "We cannot risk losing these ellls. Maintain course."

"My order stands," Tera said into the intercom. "Find Korad." Her order was a direct challenge to Tekram's authority.

Finally, the third ranking official on board, Okarian Telrak, made the decision, as required in times of controversy. He nodded to the beach and ordered the search. "Reduce speed, circle, and launch a rover."

The glider circled offshore while two young varoks, Ohlren and Markhel, prepared to launch the auxiliary land rover. Soon Tera and the two youths were skimming over the sullen waves of the shallows.

Tera watched as they examined Korad's disabled land rover. How had the boy survived in this land? Had he eaten mud turtles and *lohn* birds, or the small burrowing creatures that lived beneath the rocks?

The searchers moved swiftly along the shore. When their infra-red detectors had covered a far greater distance than Korad could have walked, they returned to their rover and sailed back to the waiting glider.

A strange quiet had settled over the captured ellls. Several of them strained at the net hooks and tried to see above the surface, but the net held them under the glider. It was as if they understood what was happening, as if they already knew about Korad's abandoned rover.

"A hydrogen pack is missing from the rover's engine," one of the young searchers reported to Tera. "There is no sign of varokian life in the area, just elllonian footprints in the mud around the rover."

"That's not surprising." Tera tried to keep her mind free of suspicions, so Tekram would not read them. "Ellls are very curious beings. They would enjoy seeing a land rover up close, if it were obviously abandoned. I suggest that we use the rover to search for Korad, then send it back to the lab. You can't argue against such a precaution."

He nodded—his blue eyes curious, but his patches restrained.

"Since I cannot help to free the captive ellls yet," Tera said, "I will accompany the searchers on the land rover. Be advised, Tekram. I regard your actions as criminally irresponsible. Mind well these ellls. If any are in discomfort, if any have strained one toe-fin when they arrive at the lab, I will have you thrown so far off Ellason you'll go into orbit around Jupiter."

"I too will prosecute, Tehr Adkarian. You have acted against orders."

"Illegal orders mean nothing," Tera snapped. "Enough." She dismissed him from her mind and turned to Ohlren and Markhel. "We will take the largest rover. Korad can not be far from here, if he has survived."

When Tekram turned away and disappeared into the ship's cabin, Tera moved close to the ellls' net and strained her patch sense toward their minds.

It was difficult to catch their mood. Their minds ran in channels of narrow logic studded with potholes of unleashed emotion. Tera finally found a memory of a webbed hand tearing a metal object from Korad's rover. She felt a diffuse memory of terrible sounds coming from a young varok being dragged unwilling to the sea. She scanned mind after mind among the captive ellls, but she could not find the owner of the vision, nor any other memory of Korad's fate.

"We are ready, Tera."

"Yes. I'm coming." Reluctantly, she boarded the rover, irresolute and torn. She felt she must find Korad, but knew she should stay with the ellls.

"Follow the most likely path toward the lab," she ordered, "until Tekram and his catch are out of sight." If Korad wasn't nearby, stranded in an attempt to return to the lab, she would turn the land rover toward the eastern shores of the Great Basin, to the caves of great-fish. There ellls might find ample rocky prisons to hold a varok.

Ahl Leaves and Lohn Bird

On secret ahl-leaves, precious to the ellls,
The varok searched for clues to link their lives,
But found instead their lack.
Their differences multiplied
And mocked the sealed archives.

Like all varoks, Korad's nature was deeply ordered, with a measured sense of time closely tied to the short, alternating periods of light and dark on Varok. Here on Ellason, the changing patterns of light were completely divorced from time. No fiery sun warmed the mists or cast a shadow. Sol was too far away to act as warming lamp to the rich oceans. Only when the mists cleared could the sun be seen on Ellason. It swung far beyond Pluto's orbit; it was hard to believe that the massive world of water was tethered by gravity to the sun.

Now, safe within Ilean's school, Korad enjoyed the quiet beauty of Ellason's living lights. Hordes of bioluminescent fish came and went with the upwelling currents of warm water. Flotillas of bright sea-moss and swarms of tiny flashing air-beasts lit the watery world with glowing sheets of light. The tireless shores were trimmed in a misty blue-green glow of their own, and the mists caught enough light from the vibrant seas to paint the flat silhouettes of the island continents with shades of silvery gray.

To Korad, the bioluminescence of Ellason was like a blanket of da-ramont wool warming his soul—or was the warmth coming from the ellls themselves? Certainly they had been generous with him, sharing the fish they caught and the *ahl* leaves they picked as they swam along. They seemed never to finish eating, or to tire of feeding him.

Korad rode between the locked arms of Ba-ohl and Navell as they led their small school south along the rocky eastern shores toward the elllonian library. The water had grown cooler, then cold and black beneath the tall rocks of a long steep cliff. Where the cliff sheered away to the east, Ilean stopped.

The Bay of Cold Deeps, Korad saw in Ilean's mind. *We will soon be near the library. We will beach you on this side of the peninsula. The library faces the Bay of Shallows on the other side.*

Korad thanked Ilean with a gentle tap on the surface of the water, one of several signals they had devised as a rudimentary means
of communication. By the time they crossed the bay and moved onto
land, Korad was very tired. His hands ached from hanging onto back-
fins, and his nerves were pulled taut by the constant contact. On the
beach they found a pool hidden behind three large boulders. Quickly
they enlarged it by digging with cast-off *al*-shells. Then they settled
into its warm water and wallowed like philosophers in a hot tub. There
was no sign of the librarians.

Korad chose to dry out. He propped himself against a rock near
the edge of the pool and tried to sleep. Whenever he began to doze off,
however, a shout of laughter or a loud splash roused him. Fascinated,
he would stare at the ellls as they talked or mated or played compli-
cated games with mud sculptures and sound pictures, until his tired
body won the battle with his mind.

He must have slept, for he found his arm being shaken by a gentle,
finned hand. Ilean stood near him, eager to be off to the library.

He got up feeling refreshed. With little trouble he and Ilean made
their way along the shore and around the end of the peninsula, until
they found a tiny beach of coarse sand. Ilean knelt in the crystal grains
and pushed her fingers through them, remembering her lessons here
with the great-fish Orlegh and Harrahn.

She motioned for Korad to stay on the sand, then she disappeared
into the rocks that rose in jumbled profusion above the shore.

She was gone a long time. Korad moved about the shore pools, looking for the tasty crustaceans that Duregal had taught him to catch.

He had gained strength since the ellls disabled his rover. Now he
could feed himself with the tiny creatures and succulent mosses of the
shore, could find warm rocks and moss to protect his body from cold
mists, could ignore the absence of sun and the plethora of moons and
enjoy the rare glimpses of stars, could live by the changing moon-light,
could savor the flashing of shore-pool lightning bugs and the glow of
mist-drinking plants that clung to moist rocks above the water's edge.
The planet no longer seemed hostile. The ellls' underwater culture
seemed natural, no longer mystical—well within his mind's grasp.

Ilean returned, laden with inscribed sheets of *ahl*, exhausted from
the effort of climbing up to the library cave and back.

Korad took the sheets and spread them out on the sand so he could see the pattern of marks and run his fingers over them. They seemed hopelessly complex.

"This symbol means *ahl*, this one means *rock*; this one is for *great-fish*." Ilean translated the marks in the ellls' sonic code, guiding Korad's finger with hers.

"Yes, these might be helpful. But what do the larger marks mean? Here and here and here?"

Ilean nodded. A knowing grin grew on her face. She understood his question all too well; she had asked the same questions. The great-fish had been precise in their answers. She held up her hand, telling him to wait. She would talk in her head so he could read it. *The ahl sheets are summary codes devised by great-fish to trigger elllonian echo-location memory. That memory is tied to the total eight-dimensional experience: pressure patterns, electro-probing and sensing, sight, sound, direct touch, smell, taste, sonics.*

Korad groaned.

Now wait, dear varok. I have never been able to receive the echoes or direct ultrasonic sounds, so I can't learn what they mean. But I know part of the great-fish Braille, the part translated to the ellls' lower sonic range. Doesn't that help? We could expand it, couldn't we?

"I don't think so, Ilean. Is there enough of the low range code here? Echo location is experienced in ultrasonics." His hands spoke his meaning and he drew great-fish symbols in the sand, until Ilean understood.

Yes. Yes. Ilean laughed. *I am coming to it. The great-fish showed me what I was missing, but it still works for me. Most of these marks are representations of underwater landscapes, to be read with the fingers. Language is symbols, isn't it? These symbols are designed to help ellls select particular events from their memory, from their ultrasonic images. The library reinforces history. It doesn't contain it.*

"You mean these symbols are nothing more than reminders? Symbols to trigger memories?"

Korad gathered the *ahl* leaves into a pile and stood over them shaking his head. He could not hide his bitter disappointment. "There is very little in these leaves that could be used as a basis for language. Varoks can't share memories with ellls. You have no patches. The symbols need to be very precise. One object at a time. One sense at a time. Only ellls know their own ultrasonic memories."

Ilean understood his disappointment. It was too much like hers.

Sadly she gathered up the scattered leaves and started back to the library with them.

"They are cruel beasts," Korad stormed. "The great-fish have thrown your disability in your face and left you yearning and hungry for a food you can never taste."

Ilean longed to comfort the varok, but she did not dare touch him, as she would a troubled elll. Duregal had warned her that strong emotions could make a varok go insane—or was it irrational?

She found a rock to hold down the leaves, then she hurried along the shore. Korad followed at a distance. Somewhere nearby Ilean had seen a gaggle of *lohn* birds waddling through the mist. She would bring her poor, frustrated varok something to eat. Perhaps he would like a *lohn* bird egg, since she had none of her own ready to lay.

Before she saw them, she heard the soft mewing of the birds. Five or six of the plump waddlers were nested in the muddy rocks at the bottom of an old landslide, where shore-pools had not formed. Cautiously, she crept up on them and began to sing the song of a hunter:

> *Wind, turn away my sorrow.*
> *Beauty is fragile*
> *And time is dear.*

> *Mist, cover my horror with the sweet taste that forgives.*
> *All who know life*
> *Must live by its own.*

> *Waves, take me away from my hunger.*
> *Save me from putting out*
> *Eyes that see too well.*

> *Rocks, crush out this life before it knows it has died.*
> *Let none of its moments*
> *Be less than full joy.*

The *lohn* birds sat motionless on their nests, mesmerized by the soft tuneful sighing that carried the elll's regret.

"Aeyull!" Ilean rolled her tongue and let the scream race past her gills. In the same instant she threw herself on a plump bird and wrung its neck in one quick motion. Then she gathered up its clutch of three eggs and walked back along the shore.

Korad was standing in her path, his eyes wide and his mouth open. Ilean looked closer and offered to help. The varok's tongue was curling and moving over his palate. A sound came from his throat. He was making fun of her song.

She laughed and offered him the dead *lohn* bird, but he shook his head. Strange noises still came from his throat: "Beauty is wicked and time plays over stones," his noises said—if she wanted to read a song into his sounds. She laughed again and sang correctly, "Beauty is fragile and time is dear."

The varok listened intently; then he nodded eagerly and tried again. "Beauty runs still and my dear one times," he sang.

Ilean whooped with delight. What wonderful nonsense this varok could sing. She laughed until great tears gathered on her brow plumes. Oh. Oh, this poor alien. He wanted to be an elll so much. And no wonder, with no gills to help him swim, no moss tiles to protect his skin from drying.

"No, no. Ilean. Remember what we must do. Don't misunderstand me." The seriousness in Korad's voice interrupted Ilean's fun. "I think we have found it." He went on and on with his Varokian sounds. "We varoks will be able to imitate that sound you made when you stalked the *lohn* birds. I saw the meaning in your mind. The sounds have meaning, don't they? All you have to do is to teach me what the sounds mean."

Ilean was totally bewildered. He was ignoring the precious *lohn* bird. Why didn't he want her gift? Wasn't he hungry?

"I wish you could understand me," he groaned.

Ilean backed away uncertainly. The varok's words had a tone of desperation in them. She decided he was angry at the fun she had taken at his expense. She looked at the *lohn* eggs in her hands. He may not want her gift, but the eggs were his, collected just for him. She pressed the bird and the eggs into his hands and turned away to the sea.

For a moment Korad didn't understand what was happening. Why was Ilean so upset? He had discovered the answer to their puzzle. Why was he standing ankle-deep in mud, holding a dead bird and its eggs?

He looked at the poor creature, cut off from life to satisfy his hunger. That was the essence of Ilean's song. She had killed for him—a deed more painful to the hunter who took great care to kill instantaneously, than to the hunted who lost no life moments to pain. *I ignored her gift, imitated poorly her lovely song, then stormed at her in my own language—and all she could do was read the look on my face and in my eyes. She was full of disappointment with herself and bombarded with feelings of rejection from me.*

Korad almost laughed with relief at his discovery. Ilean had tied a wonderful, twisted knot of logic and emotion in her one-track mind. She had invented a lover's quarrel—just when they were on the threshold of their common language.

He tried to run after her as she retreated to the sea, but the sand threw him off balance, and he fell onto the shore mud, crushing beneath him the eggs he carried. He cried out, and Ilean turned to find him desperately trying to save the remains of the eggs from the restless water.

Together they sat in shallow water and washed off the bird and ate what remained of the scattered eggs. The need for reassurance grew very large in Ilean's mind. She was deaf to half the elllonian world. Now she felt deaf to the one being who had made her feel whole.

"Never sure, poor elll?" Korad whispered, reaching out to her. "Always different—left out of the pressure patterns that shape the school, ignorant of the subtle social waves that temper personalities, blind to the sea around you, and shut off from the major fund of elllonian knowledge. The loner, the blind loner, plying seas half seen and rarely felt, only partly heard and unremembered—and not really understanding why you are so different."

He led her to the sand and held her very close, as he thought an elll would hold her. "I will help you know the special purpose that has made you different, Ilean," he sang to her in Varokian. "You have seen my mind more clearly because of your blindness. Now you will be the mother of speech between peoples from two vastly different worlds. Your song will make us brothers under that bright star." He pointed into the fine mist that danced above them under a black sky. "Look. There is the sun, Ilean. It links our worlds together. It's telling us that we belong to each other."

She followed his gaze to the bright star, and his sounds, though harsh with Varokian words, made her feel strong and whole again.

As he comforted the elll, the bare wires of Korad's nervous cage grew a calming insulation. As he had with Duregal, he encouraged

Ilean to know him through touch, as her nature dictated. All barriers
of mind and body were down between them. Ilean could now experience him as a brother in curiosity and logic, an equal partner in a
difficult quest, no longer alien. Like no varok before him, Korad understood that ellls lived less by logic than by their senses, in a world that
moved through timelessness moment by moment.

A NEW SONG

They traded gifts of self—far more than love—
And put themselves aside to learn the new,
To sing for all in turn
A new-found song of trust in life,
With verses written true.

Korad loved best the time one might call evening—when the dark-
light tulip spores changed the sea to muted rose, a spectacular sight
under a black Ellasonian sky empty of moons and full of stars. The
varok enjoyed the quiet time with the ellls, but he couldn't keep his
mind off Ilean's hunting song.

Why do you want to imitate the song? She focused the question in her
mind. *You are having such trouble with it. It doesn't have to be perfect. The
lohn bird doesn't care. It was just a song to help me make the kill, nothing more.*

Korad insisted. Slowly he learned some of the correct sounds, but
Ilean grew bored before he finished.

She tried to explain that the sounds could be of no use to them.
They were made with the tongue against gills, sounds made only for
children's games or artists' fancies.

He persisted, and at last he repeated Ilean's hunting song without
distorting its meaning.

Well, good for you. Ilean laughed. *But it's no use. I love singing songs,
but they are not taken seriously by most ellls. As a tad, I sang after Duregal fed*

me, and I sang for comfort when the school left me behind.

"Perhaps all ellls sing at such times." Korad added gestures to the Varokian words, hoping Ilean would pick up some meaning. "I think you ellls experiment with conventional sound phrases or seek new patterns when you think no one is paying much attention."

Ilean knew only that some ellls were recognized artists, who sang for the beautiful tone or for the intricate patterns of rhythm and logic they could execute in new inventions.

The songs have nothing to do with things varoks care about, she thought, inviting Korad to continue reading her. *There are no songs for water currents and life studies and stars and the ways of mist and dry-land machines.*

All that knowledge was locked into elllonian memory. The songs never spoke of such detailed, dry information. They spoke of joy; or they were tone patterns for the sake of tone; or they were thoughts organized in sound for the pure joy of expressing emotion. It was the ellls' only means of expressing their individuality, if they weren't loners. There were singers in ancient schools, ellls who felt so strongly that they burst into song, shocking their schools with their lovely sounds, but pleasing them too. These first singers were the ancestors of loners.

It took all Korad's stubborn persuasive powers to convince Ilean she must teach him all the songs she remembered. As he read her thoughts about the songs, Korad grew more and more frustrated.

"No, no. Your singing is more than just beautiful sounds," he said. They joined their small school in the enlarged tidal pool, and he continued to speak Varokian. "How can I make you see, Ilean? The songs can be the basis for our common language. All we need to do is to make up a dictionary of your sounds and their meanings. Then varoks can tell you what is in their minds, by using your song words." He motioned for her to sing.

Reluctantly, she made up a tune about stubborn varoks.

He drew the sound of her voice in the damp mud with an *al*-shell, moving a line up and down as she sang. Then he cut the swerving line with many crossing lines and redrew each segment by itself. He gestured eagerly, imitated one part of the song, then stopped. Again and again, patiently, he repeated the exercise, and she began to understand.

The mists moved in and out along the shore, and two luminous moons did their slow-motion dance across the dark sky, while Ilean struggled with the concept.

"Ba-ohl, Melo, help Ilean to understand," Korad shouted in frustration. "The songs must be split into fragments to make a language from them."

The ellls mimicked his choppy imitation of the song, until they were laughing too hard to continue. Ilean understood, and she barked angrily at Korad in sonics. "You are not a reductionist." She made a chopping motion with her hands. "You are not so crude. How can you think of chopping up a beautiful work of art?"

"We will chop it up for only a moment, only to re-form it again into other meaningful songs—into sentences," Korad insisted.

Through another moon-light change he worked with the entire school. They tried to connect specific meanings to linked song fragments—but the ellls rejected all combinations that were not poetic.

At the end of the second starlight cycle, Korad sat on the beach and pointed to the outer shore, where the mists were coming in from the ocean. He sang his imitation of the elllonian sounds, trying to tell them: "Wind is blowing mist."

The ellls nodded gravely, understanding the meaning and appreciating the varok's seriousness. Korad's heart leapt. He had spoken his first sentence to the ellls and had been understood—but soon they began to discuss in sonic code the obviousness of the poem's message and its lack of beauty. Korad could see that they unanimously rejected it as a valid song.

"My hunger is horrible." He rolled the sounds from his tongue, composing the sentence from his song vocabulary, then he looked hopefully into the ellls' minds to see if they understood.

Ba-ohl exploded. "I've heard enough insults, Ilean," he growled in sonic code. "Stop this alien from making a parody of our songs."

"I don't think he means to be insulting," Ilean said, watching Korad closely. "He wants to use the sounds within our poetry to say things, as we use sonic code."

Korad nodded, and his eyes begged her to go on.

"Varoks know what we think, Ba-ohl. They are like great-fish. But we need to know what varoks think, and, unlike great-fish, varoks can't make themselves understood with our sonic code. They can't make noises out their ears. They have tried to imitate sonics, but they can't do it. I've seen Korad try. There are some rapid codes he simply can't duplicate." She looked around at her school. "The varoks could teach us many things," she said. "We all know that now. Since they want to talk to us, doesn't it make sense to use sounds they can imitate?"

"Talk to them by singing nonsense poetry? By making fun of it? By making sounds in ugly patterns or noises with crude meanings?" The blue elll, Melo, was incensed. "Even if we agree to such an experiment for your sake, Ilean, we would never convince other schools to use such a language."

"But I may need to tell you an ugly, common fact like 'my hunger horrible'," Korad dramatized.

"Yes. Yes, I see." The skeptical elll shook her head, and, without warning, the school disappeared into the sea.

Korad was left alone on the sand, wondering if the ellls' limited attention span would doom the experiment to failure.

Soon Ilean emerged from the water. "They are schooling," she said in sonic. "They are trying to adjust to your idea. They would like to help you if they can."

"And you?" Korad gestured toward Ilean.

"I will always help you, of course. You are my alien tad—probably the only tad I will ever sponsor," she added, indulging in a moment of self-pity.

Korad shook his head to protest the last thought.

Ilean took the denial to mean he would not be her tad, so he opened his arms to her. "Sing me another song, Ilean." He hummed a little and urged her to continue the sound. "Teach me all the sounds you know, so we can find a way to avoid desecrating elllonian poetry when we make up our language."

Ilean seemed to understand, for she began to sing rolling pure tones he had not heard before—long, dry *l*'s and soft *a*'s and hums close to *m* and *n* and soft *b* and *p* and *d* sounds, mild *v*'s and *s*'s and an occasional clicking *c*.

As they sat beside the pool, letting the song develop, Korad slowly transliterated the sounds into Varokian symbols, adding *l* on *l* in an attempt to represent the ellls' difficult tongue-rollers.

> *Canl elok avalll*
> *Vana llova bol save bae aloo*
> *Kohlok ulloonl*
> *Danl e anu ool.*

Va ba lle leall, ellovas unyan oasoo.
Vaona le oowaml
Elelel belle fomahl.
Vona le dvellloo ev aom acuh elll.
E ullleoon
Ya leell lok boon
Kuoma e savolla e uem aeyull.

Korad then translated the meaning he saw in Ilean's mind. Eventually he made it rhyme in Varokian:

Beside the great ahl tree
I tend the sweet star-light,
Knowing you school far away in the deeps,
Braving cold waters
To harvest the dawn-fish.
Come back to me elll-friend while yet the school sleeps.
Tell me of waves
That roll higher than leaping,
Tell me of dark caves where lone ellls are drawn;
Then gentle me down
To the oceans rich bosom
And drown out the loneness
That aches when you're gone.

The translation, going directly to Varokian from Ilean's poetic mind, was not difficult; but when Korad tried to link individual or grouped sounds to separate nouns and verbs and adverbs, he found the task impossible. Language to Ilean was a code, an elaborate telegraphy of meanings with no alphabet. The poems were objects of beauty, whose meaning was totally lost if the coherence of each line was destroyed.

"I need to know more songs," Korad insisted. "Maybe it would be easier if I were in water with you." He worked his way into the water and rested his head on the soft mud bank. Soon, one by one, through many more moon-light changes, the ellls swam to the varok and sang for him, slowly, and with emphasis.

Gradually he compiled the sounds. Using what he had learned from the library's *ahl* sheets, he transliterated the poems onto blank sheets with a sharpened shell, and matched sounds and meaning as best he could. Only a few sound patterns were identical.

"It's not enough, Ilean," he concluded when he had gleaned all the information he could from the ellls. "I need many more songs. And a computer."

She understood all but the idea of computer, but she shrugged off his request. *We can't make up any more poems now*, her mind said. *Our emotion is all spent. The songs would be pure nonsense if we tried to invent some out of vacant minds.*

"Your minds are vacant when they are drained of emotion?" Korad filed the thought away to tell Tera. *What a contrast to us. We varoks work very hard to keep our minds free of emotion, so we can operate rationally.*

How he wished Ilean could understand him. "The library," he said, pointing to the cliff, "are there more poems there?" Painstakingly, he approximated his meaning with his improving imitation of Ilean's poetic sounds.

No. There are none in the library. Poems are for fun. They last only as long as the singer sings.

"But I have saved your poems." He held up his scratchings and sang slowly the sounds they represented, pointing as he went. "I can read them, any time I like. I have preserved them. Look, Ilean."

She nodded. *It is a good idea, I suppose, but no one ever feels exactly the same from one moment to the next. I wouldn't want to sing the same song over and over again. I don't think I could. We are always changing, aren't we? The poem I made up earlier was nonsense. I sang to you as if you were an elll; I pretended you were an elll. But now I have another song to sing.*

She led him into the shallows and swam with him into the deeps. Then they floated back again toward the shore, into a narrow inlet where the weeds were tall and the earth was soft and clean. She set his head in her lap, while she knelt in the warm water and gently plastered his body with mud. Korad had long since ceased to care whether his jump suit was wet or dry, smeared with mud, or caked with algae. It would all come off in the ocean or in the shore-pool, with the careful grooming of the ellls. He had given himself up to the school, and they treated him as a dependent, as he was.

Gentle brown god of my heart, Ilean began, hushing Korad's protest at the idealized image of himself in her mind,

Take me within your tender net.
I will walk gently on nerves anesthetized with love.
Your sound is my riddle — all but its tone,
So drift through my mind and know my soul.
I long to give you all I am,
And in the giving find that hidden realm within you
Only now your eyes betray.

The sound of the girl's lapping tones rang like bells of velvet through the varok's mind, and his patches took in their meaning. "That is not a song you would sing to a tad, Ilean," he murmured. "Can you love me so well? As well as I love you, dear beautiful creature? How can I make you understand me?"

Ilean smiled at his noises and shrugged.

Her gesture melted the iron fabric of his self-control. He grieved for the silence between them, for the anger building between their species, for the time when he would have to leave Ellason.

Finally his grief let him sleep, while Ilean kept his head in her lap, and the shallows rocked them both in its warm blanket of clear water.

Ilean's eyes grew heavy watching the ocean's surface move up and down. She didn't see the broad tail-fin of a great-fish cut the surface. She dozed, wishing Korad could someday know the great-fish, Harrahn and Orlegh and stern Ahlkahn.

– Δ –

When Korad awoke, he found himself alone on the beach, his head pillowed on a stack of shore-weeds. Ba-ohl stood over him with a furious expression.

Korad rose to his feet and faced Ba-ohl, putting an obvious question on his face. In answer, the elll's grievance ran through the varok's patches like a nightmare: *The school is very small. You are taking too many life-moments from us.*

Korad tried to signal a question. Ba-ohl's thoughts made no sense.

Ilean must be with the school more.

"The school was formed to bring us here to the library," Korad tried to indicate. "Ilean and I must work together."

You school together—alone? Ilean must be with the school.

Korad felt like laughing, but he didn't dare. "You are jealous, Ba-ohl, jealous of Ilean's pet varok. Don't be jealous of me. It is Sa-el whom Ilean has chosen as mate."

Sa-el's name was a recognizable sound, and Korad saw Ba-ohl grow confused. The varok looked deeper into the elll's mind and saw that Ba-ohl's jealousy was not connected to Ilean's mating habits. It was Ilean's time Ba-ohl missed, her life-moments. "I have taken too many of Ilean's life-moments from the school?" Korad sang in the language he already called Elllonian.

Ba-ohl grimaced with the sound of the varok's poor song, but he understood it.

"No more stealing life-moments from the school," Korad promised. "Ilean and I will work with everyone."

"A-leel." They heard Ilean shouting from far down the beach. She pushed toward them, straining clumsily against the gravity. "I have remembered something wonderful."

"Stop. Wait there. You'll tear your feet," Ba-ohl barked in sonics.

As well as they could, with the slow motion demanded by Ellason, he and Korad hurried toward Ilean. When they finally met, she laughed and leaned heavily on Ba-ohl for support.

"I have just remembered," she panted, "there is a corner of the library cave not open to students. When I was getting *ahl* sheets to study with the great-fish, I asked what was in that corner, and the librarian said there was nothing stored there but samples of elllonian art, songs and stories that had no interest to anyone gathering information."

Korad saw the image of recorded songs in Ilean's mind as she spoke. "Ilean, that's wonderful." He shouted, grabbing her hands. "We must go at once. I'll copy all the poems in the library. There is a language buried in them, just waiting for us."

"I'll go alone," Ilean said. "You'd better remain hidden, in case the librarians come with me. They might want to adjust with a school interested in the poems of other schools."

"It's too dangerous," Ba-ohl said. "If the library school ever suspected we had brought a varok here . . ."

"They would be delighted." For a moment Ilean believed what she said.

FRAYED LOYALTIES

Are those less true who take the traitor's name?
Can means be all that matter in the end
When visions overlap?
Whose cause is locked in rigid thought?
Can truth be traitor's friend?

Tera and her small varokian crew drove over Ellason's shoreline in an easterly heading, away from the lab. Great-fish had told her that Korad could be found beyond the Eastern Rocks, on the peninsula that separated the Bay of Cold Deeps from the Great Bay of Shallows.

Tera reported every observation to the Directorate, at first. Then, more and more frequently, she messaged only Amanok.

When she told him that they were crossing the Currents of Altoon, the currents that ran north between the continents encircling the Great Basin, he asked her to repeat the story of her contact with the great-fish. The transcript had been misplaced by one of Tekram's students.

"You have the detailed account, don't you, Amanok?"

"I want to hear it directly from you."

"All right. On our third moon-light change away from Tekram's slave ship, the great-fish intercepted our rover. We were cruising over the underwater caves of their northern city to invite such contact.

"It was wonderful, Amanok. Three of the marvelous beasts circled the great rocks that mark the entrance to their underwater caves. They led our rover onto the fine clay bordering the Northern Shallows and waited while we joined them in a protected cove close to shore. We stood waist deep on a stone shelf and watched the great-fish weave their intricate symbols. They used mud and rock and moss to create sculptures with their prehensile fins. I can't tell you why the message was so clear, but I'm sure they do a rudimentary mind-link.

"Their message was that ellls and varoks would soon meet, tragically, but there was now some hope for a partnership that exceeded all their expectations. Korad has found a way to join elllonian and varokian minds. I begged for more details, but the great-fish would give me none. They told me to hurry, to urge Korad and his school to return to the lab.

"When they saw how delighted I was, they actually beamed with pleasure. But then they turned away. I probed their minds, but you know how impenetrable they are. All I could do was sense their mood."

"You said, 'join elllonian and varokian minds.'"

"Yes." Amanok's lack of enthusiasm worried Tera. "I've got it. That might help. Certainly the great-fish are not the traitors Tekram believes them to be."

"Of course not, Amanok. They are eager to encourage something good to happen without their interference."

"Yes. I must sign off now, Tera. Use great caution."

She understood the message of his perfunctory farewell and turned to the task of finding Korad.

– Δ –

While her eager companions took the rover through the Northern Shallows, Tera set the infrared scanning equipment to maximal sensitivity for signs of life. The crew guided the rover skillfully back and forth through the dark rocks and over the shallows, while the scanners searched. Nothing showed larger than an occasional burrower out of its mud-rock den or gaggles of *lohn* birds alarmed at the humming intrusion.

When Amanok was free of interference, he sent Tera another signal from the laboratory. "Have you found Korad?"

"Not yet."

"He could not have gone far, Tera."

She switched to visual. Something was very wrong. She saw that Amanok's eyes were wide, as if he were near grief for the boy. "The great-fish have purposes of their own."

"What are you suggesting? Why would they send me so far from the lab? Who's nonsense are you believing, Amanok? Tekram's?"

"Not his alone, Tera. Listen to me. The great-fish have not been cooperative."

"Oh yes they have. They told me exactly where to find Korad."

"He could not have crossed the currents, Tera. Think. There is no hope for him."

"He could have had help from the ellls. I'm sure he did. If only you could see my mind, Amanok. You would know the great-fish gave us all the help they could. They were excited about what Korad has done." She spoke carefully, so he wouldn't mistake the transmission. "Amanok, they said Korad had a 'school' of his own. A *school*, Amanok."

Silence.

"Amanok?"

"I am here, Tera." He sounded very distant. "What you have just said—I won't mention it to the lab Directorate."

"Why? Amanok, this is more than we hoped for. What is going on there?"

"The Directorate is meeting now. Signing off, Tera."

Amanok had no choice but to cut off the transmission. If he said too much, he would do Tera harm. The lab had become a political entity, on a planet that had never known politics. It was ludicrous to think of such a thing—Amanok had always known laboratories as places of study for experts gathering information—but information could be distorted when used in service of politics over truth.

– Δ –

Tera took the controls from the sober young varok Markhel. The challenge of skimming across the powerful currents of Altoon would keep her occupied.

A full moon-light cycle passed before they came to the Eastern Rocks. Tera surrendered the controls to Ohlren, a bright-eyed botanist from the shores of Varok's largest inland sea. While she rested, Ohlren guided the rover along the straight shoreline running into the Bay of Cold Deeps. Soon a call signal came in on the communications panel. Tera ordered the rover stopped.

"Tera to the varokian observation laboratory," she answered, "reporting from the entrance to the Bay of Cold Deeps."

"This is Mah Harahk, Tera. As director of the laboratory, I have a sad chore. I must order you to abandon your search for Korad. Return here at once. We believe we will soon be under attack. There is an unusual gathering of ellls in the Far Deeps. It is moving this way."

"Good. Perhaps we can meet them as they enter the Basin. I have been contacted by great-fish, Mahar. They told me I need not look beyond the Bay of Shallows for Korad. They urged me to find Korad and his school as soon as possible. Note the phrase, Mahar: 'his school.' Korad must have made a real breakthrough for the great-fish to use such an elllonian term in reference to a varok. They were being quite serious."

"Serious or not, the great-fish are not to be trusted," Mahar said. "Do not pursue the ellls out there. We believe you are in danger from all ellls now—and perhaps from the great-fish."

"Impossible." Tera laughed grimly. "I can tell from your tone and your nonsense that Tekram has arrived with his catch." She spoke with precision. "I assume you released the ellls he captured."

"The ellls are undergoing study as a school," Mahar mumbled. "It is an invaluable opportunity."

"You are studying nothing but the effects of torture. Tekram's capture of these ellls is a criminal act. I will not hesitate to name you as Tekram's accomplice if you don't immediately order their release."

"Amanok has already reported the capture to the authorities on Varok. The lab is divided. It is all we can do to maintain rationality, while we prepare to defend ourselves. You must understand that we have no hope of communicating with ellls here. The ellls of the Northern Shallows attack on sight anything varokian. We have lost Kah Larian, yanked from a fishing rover and drowned. Maklan was killed in the channel making repairs on the satellite monitor. I could name several more, Tera. We have lost eight varoks to elllonian belligerence. All were unprovoked incidents."

"Unprovoked?" Tera could not believe what she was hearing. Anger took full control. "While Tekram hauled an entire school of ellls in steel nets through the waters of twenty-four other schools? And then dragged them through the cold waters of the Viortahk to an alien chamber of horrors? Every ell in the Great Basin knew of that tragedy within a moon-light cycle."

"It was no tragedy, Tera; no ellls were lost from the school."

"It was a tragedy to the ellls, Mahar. Do you understand so little about them? I know, directly from their minds, that captivity, even for a moment, is torture to them."

"You exaggerate. You romanticize, Tera."

"Don't tempt me to resign, Mahar; I won't do it. I will report to Varok directly from here, if I have to. And I will continue my search for

Korad. Trust Amanok and your own good judgment, Mahar. Tekram has led you all on a paranoid fantasy."

Tera flipped off the radio and leaned back in her couch. "There goes my career," she said to the two young varoks staring at her from the rover's controls, "but not my integrity. Amanok and I are not wrong."

Slowly, so casually that Amanok would have laughed, she pulled out the laser pen she carried in her pocket and aimed it at Ohlren's hands resting on the rover's controls. "You haven't any choice, of course, my dear boys. You must help me find Korad. But don't worry. You will not be accused of any wrong doing, for I am quite serious about shooting off your hands if you try to turn this rover back to the lab."

They nodded, and she saw relief in their minds. Ohlren kept the rover on course along the coast, toward the Bay of Cold Deeps.

The Library

> *"Stay my hand, so I won't trespass here.*
> *"An unintended danger leaves its scar,"*
> *The varok told the elll.*
> *"I'll bend your songs to shape your tongue,*
> *"And fathom who you are."*

Feeling puzzled, a frown creasing his glabrous face, Korad sat staring at the rock in front of him, just off the path to the library. The last stack of *ahl* sheets, poems borrrowed from the ellls' collection of songs, lay in his lap. His growing dictionary of sounds and meanings wove a hopeless tangle in his mind. "Many sounds are used for only one meaning, but there are too many small differences. Look, Ilean, see if you can understand my question. This sound, *fomoh*."

Ilean smiled at his pronunciation but the meaning was clear in her mind.

"*Fomoh* seems to mean 'leaping' in several of these poems, but here, in your love poem, it is sung *fomohl*." Korad shrugged, hoping the elll would catch the question.

She did, and laughed aloud, forgetting that they were hidden in the rocks above the Bay Of Cold Deeps.

Ilean could not believe that the librarians were dangerous, but the varok was adamant—he would go no closer to the cave. The great-fish had said the librarians were sworn to defend the library and all knowledge of its existence against the varoks.

"It is *fomohl* not *fomoh*, because it must rhyme with *oowaml*, 'waves,'" she sang. "You are too literal-minded. This is—or was—poetry, a work of art meant to be beautiful, not accurate."

Korad nodded and shook his head. "*Pem a*," he intoned in their evolving song language, 'like you.'" He pointed to her and to her gills. "Sing for me the sound that means you, yourself, the blind loner, the sound the school sings to call you, the sound the great-fish taught me. I want to hear it from your gills, like a song."

Ilean shook her long blue plumes off her neck; then she spoke quietly, with rolling tones. "Ilean. I am Ilean."

"Ilean," Korad repeated, with more accuracy than he had achieved before. He took her hands in his and studied the huge black eyes that danced mischievously like veils shading her mind. The moss felt thin on her palms, like the richest suede. "Now you must sing my name," he said, using what he could of their song language. "The sounds are in your tongue, near the back of your gills. I know they are, Ilean. Say Korad. My name is Korad." He pressed her hands to his chest, and waited.

He heard it first in her mind, *Korad*. Then the sound caressed his ears like the touch of a muted finger cymbal, "Korad."

"You see?" the varok said aloud, forgetting their danger from the librarians. "You can make varokian sounds. You will be able to speak Varokian, as well as our new language. We will call it Elllonian."

It was clear that Ilean did not understand, but no matter. Korad saw that she loved the strange blue light in his happy look. It made his eyes dance with glimmerings, like the crystal deeps of the Great Basin. *A nice reflection of myself, he thought, a nice bonus. Now—back to work.*

"Look, Ilean. Here is the second verse of your poem." Korad scratched a line of patterns on the fresh *ahl* sheets she had taken from the library:

Vona le cowaml
Elelel belle fomohl
Vona le davellloo ev aom acuh elll

He wrote in his Varokian transliteration.

"Not *elelel*," Ilean laughed, "*E lelel*."

"Aha." Korad shouted. "And the first line must be 'Vona le e oowaml,' right? And again in the third line: 'Vona le e davellloo.'"

"*Davel lloo e vaom acuh elll*," Ilean corrected.

"All right. Now listen to all those *e* sounds, Ilean, and think about the meaning. In Varokian, these would use different words: 'Tell me of waves that roll higher than leaping. Tell me of dark caves where lone ellls are drawn.' Ilean, you ellls use the sound of *e* to mean many different things. No wonder I'm having trouble finding words."

Patiently, he went over the point in sonics, in their new language, with drawings, with pointing, and with exasperated sighing, until she finally understood.

"*E* is only a connecting sound," Ilean insisted, rather more sternly than Korad expected. "The meaning is quite clear. It is a good poem."

"It is a beautiful poem," Korad said, grasping her hands again. "But in precise language there are times when each word, *than* and *that* and *where* must be defined and sounded differently—maybe *e* for *of* and *eke* for *that* and *eh* for *where*—or whatever is closest to elllonian poetic usage."

Ilean could not understand the various *e* sounds Korad made, until he repeated the poems, making them all different:

Vona le e oowaml
Eke lalel bell eke fomohl
Vona le e davel lloo eh vaom aeuh elll.

"You have ruined my poem." Ilean shouted. "The sound is terrible."

"Hush. Hush." Korad whispered, remembering the librarians on the cliff above. "Try *em* for *eke*. Would *em* do for that? *Em lalel bell em fomohl*?"

"That's better, but . . ."

"You can sing any way you want, as always, Ilean. I only want to change Elllonian speech. It needs to be precise." He tried to illustrate his meaning by singing the original line, then tonelessly wording the revised version in a business-like manner, as if it should be used only between ellls and varoks.

"I see," Ilean said, her sonics nearly failing her. "I suppose it is very necessary to be very accurate when dealing with very very varoks." She snapped her gills, still not happy with the alteration of her poem. "Ellls won't use a language that ruins their poetry," she grumbled.

Korad longed for the time when he could tell Ilean how elegant spoken language could be, how soft and unique the Elllonian sound would be, even when spoken, how beautiful its precision and logic. "I like its sound," he tried to say. "The logic of the language will appeal to ellls. I know it will."

He released Ilean's hands and motioned to her to return the last sheets of poetry to the library. "I had better help you up the hill, at least part way."

They loaded their arms with the precious bark and stood up into clear air. The mists had been driven onto the land by a warm wind off the Great Chasm. The sky above them sparkled with stars, and the sea below glowed with its inner life. Korad felt as if a light-period had begun, much as it would on Varok. All that was missing was Varok's ubiquitous lightning, dancing on the upper horizons. He longed to take Ilean there, to take her over the high rocks of the Vahin Teral and into the great Forested Sea."

"Stop. Be still," Ilean commanded. "The librarians."

Korad piled his *ahl* sheets on top of Ilean's and ducked behind a large rock near the edge of the cliff, while she went unsteadily onward.

There was no path here, and the pebbles pushed roughly through her moss slippers. She didn't dare stop. The muscles of her thighs would easily cramp with the strain of starting up again. She moved slowly, rhythmically, gradually working across the rocks to the path she was expected to take between the great-fish's favorite beaching shallows and the library.

Before she reached the path, she saw two librarians watching her. They stood tall and dark on the path where she should have been.

"Hurry," one of them demanded in sonic code. "We have heard the sound of varoks nearby. They must not find the library."

Ilean pushed harder and finally reached the path. "I was return-ing these poems," she gasped, "when a strong wind blew some of the sheets out of my arms. I had to climb far down to get them all."

The ellls said nothing. They led her at a fast pace up the hill and into the library cave.

"Now." The lead elll turned toward Ilean when they were well inside the small alcove reserved for works of art. "There is no wind to bring strange odors into this room. As we suspected, you smell of varok, even stronger than before. You have not been studying with great-fish. You have brought a varok to the *ahl* sheets. You are a traitor to ellls."

"He loves our poetry," Ilean cried. "He and I are making a beautiful language, so that ellls and varoks can speak together."

"Then it is true; a varok has seen the written code. Don't you realize how that helps them against us? Don't you remember the tales of ellls taken to other worlds, their life-moments stolen, made unbearable by isolation from their schools? We must share with the varoks nothing, or they will take everything we are."

"But they want to be our friends. They want to help us. We have made the varok Korad a part of our school. He sings my name like an elll."

"You are the tad of Duregal the murderer. You are a traitor to all ellls." As they spoke, they backed away.

Then they moved quickly, pulled a mat of *ahl* vines over the entrance to the art room, and shut her in. Their action was so strange, Ilean did not recognize what they had done.

When she found herself entirely enclosed and unable to unfasten the mat from her side, she exploded with rage. "You are no better than the varoks who take ellls captive. Scum of Ellason! This is no library. This is a den for self-indulgence. A garbage pit meant to rot elllonian history. You want to keep ellls captive in their own minds. You are afraid to face what lies beyond Ellason."

– Δ –

Korad had moved as close to the entrance of the cave as he dared. When he heard Ilean's screams and saw one elll leave, he inched cautiously toward the dark opening to the library. When he saw no ellls, he entered.

The vault of the cave rose high above him. Row upon row of *ahl* sheets lined every face of the huge cavern. Stacks of sheets covered large steps carved in the rock. Heaps waiting to be catalogued leaned against large desks of *ahl* wood. Varoks had never imagined such a wealth of information could be gathered by ellls.

"Korad."

Ilean's quiet call shook the varok back to the moment. He ran to her and unfastened the mat of vines holding her captive.

"Were you seen?" she asked.

"No." Korad shook his head. The sound of something heavy being dragged across the floor came from one of the smaller side passages behind the main cave.

"Hurry, Korad. They are coming back."

"They are already back." An angry bark echoed through the cave. "We have Ilean. Destroy the varok."

Three ellls emerged from a side cave wielding long knives of *al-shell*. They rushed at Korad. He ran out of the library and down the treacherous slope that faced the Great Bay of Shallows. He skidded, fell, then rolled to a stop. For a moment he lay bruised and disoriented near the shore, then he dared to look back. Ilean was nowhere in sight. He shouldn't have risked entering the cave. In misery, he realized he had no choice but to stay away from her. With him gone, the librarians' anger would quickly dissipate, and she would be safe.

An ominous undertone, the quiet hum of a varokian rover spread over the sea.

"Aeyulll."

A cacophony of sonic cries erupted from the low eastern cliffs. They echoed over the rocks in chilling tones, as if the heart of Ellason were crying out in agony. "The varoks will take the library. Their machines are coming. The library is discovered!"

As it rounded the peninsula and approached the sand where he lay, Korad saw the flurry of water and spray the rover left in its path. He did not see who was in the rover, however, for, when it appeared, an enormous explosion ripped open the bowels of the mountain and sent a cascade of rock and *ahl* leaves flying to the beaches below.

Cleansing in Fire and Light

"I did not know the depths of fear,"
the varok thought,
"until I saw a strange new people throw away
The history of their race
To keep it out of alien reach,
Secure from sore display."

In her rover below the library, Tera was shocked to hear the percussive reports of incendiary bombs. Explosives? On Ellason? For a terrible moment she thought the entire cliff would come down. Rocks and dust and flying debris flew outward, and a hundred landslides started down the mountain. As the rover hurried to shore, she spotted the warm infrared image of a varok on the beach south of the peninsula. It had to be Korad. He was off to one side, apparently unhurt, but he was starting up the cliff.

"Korad, wait!" Tera shouted as loud as she could, but he kept climbing upward, toward the gaping wound in the mountain's side.

"I'm going after him."

Tera's two companions beached the rover. They knew better than to argue with her.

When she reached the crumbled remains of what had been a huge cave, Tera found Korad surrounded by flat stones and fallen chunks of solid rock. He was stamping frantically at burning *ahl* leaves and calling for Ilean, weeping as if he would never regain control, his mind consumed with grief.

It didn't take much imagination to see what this place had been—or what it could have meant for elll-varok understanding. With a cry of dismay, Tera ran to put out the fire that was racing over the few shelves left standing.

Too soon, she was nearly overcome with the smoke. "We've got to have air." Tera stumbled to the cliff's edge, pulling Korad with her.

"Only one breath," Korad agreed. "We've got to save the *ahl* sheets."

Tera nodded and turned her forearms up until Korad recognized her welcome. "Your discovery will be honored," she said.

"And its secrecy will be respected," Korad warned.

"Of course." Tera's mind was open to the youth.

"We've got to put out the fire."

They returned to work. With large sheets of baked moss stripped off the library floor, they smothered the remaining flames among the *ahl* leaves. Then they put together what remained of the library. Only a few sheets and a pitiful heap of corners and remnants were left of the ellls' vast store of information and memory references.

"No ellls got caught in the blast?"

"I checked. Ilean must have been taken away. Ba-ohl and the school will find her."

"Our scanners showed no one but you on land."

"Yes. Yes, of course." Korad collapsed to the ground. "Why? Though I know very well why, Tera—or think I do. We varoks have approached Ellason with all the finesse of a harvesting machine. We have treaded on their life-moments as if they had no value. We can't even begin to appreciate what that means to them. With all their ten senses, they are a hundred times more aware than we are with our six. If the lab had found this library, would they have left it alone?"

"Korad, this *ahl* bark is not fragile at all." Tera was staring at the piece she held in her hands. "Look at the ash it has left. It did not burn easily. It melted, or reacted." Tera tried unsuccessfully to make a tear in an undamaged piece of the bark. "It is impregnated with a preservative of some kind. Ellls are not as primitive as they seem, are they, Korad?"

"'Primitive' is not a good word for them. No. Look at this, Tera, and tell me what you think it is." He handed her a large fragment that was etched with a complex diagram. Part of the labeling in sonic code was still clear.

Tera stared at the diagram. "Korad, this cannot be what it seems."

"Why not? Ask yourself carefully—why not?" Korad stared hard at his superior, then he fell to the pile of scraps, searching for something more.

"There is no evidence to indicate that ellls can build a thing like this," Tera said, studying the diagram. "This is a plan for an electric generator, powered by differences in natural sea water temperatures, an enormous device capable of producing electricity in the middle of Ellason's oceans."

"Perhaps the ellls have chosen not to use electricity—yet. They hate machines. They prefer to feel everything they do, rather than let some electrical device do it for them. They have invented gardening tools, Tera, and toys and ingenious musical instruments you would love. I've seen them in the art room of this library, heard the ellls play them from a distance. And their poetry is exquisite—a melding of sound and meaning that has nothing but pure aesthetics for its measure. It took some time to convince Ilean that we could convert their songs to a workable language for speaking with us varoks."

"The great-fish said you had succeeded. Congratulations, Korad."

"Yes. Congratulations—for what?" Korad controlled his sorrow with difficulty. "It is all gone now—all hope. The destruction of this library was the final act of rejection. My intrusion here will never be forgiven."

"The librarians sound like an extremist lot. But they are no worse than the ellls of the Northern Shallows. Varoks are not safe working outside the lab. And more trouble is on the way. A collection of schools is heading toward the lab from the Far Deeps. Everything will be lost if that main force of ellls arrives to reinforce the terrorists."

"That is no main force." Korad felt a new surge of hope. "The schools from the Far Deeps are led by Sa-el and Duregal, ellls of Ilean's school. They must have convinced the ellls of the Far Deeps that they are needed at the lab. They will stop the troublemakers, not join them."

"Can you be sure, Korad?"

"Of course," he said. "There is only one large school heading toward the basins, right? Not two? That is good news, Tera. Now, when Ba-ohl finds Ilean, we can relax and take our time with what we have found here. Perhaps we could win over the librarians."

He began to rummage among the *ahl* leaves again, drawing out a large piece to show her. "Look at this, Tera, if you doubt that ellls have a technology as selective as varoks. I would say that their technological mentality is far more selective, far more intelligently reasoned than ours."

"I see." She was looking at the graphic design of an ocean transport system run by currents. "The ellls know more hydrodynamics than varoks would like to admit. What about metallurgy, Korad? You must have seen evidence for knowledge of metals."

"Very little," he said, "as you would expect from a water-bound society. But not all the diagrams and symbols are as obvious as these. Much of the library was composed of cues for echo-location memory."

"Perhaps the ellls are not as water-bound as we assume they are."

"They are water-bound by choice. It would take severe social pressure to push the ellls onto the beach long enough to forge iron. Land is good for nothing but academic experiments and specialized gardening, and escape from *eefl*."

"Well, metal or no metal, we have greatly underestimated the ellls. I think we should take these fragments back to the lab, as quickly as possible."

"The ellls have abandoned the library," Korad agreed. "I don't see why you can't take them." He stared at the lovely old varok and saw in her eyes a reflection of his own exasperation. "They sacrificed too much in order to preserve their species' secrets."

Tera had difficulty understanding that.

"They feared too much, cared too much for their secrets, but we also care too much, and for our own reasons. If we can do real communion with ellls, we are somehow cleansed, isn't that it, Tera? They are our link back to the natural universe. If only they would love us, we could love ourselves better, perhaps struggle less with our need to control—perhaps live out more fully our need to be part of the whole. It's almost disappointing to learn that they understand so much, isn't it?"

"Almost." she smiled at the young idealist, remembering herself at his age. "Now, no more delaying. I will help you find Ilean. I know you won't leave her until you know that she is safe."

Korad looked up with surprise, forgetting how words were often unnecessary in varokian company. "You read me well, Tera," he said, "but not accurately enough. I will never leave Ilean."

"'Never' is a very large word, Korad." Tera smiled uneasily. "Do the ellls have a poetic sound for 'never?'"

– Δ –

Far across the Great Basin, Amanok stood on the laboratory dock staring into the restless water. He had come to the captive ellls, haunted by the muted sounds of their sonic code. Were they never quiet? What did it mean when the sounds soared out of hearing? Certainly the ultrasonics of the ellls' echo-location was not tied into the rudimentary sonic code. Or was it? Why else would it be contiguous, especially here, where there was no reason for echo-location.

If he could only understand them better! Perhaps, working with them, he could devise a way to release them.

Amanok could understand something of their conversation, but he soon realized that he was relying too much on his patches. He was reading their minds, not translating their sonic code. Ceaselessly, they talked of escaping the steel nets that enclosed them.

He tried to tell them, in their own sonic code, that help was coming, but his efforts were misinterpreted or not understood at all. The elllonian code was a far more subtle language than he had realized.

Dear Tera, come back soon. This lab has gone mad without you. During their last radio conversation, Amanok had neglected to tell her of the Directorate's battle for control of the captive ellls.

When Tekram had arrived with his catch, several of the varoks had assumed that the ellls would be released. The Directorate said no, and no varok would risk his career by opening the nets. Amanok was not able to release the pressure catches by himself.

When Director Mahar opposed Tekram's plan to "train" the ellls, and a full-blown debate blossomed, attention was drawn away from Amanok's sentimental inclinations, and he was ignored. His serious attempts to release the ellls were not discovered.

"I carry this fake innocence with me like a bad odor," he said in Varokian to the indifferent ellls beneath the dock. "It cannot last long, my friends." He knelt down and peered into the water but could see nothing but the nightmarish vision of elllonian fingers grasping at the cage. "If I could tear away these nets, I would." Amanok dipped into the water to touch the elll's fingers.

Instantly the school converged on him. His finger and hand were pulled violently through the mesh. A powerful webbed hand shot up through the mesh, caught hold of the belt buckle of his tunic, and pulled him off the dock into the water.

He cried out and grabbed for the dock as elllonian hands caught his clothes in many places and worked in concert, dragging him lower and lower in the water along the steel mesh. He tried to pull the tunic over his head, but the ellls' hold was too firm.

With one free hand, he reached for the laser pen he carried in his back pocket, but when he brought it out to sear the elllonian fingers pulling him to a certain drowning, he found he could not press the deadly trigger. Instead, he turned it toward himself, just close enough, he hoped, to tear his tunic and nothing more.

The burning was cooled by the water. He hardly knew where the laser struck, until the tunic fell away, and he was able to scramble to the surface away from the ellls.

There the smell of his own seared flesh boiled through his nostrils and sent him into a rage. "I am your friend. Your friend!" he shouted in Varokian. "Who will free you if I don't? Who has put his life's career in jeopardy for you?"

Groaning with pain, heedless of the ellls, he leaned over the dock again and splashed water on two long burn wounds that crossed his body. When the pain eased, he found himself staring into the eyes of a young ell. There was regret in the ell's mind beneath the anger and pain of captivity. Amanok held up his hand to indicate patience. The ell smiled.

He slipped off the dock and grasped the side of the steel net, where the ellls could easily grab him again. They backed away, all but the young one, who put a finned hand over Amanok's varokian fingers. For a moment their eyes locked.

The varok's eyes seemed very small to the ell, dangerous, but friendly, like the deep blue waters over the Great Chasm, the source of life but deadly up close.

Amanok saw, in the ell's mind, relief that their rage had not made killers of them, but that the captivity now threatened them all with madness. Their appeal tore at Amanok's reason and pulled him into an irrational passion born of confused yearning, empathy, and frustration. He nearly drowned before the emotion lost its deadly grip. The ell pushed the varok toward the surface, and he saved himself, but many ellls saw the grief at his helplessness, and some did not forget it.

Bay of Cold Deeps

If in the mind's true bent an angle sharp
Distorts the straight line flowing from our youth,
Then where can trust be found?
The line is spoiled; the dent is firm
'Til forged again in truth.

What horror now: To look in tortured eyes
And fail to stop the pain of those defiled,
To understand too late
That though communion is at hand,
It won't be reconciled.

The Bay of Cold Deeps shone like a great dancing crystal. Its inner lights of red and purple flashed like necklaces of amethyst among the curtains of brilliant moss green.

Korad was no longer enchanted with the glowing sea. The vibrant waters seemed strange and empty. His small school was not on the beach, where he and Ilean had left them. The librarians were gone. No elll was to be seen, either by eye or by infrared scanner.

"Am I to sit in this vile boat doing nothing?" He shouted at Tera as the rover cut its last swathe across the bay. "The ellls could not have gone as far as we've searched. They had no reason to run. Why can't we find them? Must I go back to the lab with nothing but fond memories of schooling with ellls? Were they toying with me, Tera? Was I imagining everything?"

"Easy, easy, my friend. We have been searching like mad *eefl* with our technical noses tuned too high. Let's just sit here and wait and watch. You said ellls hate machines and mechanical noise. So let's not use any. You did fine with them when you were quite helpless. Perhaps your school thinks you prefer a fancy machine to a living raft of ellls."

"Of course. I should have thought of that. It is very difficult to re-member how alien minds work when you're surrounded by familiar comforts. Once I had met the ellls on their own terms, I assumed they would follow me, like hand-raised daramonts, right into my mecha-nized existence, no questions asked. I'll swim to the shallows near our beach and wait for them there, in their element."

"Must you swim?"

"Take me in a little closer, Tera. I can swim farther than you might imagine. If the ellls spot me with their echo location and know I'm separated from this varokian hardware, they will take it as a show of trust and come to me."

"If they are anywhere in the bay."

The rover skimmed back across the water, until the rocky inlet near the end of the peninsula was just visible. "I can make it from here, I think—if I have to—if they don't find me."

Tera ignored the doubt she saw surfacing in his mind. "We'll be watching. Use this strobe signal if the wrong ellls find you." She strapped a small signal light to Korad's wrist and watched him drop off the rover into the water. "Shouldn't you use lifters, Korad?" she called.

"It's all right, Tera."

Korad smiled up at her from the water. Apparently, he didn't mind having a mother-surrogate fussing over him. His lithe young body was silhouetted darkly against the glowing life in the water below.

"I have grown stronger in my travels with ellls. Ellason will have to pull harder than this to take me under."

"Take what care you need, Korad." As the youth slowly churned away, Tera did not hide her fear from her captive crew. Ohlren smiled to reassure her, but Markhel looked grim and nervous. When she returned to the scanning controls, she found Korad on the infrared scanner, a large warm dot in the cooler sea around him. If any ellls approached him, she would know immediately.

Tera reached for her transmitter, hesitated, then sent her signal. "Amanok, from Tera, Tehr Adkarian, personal answer requested."

"He will be at a transmitter shortly, Tera. When will you return to the lab?"

Tera had no idea who was asking the question. The radio signal was impersonal and anonymous when the visual transmitter was off. "I have found Korad," she said. "He has established contact with a school of ellls and discovered a language we can use with them."

"Details please," the crackling radio commanded.

"We will make a full report as soon as . . . practical. Korad is now with the ellls. When he returns we will evaluate his progress and decide what to do."

"You are to return immediately. All varoks are needed to defend this installation."

Tera's face hardened into resolute varokian walnut, all emotion held firmly in check. "Your best defense is to release Tekram's elllonian prisoners and attempt to make restitution for the life-moments you have stolen from them. I await word from Amanok."

She shut down the voice transmitter, turned on visual reception, and refused to respond to any more anonymous commands. Finally, Amanok's unhappy face appeared on her small receiving screen. "Tera, let me see you," he said. "Turn on your visual transmitter. Have you really found Korad?"

Tera threw open her transmitting beam. "I am watching him this moment, Amanok. He is a small speck on my infrared scanner, swimming in an empty sea toward a rendezvous with his school."

Amanok did not reply.

She was alarmed at his silence. "I will speak freely, as if this transmission were private."

"It is not private, Tera," Amanok said, with a look of warning.

"Nevertheless—" Tera paused, then decided to go ahead. Her information could do nothing but support their cause and undermine Tekram's aggressive policies. "The ellls are far more—shall I say intelligent or sensitive?—and capable of historical orientation than we guessed. Korad and I have seen a library, *ahl* leaves preserved in a dry state and embossed with symbols like Braille, coded information that approximates great-fish signals. There was a whole library of information preserved by a sophisticated impregnation process. The ellls are organic chemists, Amanok. And technicians. In the remains of the library we found plans for a power generator based on differences in ocean temperatures. It would work well to produce electricity near the hot waters of the Great Chasm."

While she talked, Tera kept a watch on the infrared scanner, continually centering and magnifying Korad's slowly moving image.

"The ellls are not only electrical engineers, Amanok, they are poets, singers of great artistic sensitivity. I have not heard them yet, but Korad describes the beautiful dry, rolling, lapping sounds they make. Their tongue works against the rudimentary gills in the back of their nasal-gill passages. Korad has defined enough meaningful sounds from the songs to serve as the beginning vocabulary of a common language.

Varoks can imitate the sounds. At last, we can communicate."

Amanok gave her no response. For a moment she sensed that irreparable damage had been done. What was happening at the lab?

"That would be good news, Tera, but Korad's discoveries will do us no good," Amanok said. She took the cue and decided to forge ahead into the quicksand.

"Surely the lab is not holding ellls captive. It has been too long, Amanok. The lab must understand that. We have ignored the most important of all elllonian characteristics. Ellls sustain an enormous sensual input. They are creatures of the moment. Loss of life's moments is the worst possible tragedy for them. You must release the ellls, Amanok. Regardless."

"I have tried." Then Amanok stepped into the quicksand with her. "I can't do it alone. The nets are too strong, and I can't destroy the net without doing harm to the ellls. It is hopeless. Put away all thought of communication with ellls, Tera. It, too, is hopeless. The Directorate is concerned with the lives of varoks now. They expect the lab to be attacked. What you have told me about ellls being organic chemists is not good news. It will only exaggerate the growing fears here. I assume you know about the schools that are converging on the Great Basin from the Far Deeps?"

"That is why I called, Amanok. Those ellls are *friends*. They want to stop the violence. Part of Korad's school is ready to learn his new language. They believe varoks can help them save their way of life."

While they talked, Tera saw that Korad's progress toward the beach was slowing. She tensed, staring hard at the numbers clicking off his rate of progress. Unknowing, Amanok talked on.

"How can I convince varoks under attack that an entire fleet of ellls is friendly?" he asked. "Now the Directorate will imagine plastic bombs, explosives made of every kind of Ellasonian nitrogen source—incendiary devices. I won't ask why you spoke of the 'remains' of the library, Tera. I see trouble in your eyes, dear woman, and I long to read your thoughts. Don't speak them. You have told me too much already. A transport space cruiser is coming from Varok with 'reinforcements.'"

"That's insanity, Amanok. The ellls coming from the Far Deeps want to talk. To varoks. Now. Won't anyone there hear me?"

"There is one on the space transport that will listen, Tera. Vohren is coming."

"Vohren? Voh Renak, my consummate mate? Why is he coming here?"

Tera searched Amanok's eyes, imagining the questions that must be going through his mind. Was Vohren sent to help control me? To drive a wedge between us, weakening our opposition to the lab's policies?

"Is that it, Amanok? How I wish I could read your mind, my dear friend. Vohren will accept our friendship. See it in my eyes."

A change in the scanner drew Tera's attention. Korad's image had stopped. He was no longer moving through the water. Was he too tired to go on? Fear took a cold grip on Tera.

"It doesn't matter whether Vohren agrees with us or not, Tera," Amanok said. "Your friendly group will have to fight their way through a great many schools of maddened ellls in the Great Basin in order to get to the lab. There is no talking to ellls near here."

"Don't give up on them, Amanok. Please. Ellls are not natural killers. Their anger is quick to die. They live one moment at a time. They don't give up their life-joy, unless cornered in all six directions." Tera looked down at the scanner, as a group of images flashed quickly toward Korad. "I must go."

"One last thing, Tera. Vohren was told you were in danger and alone, and that you and I were of one mind."

"Fools," Tera declared. "Why did the lab worry Vohren with such talk?"

Korad's image in the scanner disappeared in the midst of the swirl of ellonian patterns. Should she go to him? If the ellls were those of his school, her rover might frighten them away again. If they were the librarians—her mind was torn with indecision.

"Release the ellls, Amanok. I am with you both. Find me in Vohren until I return." She turned off the radio.

Images swirled in the infrared scanner. The ellls did not go toward the beach, as she expected. A second set of ellonian images came into her scanner's view.

"Full ahead." she commanded.

Her varokian team sent the rover leaping toward the converging schools. As they cruised toward the rocky beach, she struggled to remain calm. "Korad, Korad, what will my coming do to you?"

There could be no clear answer. One of the schools must be the librarians. She had to help.

THE BATTLE FOR ILEAN

Their fear made masks of faces raw with doubt,
Then gave them nerves of steel—a devil's gift
That stoked the fire of grief—
As into blood they plunged their hands
And set their souls adrift.

Just minutes after he left Tera's rover, Korad's aching limbs fought the current. The beach seemed too far away. He no longer looked for ellls. He struggled to keep afloat. He knew he must relax or he would never make it to shore.

A *lohn* bird rose from the rocks on pumping wings to investigate. "Curious sadist," he swore. "Throw me an egg or worse, why don't you?"

The *lohn* bird startled, turned, and lumbered back to shore.

Korad felt the swift brush of many ellls swimming by his legs. He sang out a phrase of welcome from an ancient elllonian song, but the ellls turned, closed in, and pushed him underwater.

Immediately something brought him up again. He gulped air and looked around. Ilean's grief-stricken face flashed by in the water, then she disappeared with an unfamiliar elll, and her now too-familiar scream split the mist. "Aeyull!"

Like a surreal underwater movie, the images of plumes and foam and dark streaks in the luminescent depths flashed before Korad's eyes. He used his last strength to fight off arms that threatened to strangle Ilean. He felt himself torn away, grabbed about the neck, then suddenly released again. He turned and chopped at Ilean's attacker with the rigid side of his hand and finally saw her swim free, just as he lost self-control to rage.

He thrashed out blindly at another elll that moved in to defend the first, but his arms were pulled backward by a powerful grip, and he was taken in a semi-conscious state out of the fracas, towed into the shallows, and left alone to recover.

As soon as his mind cleared, Korad stumbled back into the waves. A circle of disturbed water rent the bay.

"Back you fool." A sharp barking sounded. "Go to your boat." It was

Ba-ohl, pushing him roughly back toward the rover.

"Ilean. The librarians have her." Korad shouted in the new language.

"She will be all right," Ba-ohl sang. "The great-fish have come." Then he was gone.

Far out on the waves Korad saw Tera leaning over the bow of the rover, cautiously approaching the circle of struggling librarian ellls and great-fish. He shouted and waved, but she was intent on what was happening in the water. As the rover approached the struggle, Ilean leapt across the bow and pointed toward Korad.

Korad waved his arms frantically, trying to indicate that Tera should take Ilean onto the rover.

– Δ –

Tera saw Korad as a frail brown figure in the mist, pointing up with one hand and motioning the curve of a leap with the other.

"If only minds could be read at this distance," she grumbled. "Take the rover in closer," she shouted to her crew.

At the rover's approach, the ellls scattered and rejoined their battle farther off. Tera saw the long surge of great-fish fins cutting the surface. The librarians had not attacked the rover, nor attempted to board it. The great-fish would know how to stop the battle, if it could be stopped. Korad was still urging her on—to what? She decided not to take the chance of misinterpreting his hand motions, so she directed the rover to shore.

From a rock in the shallows, Korad stepped on board and confirmed his message.

"We've got to get close enough to the ellls to take my elll-friend Ilean aboard," he said. "Once she is out of reach, the librarians' rage will subside, and Ba-ohl and the others will escape. The great-fish have not been able to stop the fighting."

"Will she come with us?" Tera wondered. "If we could get her to the lab, perhaps she could put a stop to the insane things happening there."

"She will come if she knows I am on the rover."

Korad called Ilean's name over and over as they cruised quietly toward the warring schools. When they were on the edge of the turbulence, he dove overboard before Tera could stop him.

In the water he found himself immediately surrounded by great-fish, intent on guarding him against two murderous ellls from the library. Illean was not to be seen.

Soon he became aware of the peculiar ethics that governed the battle: Whenever the ells saw that a great-fish might be harmed or that their shell knives would only wound, not kill outright, they quickly aborted an attack, reeled, and searched for another chance.

An insistent nudge from a great-fish caught Korad's attention. Back-peddling with fins twice his height, a great-fish tapped the patches behind Korad's ears with the tips of his tail-fin.

Obediently, Korad probed the great-fish's mind. It was a strange sensation, being ushered into such diffuse thought, like being lost in a three-dimensional web of interlacing searchlights. At last Korad managed to find the central idea: "Sing," the great-fish commanded. "You must sing."

Korad called Ilean's name over and over again, using his imitation of elllonian song. With great relief he saw her coming toward him, escorted by more great-fish. "Come to me, elll-sister," Korad sang. "Our love will bring peace between strangers. Our mind as one mind will end anger."

Ilean joined the song. She clung to him and shared his weight with the great-fish, and the sea around them grew gradually calm.

The ells re-formed into two schools—waiting, listening. The angry mood was broken. More killing was impossible now.

Ilean and Korad sang their song again, and from above the waves, in the rover, Tera took up the counterpoint, calling Ilean's name as Korad had. Still singing, embellishing the song, Ilean helped Korad board the rover. Then she swam away between great-fish, past the librarians, to find Ba-ohl and her school.

"I must go with Korad," she told them.

"We will adjust." Ba-ohl tried to speak calmly. "Loners take their time where they will."

"My time belongs to Korad and the new language. You have seen that, Ba-ohl. I would only bring you a tortured state of partial adjustment if I stayed."

"Go then. Quickly. You are taking my life-joy. I'll go to the Far Deeps and bring Sa-el back to you. Then we will see how your moments are spent."

With a shudder of regret, she left Ba-ohl and rose to the surface. Gliding slowly to the rover's broad side, she reached up to Korad.

He pulled her onto the deck and kept her wrapped in his arms, while her school rose to the surface, sang their adjusting farewell, and moved off. The great-fish were already gone. Ilean was safe.

Tera interrupted their reunion with an urgent request. "You must call Ba-ohl's school back for a briefing, Korad. They must know what has happened in the Great Basin and around the lab."

Using poetic sounds for "stop" and "help," Korad called out across the water, and the ellls circled back toward the rover. The librarians kept their distance, watching.

In a mixture of poetic sound, sonic code, and sign language, Korad made Ba-ohl understand that the varoks were being attacked by ellls angry at the capture of one school, Falll's half of their original school. Sa-el's contingent of schools, coming from the Far Deeps, were in danger because some varoks believed them to be another attacking force. The varoks were very frightened, he emphasized. Sa-el's school must be stopped before it entered the Great Basin.

"Go and find Sa-el and the joined schools," Ilean told Ba-ohl. "Tell them to await the varoks in the Bay of Altoon. If they come farther, the varoks will mistake them as enemies."

Until that moment, the librarians had been circling in the water considering the situation, as if they might follow Ba-ohl. But with Ilean's last command, they turned south and cut swiftly back into the luminescent water of the Bay of Cold Deeps.

It was finished. The plans were made. At Korad's signal, the rover came to life and turned west, while Ba-ohl headed his small school north toward the Currents of Altoon.

ATTACK

The tragedy of tragedies is this:
When good will, taken wrong, its good intent
Left broken on despair,
Turns full upon itself in flight,
Destroying all it meant.

While Tera's rover took Ilean and Korad to the varokian laboratory, Sa-el and Duregal swam at the head of a large gathering of ellls.
They had reached the cold gray of the Far Deeps, where the water was
brightened by the warm glow of the Northern Crossing. Most of the
ellls there were horrified at the rumors of violence in the Great Basin.
Now the rumors had grown from subconscious threat to undeniable
fact. The ellls cared little whether the violence was directed against
themselves or against aliens. Violence in any form meant the loss of
life-moments, at least the degradation of life-joy. It must be stopped.

Word of the joining of schools had spread rapidly through the Far
Deeps, and ellls had converged on Sa-el's throng from as far away as
the Shallows of Ni.

At first Sa-el did not realize that his loner tendencies were serving
him well. He enjoyed his unique status as guide and source of information, leaving to others the gathering of food, the protection of the
school's fringe ellls or laggards, even communication with the great-
fish, who passed near the school at regular intervals. He swam before
all of them, choosing the safest path back to the Great Basin. Thus, he
fed his ego with a vision of a mighty school of ellls gliding through the
universe of consciousness to a new awareness.

"Now I lead all ellls—beyond the struggle to secure their gardens
from others—to that larger destiny." He voiced the last thought aloud,
startling the female resting beside him.

It had not been easy, he told himself, to collect enough schools willing to go back to the Great Basin and face both the varoks and the
varok-hating ellls.

"Sa-el." His name echoed dully in ultrasonics from deep within the
massed schools. Sa-el answered in the high range, took leave of the female, and made his way to the center, where he joined Duregal and six

elders. They were discussing the approach of another school of ellls.

"We have felt fear in the pressure patterns of this new school, Sa-el," one large old elll declared. "We had better swim in closer and ask them to join us, whether or not we can find enough food for them all. Every willing school should be welcomed into this venture."

"We can't take on any more schools," an older female insisted. "We are having trouble finding forage now. If our ellls begin raiding gardens on the way to the Great Basin, we will lose our advantage. So far, we are respected for our courage in seeking out the aliens."

"On the contrary, I believe many are against us," Duregal said. "Dissident schools have not stopped us, but many fear our talking with varoks. They believe that all the oceans will change, once varoks are befriended by ellls."

Sa-el's eyes narrowed with anger. "The oceans are already changed, because ellls are too stubborn to listen to their own minds. Schools attack schools, ellls raid others' gardens, tads are abandoned. We have seen the end of elllonian life as it was before the schools became too large and too many. We have not come together merely to talk with varoks. Our purpose is to save the ellls of the Great Basin from warring among themselves, and our real purpose goes far beyond that.

"We seek a new way of life. We believe in what the great-fish have promised: the varoks' good will and willingness to help us. Any who can't believe that, any who have lost faith in our need to learn should leave this greater school, for it is certain that before we are finished with the Great Basin ellls, we will be defending varoks."

"Be practical, Sa-el," the old blue elll demanded. "Can we hope to find food for more ellls or not? We will not find much in the currents of Altoon. What about the Great Basin? What will we eat there? Food from the gardens of varok-haters?"

"Listen," Sa-el cried sharply, and a wave of silence raced through the immense school, as the ellls hovered in the water. Nothing could be heard but the creaking of the mud-walkers, nothing felt but the odd pulsing of an approaching school.

"The new school is warning us off," Sa-el said, looking to Duregal. "Why? What is that below?"

A fleet of ten great-fish soared up from deep water. They sent a frantic message that traveled as an expanding ripple through the school: "Flee! Follow us into North Bay. Flee!"

Their great forked tails whipped around, and they led the ellls in a wild race against an unseen terror. They ran around the eastern peninsula, to the protected bay where their caves offered shelter.

"Dive!" The command came as an ultrasonic scream, as well as a pressure signal, flashed crudely but effectively by the enormous waving span of fully extended great-fish fins.

Some ellls were leaving the shallows, swimming hard toward the deeps, when a loud crack pierced the water. A cascade of mind-numbing echoes exploded off the rocks like acoustic bombs, cutting the school apart and scattering the ellls in every direction.

Then all was quiet.

Some ellls dove to the safety of the great-fish caves. Those at the head of the school, those who refused to follow the great-fish to deeper water, were killed outright. Some left the shallows in terror and crawled onto the beach.

Like an eagle skimming the water for fish, a Varokian space cruiser pulled out of its dangerous loop and rose into the mist.

V. ESCALATION

Ellason's gravity (1.4 Earth's) proved too much for some organisms trying to live out of water. Many gave up their dry-land ventures to continue their evolution. Thus, in the shallowest waters and near the warmest spots of the vast oceans, oxygen breathers joined the race for life.

Much later, clever swimmers found temporary refuge from predators in moss-covered rocks. Together with stereoscopic infrared vision and frontal gills, their newly evolved optional lungs contributed more oxygen to their ever-growing awareness, hence their inventiveness. Their prehensile fins extended into powerful limbs that withstood Ellason's gravity. The tips of those appendages became ever more dexterous. Their senses tuned to the demands of foraging on the dim land, to the challenge of farming in warm sea currents, and to the excitement of schooling during the violent storms those warm waters created. Thus, over a span of four and a half billion years, ellls came into being and named their planet Ellason.

—Aman Telariahn (Amantel), Varok, 2072 CE Earth

GUARDIANS OF LIFE-JOY

The gentlest of ellls, confined in time,
As one pure moment follows blind the next
By senses overdrawn,
Are soon o'ercome by moments' loss,
Their flooded souls perplexed.

Those ellls who dared to look out from their shelter in the rocks saw the sky go black over the beaches of North Bay. Some saw the Varokian cruiser disappear into the upper mists.

Soon after the sound attack, hundreds of great-fish gathered in the waves, cutting broad arches through the water in their search for lost and injured ellls. They set up a nursing station in the underwater forest that sheltered their caves from the cold currents. In the soft mud beneath tall, big-leafed *ahl* trees, they gathered together those ellls suffering disorientation or severe pressure shock. Those whose moss skin or hexagonal line networks were disrupted were gently suspended in sea vines tied to the long branches of swaying *ahl*.

The great-fish administered what herbs and anesthetics the ellls carried, but there were not enough. A crude lab was fashioned on the rocky shore, heating vessels were made of large shells, and herbal sea plants were gathered by the ellls physically untouched by the sound attack. Using shore-tossed *ahl* branches as fuel, the chemists among the ellls distilled medicines, hoping that some life-moments could be saved.

$$- \Delta -$$

Sa-el swam slowly out of the deep rocks, where he had taken refuge from the cruiser's attack. A sharp pain ripped across his thigh, and he knew that three hexagonal tiles had come loose from his leg. Sea water seeped beneath the tiles, covering his thigh with excruciating pain. He tried to call out, but the sonar code fell with dull thuds on his larynx. His head ached and he saw nothing. Frantically, he searched for the feel of pressure talk on his tiles. There was no sensation.

He felt isolated, floating blind in a space defined by the pain in his leg. The water seemed empty and silent, as if he were the only elll alive of all the joined schools. He decided he was deaf and lost from the school, as Ilean had been.

His ultrasonic echo-reception showed him the round depths of a great-fish cave not far ahead, and he made an effort, hoping he could glide there before *eefl* made a meal of him.

Why had the varoks attacked? They didn't mean to kill. Sound is not used to kill. They meant to destroy life-moments. That must be it. They meant to prevent the joining of schools.

In a rage, Sa-el gave an extra stroke and entered the great-fish cave, ignoring his pain. As a result, the searing ache of his wound tore through his mind and imposed the dreaded relief of unconsciousness.

– Δ –

Duregal paced the waters, aimlessly calling for the school. When he regained some focus, he realized that it was badly disrupted and needed to congregate immediately. A deadly variety of *eefl* was known to hunt the waters of this bay.

Duregal swam along the shore calling in ultrasonic, overlapping his path as best he could, until other ellls joined him in the search. As they re-gathered and extended the call, they began their adjustment to the trauma. They formed a core for the lost to rejoin, swam in formation to protect the injured, calmed the tads, and built a new pressure pattern that comforted everyone.

Then the eldest led the strongest out onto the rocks. Working in groups of six, they retrieved from the rough beaches those ellls too wounded or stunned to return to water by themselves.

By the time he reentered the water, Duregal found in a thick *ahl* forest a nursing station set up by great-fish. The larger school circled the station, while the great-fish and nursing ellls applied herbs and *ahl* bandages to ellls with damaged pressure systems. Those temporarily deafened found useful counsel with elders among the great-fish, but those crippled with rage found no solace or relief.

Treated ellls returned to the circling school, and an accounting was made of all who had been a part of the whole. Gradually, Duregal became aware of a large gap in the school's patterns. Sa-el was missing.

– Δ –

When Sa-el regained consciousness, he secured his leg tiles with a packing of soft mud and *ahl* leaves tied with vines. He lay on the floor of the great-fish cave, wondering how he had become separated from the school. He still could not catch their ultrasonic signals.

He slept for nearly a moon-light change, then awoke, realizing he was too hungry. The mud-pack had come off his leg wound. It was throbbing and sore again. Sa-el made another pack, then pulled himself out of the cave and floated to the surface. Using one leg and a broad two-handed stroke, he guided himself toward the *ahl* forest. Soon he heard ultrasonic inquiries, but he was unable to answer. He moved on, sure that someone would find him soon and tow him to safety.

– Δ –

Duregal sent an alarm through the school with a request for help. Soon a silent elll was located near the surface, approaching the school from the shore.

In the echoes of his ultrasonic probe, Duregal saw the unmistakable silhouette of Sa-el, swimming lamely toward the *ahl* forest. Another shadow marred the fringes of his image, however. Duregal refocused and checked his impression: an *eefl*, closing in on Sa-el.

Duregal pushed off for the surface and leapt into a running pattern that threaded the waves. When he saw the *eefl* pass beneath him, he dived deep. Then he turned to the attack and missed the shell knife he had been carrying.

Vaguely he sensed Sa-el's warning to stay away. "I am wounded anyway, old friend. I might as well be *eefl*-fodder."

Duregal snorted a negative code in reply and screamed in ultrasonics for help as he dove under the *eefl*. His only hope was to cling to its broad underside, avoid the long, whip-like grasping sucker, and force the beast to the surface. He grabbed for the flat edges of the *eefl's* fins.

"Run for the *ahl* forest," he shouted to Sa-el.

The younger elll ignored him and dove beneath the *eefl*, then thrust upward as best he could.

The *eefl* tried to shake off the two ellls, but the rigid triangle of his body gave them the leverage they needed.

"We've got him," Sa-el said, adjusting his grasp. "Watch it. He's turning."

The *eefl* spun end over end, throwing the ellls off his broad fin. Duregal fell against the mid-section of its lethal tail. It snapped around the old elll on contact, immediately crushing away his life.

Before the poisonous sucker could find its meal, however, Sa-el drove two long shells into the *eefl's* brain, and the beast fell with Duregal's remains to the bottom of the sea.

The ellls who had answered Duregal's call for help saw that they were too late. They returned their shells to their vine belts and tried to calm Sa-el. It was no use. He continued to circle, maddened with rage.

As they led him back to the school, the rescuers could not find a way to help him adjust to the loss of Duregal. The elder's death was not leaving his mind as a fact accomplished and irreversible, as it should. Instead it burned its way through his thought channels and lodged like a hot *challall* coal in his pressure memory. The school decided Sa-el must be a loner, with a loner's strange capacity to retain extreme emotions.

When they were in view of the nursing station, the youth spoke cautiously, watching Sa-el's eyes. The elder elll stared oddly at the youth, then swam off through the forest and began madly pacing back and forth over the dead, ignoring the injured ellls in his wake.

"Duregal!" he screamed. "All this horror was yours—because of varoks. Varoks must pay in like torture!" Then he cried out a vow of revenge against monsters worse than *eefl*, demons who had destroyed his leg and prevented him from saving the gentle sufferer, Duregal: "Death to all varoks. For all you suffered, varoks will pay life-moment for life-moment."

Song of Release

From too much time eternal shot with grief,
I heard a cry of hope from alien tongue
That told me I was free.
"Just free?" I cried. "What good is that,
"When all my life's unstrung?"

Moments before the varokian cruiser's attack, Tera's rover approached the narrow raised walkway that followed a deep channel cut into the barren mud beach. A huge mass of square stone was set into the cliffs at the end of the dock. "The ellls must be held beneath the dock that connects the lab to the sea. Can you walk that far, Ilean?"

"I think so." Ilean sang the affirmation in their new language, then went on tonelessly, as she imagined speech should be. "I have moss shoes. The mud is soft," she laughed, "and this is a ridiculous poem."

Tera and Korad laughed with her.

"Not nearly as ridiculous as my attempts at Elllonian," sang Korad.

"You do have your own accent," Ilean admitted. Suddenly she stiffened with the sight of two varoks in full braces coming toward them from across the beach.

"So. They are guarding the lab in earnest." Korad stood beside Ilean. He looked frightened, but intensely controlled. "Let's go on into the channel. We can approach the ellls' prison by water."

Tera nodded and shouted to the guards: "No need to come so far. I am Tehr Adkarian, just returned from the east. I will report to Mahar soon."

"That is an elll with you," one guard shouted.

"Of course. This is Korad's friend, Ilean," Tera answered. "She will teach us the language of ellls." She turned back to the rover, ignoring the varoks' next question. She took Ilean's hand to reassure her, and with Korad's help translated what had been said. "A foreign tongue should not be used in the presence of others who don't understand it," she said. "That's an old Varokian law."

"A good law. I will remember it." Ilean watched the guards retreat into the laboratory. "But it must be inconvenient, if you want to hide something from a stranger."

"We will not hide anything from you, Ilean," Tera said. "We are your school now."

Ilean tried to smile at the kind remark, but she was still a little uncomfortable with Tera. She didn't understand why. Though she liked the warm, round-faced varokian woman, she harbored an internal sternness that was unlike Korad.

"You should return to the lab now," Tera told the two young crewmen. "Make your report as you must. You have been valuable friends. You know I will not blame you if you take the safest path. To ally yourselves with me, when ellls have made the beaches unsafe for varoks, is to jeopardize your careers. I think I have provided your minds with adequate defense should you undergo a mind-probe. Good luck."

"We will undergo no probing, Master Tera," Ohlren said, emphasizing her honorific title.

"I pray I will soon have time and chance to know your minds, dear friends. We hope to arrive at the lab shortly after you reach there. I would counsel silence. Use as few words as you can—at least until we arrive."

The two turned away, but the sight of their affected slumping into their braces made Ilean laugh.

"We are very tired, Tehr Adkarian, from our ordeal," Markhel said, smiling over his shoulder. "We won't be able to talk to anyone or undergo a scan like this, incoherent with fatigue, don't you suppose?"

They went off then, the stiffer one trying to caution the other to forget the fib before it gave them away.

Tera gave Ilean's hand a squeeze and smiled at Korad, as he explained what was happening. On the trip back across the Great Basin in the rover, the two young crewmen had only pretended to be captured by Tera. Now they were acting as a distraction, giving her an excuse to delay her arrival at the lab, so that she and Korad could release the captive ellls.

Ilean felt Tera's hand tremble before it released hers.

A light mist dusted the smooth caramel-colored beach as they restarted the rover. Korad took it far out over the cold shore-waves of the Viortahk before he turned it back and headed for the artificial channel entering the laboratory at the far side.

"We can't hope to evade the scanners," Tera said. "The beaches will be under surveillance. The guards who recognized us have identified us. That is why we have not been intercepted."

"Then we'd better approach the docks as if we were arriving normally," Korad said. "We should not have sent your crew off, Tera."

"They'll think of some excuse for walking. Perhaps they escaped at the first chance—when they were close enough to the lab to walk."

Ilean liked the way Tera screwed up her face, as if she didn't believe what she was saying.

"I'm afraid you're right; we're poor conspirators, Korad. We had better rush in and get the ellls away from the dock as quickly as possible. We will have little chance if Tekram decides to welcome us home."

With a surge of power, the rover moved quickly up the channel. It was nearing the docks when a piercing noise made Ilean slam her hands over her ear plaques. Korad leapt for the rover's controls and shut them down. "Ilean, what's wrong?"

A terrible noise is shaking my skull apart, Ilean spoke in thought.

"I don't hear anything," Korad said. "We must go on. Someone is coming out of the lab."

The squeal changed to a low rumble, giving Ilean some relief. She lowered her hands from her ear plaques and touched Korad's face, tilting his eyes skyward. "Look," she sang, "more varoks are coming."

Tera looked up with them. It was the space cruiser from Varok. Where the mist parted, its long hull glinted dully in the black sky. Its glide wings, extended to embrace the land, gave it the appearance of some great mechanical bird floating in on silent batteries. It was in full glide when Tera alerted Korad to something strange.

"The angle of approach is too shallow, Korad. The cruiser is not coming in from Varok. It's trajectory is from Ellason."

Ilean heard the alarm in her voice.

"I agree. It must be on a suborbital path," Korad said. "But why?" He was staring into Tera's mind, Ilean guessed, and he was obviously horrified at what he found there.

"Why else would they land?" Tera asked. "I was not believed. They have attacked the ellls."

"Perhaps they have been consulting with the great-fish across the Great Chasm," Korad tried.

"Then their trajectory would have brought them from the south. They are coming in from the northeast, Korad, where there could be nothing of interest but Sa-el's massed school."

"I hope you're wrong, Tera."

Such a heavy sadness settled over him, Ilean cried out in empathy.

"At least we can use the diversion of the landing to set the captive ellls free," Tera said. "The varoks from the lab are already on their way to greet the ship. At the moment we are of less interest."

Korad turned their rover to full power, and ran it for the dock. As it bumped to a stop, the ellls imprisoned in the steel net backed away from the near side of their enclosure so they were not visible from the surface.

"Good," Korad declared. "We won't take time to make friends now. Attach the explosives to the lower section, Ilean." His instructions to the captured ellls were a tortured mixture of Elllonian, Varokian, and hand signals: "We'll burn a hole in the net down low, so it won't be discovered right away. You ellls, stay safe on the far side."

Ilean nodded. "Stay back. Stay there."

The elll dove off the rover, clutching Korad's laser pen and an *ahl* leaf smeared with the rover's emergency marine torch gel. The water all around her was murky with elll waste. She shuddered and moved quickly to the bottom of the steel net, all the while shouting in sonic code the one message that must get through to the tortured school: "We have come to set you free. Stay back from the explosive. Stay back, then swim free."

"It is the varok-elll," one huge elll screamed, drowning out her cry.

"The traitor."

"Grab her!"

In a fury, the school rushed at Ilean and rammed grasping fingers through the net.

She pulled away, and felt a handful of plumes torn from her hips. "Stop hurting me, you fools," she screamed. "I have come with explosives to open the net." She held up the laser pen and the leaf smeared with gel. "My varoks have come to set you free. Back away."

For a moment the ellls waited, as if they were listening, then the full impact of what they had suffered became clear to Ilean. Not only was the water fouled with their own waste, rotting flesh tainted their food trough. Their plumes stuck together in clumps, and their eyes stared ahead unseeing, like the unlit eye sockets of a dead mud turtle.

Desperate now, Ilean moved closer and tried again to paint the steel net with the explosive gel, but, again, several hands shot out to grab her. One elll managed to get a deep hold in the plumes of her left hip. She couldn't pull loose. More hands reached through the net. Ilean turned the laser pen on the roots of her hip plumes and cut herself loose, trying not to burn the hands of her attackers. Pain flooded her sensory channels and she nearly fainted. Still clutching the explosive and the activated laser pen, she swam upward.

The pen's light waved oddly in the water. Dodging its beam, Korad grabbed for Ilean's hand, turned off the dangerous light-knife, and with Tera's help, pulled Ilean into the rover.

"By Harrahn. What have those devils done to you?" Korad swore when he saw Ilean's torn plumage.

She took his hands and pressed them beneath her chin for comfort. "The school will stay back now, Korad. At least some will. They have gone mad, Tera. Don't blame them. It is terrible down there. Those that don't stay back can't understand; they have lost their lives already."

Korad started to protest, but she clutched at his hands. "We may have to sacrifice some, because others can still be saved."

She felt both varoks look deep into her mind. *If we are to be true partners, Korad, varoks must understand us better. Our minds cherish each moment. The death of life-joy is more tragic than physical death. Death is logical. It is the end to life's experience. It is painless nothing, merely an ending – compared to the horror of lost moments.*

Korad's eyes and Tera's touch told her they understood.

"I had better go down with you, Korad." Tera handed him an oxygen packet and clamped another over her mouth and nose. Then she took the fueled *ahl* leaf from Ilean, handed Korad the laser pen, and slid off the dock. Ilean followed.

As the three entered the water, only a few ellls refused to give up their mad clamoring. Most backed into the farthest corner of the prison.

"When you are free, run for the deeps," Korad sang. "There are still unfriendly varoks in the lab. They are afraid of ellls who kill. They are afraid of you. Now you hear a new song. I sing Ilean's spoken song. It will bring new understanding between us."

The ellls did not respond to the strange song, but Ilean repeated it in sonic code, and the varoks saw a glimmer of hope surface in their minds.

It took some urging, but at last Korad convinced Ilean to return to the surface and tend her wounds.

When she was safely back on the rover's deck, she started pulling burned plumes from her back. She was so focused on signs from below, she was startled by the appearance of a huge varok on the dock just above her.

Ilean had never seen such deep eyes, nor hands so powerful. His brow lines folded with ferocious intensity as he leaned over her.

She tried to clear her mind of what she knew was happening beneath the dock, but like a million devils alive within her, her thoughts kept inventing the very pictures she tried to shut out.

Suddenly she jumped at a clanking noise below, expecting the explosion, and she knew the huge varok understood the entire situation. A kindly smile unknit his brow line, and he climbed into the rover. Just then Tera broke the surface and clambered onto the dock ahead of Korad.

The muffled roar of the underwater explosion shook the dock, and with a little help from the huge varok, Tera and Korad tumbled into the rover.

Within seconds the surviving ellls surfaced, waved their thanks, and sped off.

Tera gave the varok a welcoming sound, "Thank you, Amanok. Thank you," and urged him to start the rover's engines. A quiet surge of power made the water tremble. The rover followed after the released ellls at a discreet, watchful distance, until the school reached the relative safety of the first islands of the Viortahk. Then Amanok swung the rover back toward the lab, along the eastern shore.

"Can you take it from here, Tera?" Ilean felt the surge of emotion between the two varoks, as they beached the rover some distance from the lab. "You went back to watch a school of ellls heading out through the Viortahk, didn't you? That's what your two young crewmen told the lab officials, and we have good reason to believe them now, don't we?"

What were they plotting? Ilean promised herself she would learn Varokian as soon as she could.

"Amanok, you old fool," Tera laughed. "No one will believe that story well enough for you to avoid a mind-probe."

"But it is true enough to give us a little time—enough time for Korad and Ilean to present their case to minds fresh from Varok."

Amanok turned to Korad. "Congratulations, my dear son. I see that you have been more than successful."

Korad nodded to the senior varok with an openly grateful mind.

"I will leave you here now," Amanok said, "to make your entrance. I am away hunting mud-turtles, if anyone should ask. My greetings to Voh Renak, Tera," he said, and Ilean saw grief in the varok's dark eyes. "Call for me, if the time comes."

"Amanok." Tera followed him onto the beach, and they stood sharing minds, their forearms pressed together. Ilean did not miss the intensity of the moment.

When Tera turned back to the rover, Ilean saw no more sternness in the varokian woman, only a deep and ripening vulnerability, like an elll separated too long from the school.

THE TEACHER

When reason lost the battle for their minds,
And varoks desperate sent the ellls in flame
To horrors never meant,
They closed their minds upon themselves
To question not their aim.

With the captive ellls released and safely past the Viortahk, Ilean could enjoy driving the rover. On their way to the lab, it had taken her only three lessons to feel comfortable at the controls, so she was the natural choice for driver as they rode across the last stretch of beach to the launch area.

She didn't like the look of the huge Varokian space cruiser. It lay like a broken great-fish on the broad expanse of hard mud. It represented everything ellls had rejected in their lives: metal and technical power, dependence on things outside the school. She concentrated on driving and tried not to think about it. She was here to help, not criticize.

The mist had retreated from the lower hills, leaving the gentle slopes blue with *challall* weeds. Ilean wondered if the varoks had ever tried eating the delicious *challall*. It grew in odd patterns, as if it had never been cultivated here, as if it would soon crowd out the square monolith that Korad called the lab. She glanced at the alien building with more curiosity than apprehension. This was Korad's home, his garden, the center of his school.

What frightened her most were the many varoks flowing back and forth on foot and in small shuttles between the laboratory's loading docks and the space cruiser. She shuddered involuntarily and moved into Korad's arms.

"Where is the wet-sweater we made, Ilean? You'll feel more at home with us dry-land bipeds if you have it on."

"Stay close to me, Korad," Ilean sang quietly. She felt very fragile out of water, like unfired porcelain that one could crush with a hard look.

Tera found the moss sweater, and Ilean pulled it over her head, while Korad held the rover on course toward the crowd gathered to greet the new arrivals from Varok.

"I'll drive the rover right into the middle of them." Ilean laughed with a sudden mischievous urge as she took back the controls. "What a surprise they'll have—to see an elll wearing clothes driving a rover to greet their space cruiser, as if it were nothing at all."

"That's the idea," Tera said. "My consummate mate, Vohren, is on that cruiser. We'll go directly to him and introduce you as the good friend you are. The Directorate can stifle their curiosity and their demands for a while longer."

Quickly they sped over the beach to the landing pad.

Ilean was concentrating so hard on guiding the rover and looking relaxed, she barely noticed the stunned expressions on the varokian faces as she maneuvered through the crowd and came to a stop beside the space cruiser's passenger ramp.

A tall varok with bright, dancing eyes peered down at them. "Good timing, Tera," he shouted. "You are safe and fat as ever. I thought I would have to save you from starvation in the rocky haunts of the evil ellls." He ran down the ramp and held out his arms. Tera embraced him, and their minds locked.

Korad climbed out of the rover, offered a hand to help Ilean disembark, and kept a protective arm around her, while he told her about the reunion she was witnessing.

Curious varoks had closed in behind them. "Remarkable," one said.

"The elll and Kor Adtalorian seem to be in mental consummation."

Suddenly Tera pulled back from Vohren's embrace. She was trembling with rage. "What is this terrible memory I see in your mind?"

Ilean startled and huddled against Korad. She had never seen Tera so angry, nor Korad. Why was he staring that way at Tera's mate?

The crowd around Tera grew quiet as she walked over to Ilean and enclosed her in her arms. "This is the proof of the love that can be between ellls and varoks, my friends," she announced loudly. Her voice shook. She turned and tried to smile, but her tears blinded her.

She ran a hand gently over Ilean's puzzled face. "Give welcome to Ilean," she commanded. "Welcome Ilean and Kor Adtalorian, founders of the elll-varok language we shall call Elllonian. Ilean—consummate mental sister to Korad, Master of Varoks—is here to teach us the new language, to teach us the history and lore of ellls, to teach us the nature of beings we will no longer try to mold into reflections of ourselves." Her voice rose to an angry shout. "She is here to teach us to listen to minds that see with more lenses on reality than we can understand. Welcome to Ilean, bravest of ellls, honored guest."

The crowd of varoks stood shocked and silent as Tera's impassioned tone accused them all. "In Vohren's mind I have seen what you have done to try to stop Sa-el's grand school. No doubt you stopped them, all right, with your vicious attack. But why? You have no idea what you have done. Why do violence to a school that was coming here to stop the attack of violent ellls?"

Ilean heard her name and saw Tera's angry look aimed at the varok behind her, the one called Tekram. His face was frozen into an unreadable mask, but he was trembling. All the other varoks stared at the delicate blue elll, her body plastered against Korad's.

Tera looked back and nodded to Vohren. "Find Amanok. Go to the ellls in the Far Deeps and see what you have done. Take medical supplies—everything we have. There must be many terrible injuries. The young officers Ohlren and Markhel should go with you—to keep you out of trouble. Hurry."

She turned away, linked arms with Korad, and pushed into the crowd. It gave way before them. Silently, a spontaneous tribute traveled through varokian scientists. Many of their right hands spiraled upward, saluting Korad's accomplishment and the elll who chose to trust him.

Ilean wept quietly as they moved into the lab. Something terrible had happened, and Korad would not tell her what it was.

Once they were in the privacy of the varok's room, he turned away from her and threw himself on the g-brace.

"Please, Korad, what has happened?"

He had to look at her, and the pain in his face was awful to see. "How can I tell you? How can I *not* tell you? How can you stay here? I can't let you go, not without a school to protect you. Ilean, Ilean." He shook with the effort to stay rational, but could not. He lost hold and fell into an inescapable pit of grief for what the Varokian ship had done.

Ilean shrieked with terror when she saw the life-awareness slip from his eyes. Desperately she clutched at him, tried in vain to sing to him. Nothing she did aroused the varok from his passion.

Tera found Ilean sobbing over Korad. The elll refused to leave his side. She would not listen to Tera's explanation. It didn't matter that this loss of rationality was a normal varokian reaction to extreme emotion. It didn't matter that he would soon emerge, rational and whole. He was losing life-moments now. He was as good as unconscious. He could never recapture the life-joy of these moments. It was forever lost.

When the lab officials learned that Korad had gone irrational with remorse over the cruiser attack, no one spoke of him, or of Ilean. It was clear the elll knew nothing about the attack. The Directorate ordered Tera to watch all the elll's movements and to report any interchange between the elll and Korad. Tera agreed to the task so that a less sympathetic person would not be given the job.

Ilean stayed at Korad's side. Twice every light cycle Tera brought her food. The elll ate very little. After several cycles Tera noticed, in spite of Ilean's wet-sweater, her skin looked painfully dry, its moss crumbling from lack of moisture.

"You too are losing life-moments." The gentle varok counted on Ilean's growing understanding of varokian. "If you don't return to water, you will be too sick to live your moments as you should when Korad awakes. Come with me, just for a while, and take some moisture."

There had been no word from Vohren and Amanok, probably for good reason, Tera decided. All they could do was confirm Tera's worst fears as they tended to ellls injured in the space cruiser attack.

When at last Ilean followed Tera to the lab aquarium, she would not enter the water without the varokian woman beside her. They swam slowly back and forth across the sea pool, never touching, always close. When they began to swim as one, Ilean sang to give them both comfort.

Winds of time blow gently through my mind.
Ease me past all troubled days,
With shadows moving swiftly o'er the deeps,
Telling me of ellls who once have been,
Of knowledge found
And songs renewed,
Of races never won;
Telling me of great-fish strange and wise,
Of tales beyond the coldest deeps,
Of lessons etched on tiles that bind the school.
Winds of time blow gently through my mind.

Tera asked her to sing it again, so she could record it. "Ilean, this is how we will teach the varoks your language. This is how we will teach them about ellls. Please don't be afraid of the machine. It can only listen and repeat what you sing. I will tell the varoks what it means and what it doesn't mean. I will take the meaning from your mind. Korad will be pleased that you have been brave enough to go ahead with your teaching without him."

Ilean understood that Tera would use her songs to teach Korad's song-language to the varoks. Soon they would realize how little they knew about ellls.

"You can't know what you don't know," Tera said, speaking from experience, "until you know enough to understand how little you know. I want you to compose songs about ultrasonic echo memory and pressure patterns. There you have experience—a blindness that we share—and knowledge of some things neither you nor any varok has ever experienced. Your loss is the path that will give us common minds. Will you do it, Ilean?"

Ilean laughed. "The songs, yes, I understand." Tera saw in Ilean's mind the determination to teach the new language.

It was not easy. She was forced to rely on the lessons the great-fish had taught her. Now she realized, without her blindness, she would not have been able to separate herself enough from elllonian sensations to describe them.

After a few attempts, Tera discovered that the elll's songs were very difficult to translate, for there were no varokian equivalents for echo memory and pressure signals, or for the more subtle messages that the sonic code could convey.

"How did the great-fish succeed in making you understand pressure patterns and ultrasonic echo memory?" Tera asked. "Somehow they defined sight to the blind."

"I bumped my head in the tunnel to their caves," Ilean said. "How do we bump varok heads?"

Tera took her hands in her own. "I know you can do it. Already your songs are giving the stubborn varoks of this laboratory an impression of something beyond their understanding."

Ilean warmed to the challenge. She learned that most varoks had too few senses to understand the ellls' horror of captivity and the disruptive power of noise. At the same time, she understood, like the great-fish, that varoks had something to teach, something about oceans that were too small for too many ellls, something that the great-fish had seen coming long ago but couldn't stop. Tera's encouragement rekindled her sense of life-joy, but it soon became endangered again as she began to fear that Korad would never regain consciousness.

– Δ –

When the captive ellls returned to their gardens beyond the Rocky Shallows, some could not resume normal schooling life. The bitter half of Ilean's old school found their gardens empty and devoid of purpose. Adjustment was impossible with those who never recovered their life-joy. They began to neglect their gardens, and they wandered throughout the Great Basin gathering stories about the varoks and puzzling over what they heard.

Too many questions pulled through the others' minds. True to their nature as ellls, their hatred for varoks soon dissipated when they were free, but unfamiliar thoughts haunted them. They remembered one old varok, Amanok, crying like a lost tad for them. The varoks, friends of Ilean, had put themselves in danger to set them free.

Simple ways had been discovered for turning off the varokian noise makers, so their sound no longer fed fuel to the widespread elllonian anger. The loss of ellls killed in attacks on varoks was forgotten, once adjustment to their absence was complete. When healing began and pain dissipated, injuries no longer rankled. Only those ellls made permanently neurotic or crippled in past encounters with varoks were able to sustain their anger at a dangerous level.

Eventually the former captives made their way into the Northern Shallows to look for Sa-el or Ba-ohl or Duregal. They weren't sure which, because the stories that now passed between schools were contradictory. Some said Sa-el was gathering a great school from the Far Deeps, in order to battle the varok-haters of the Great Basin. Some said it was Ba-ohl who was now leading a great school to a secret rendezvous with varoks. Some said Sa-el would drive the varoks from Ellason. Some said Duregal was leading a great school, and Ba-ohl was trying to stop them. Others said Duregal was no more.

The former captives were determined to find out for themselves which story was true. They wanted to join whichever effort seemed most likely to lead them back to undisturbed gardens.

Three Minds in One

Though all your thoughts were centered here in mine,
And we saw more than I alone could see,
I could not know your soul,
Until we shared a grief
That tore away reality.

While Ilean grew into her new role as mentor to varoks at the lab, she struggled to maintain hope for Korad's recovery. Tera could not reasssure her honestly.

Meanwhile, the great-fish sent Vohren and Amanok back to the laboratory from their rescue mission in the Far Deeps. Amanok hated feeling so helpless, unable to do anything for Sa-el's injured school. Their medical supplies had helped those ellls injured by the sonic attack. Their varokian presence had not.

At first Tera had little time to work through her shattered reunion with Vohren, and no time for Amanok. Work with Ilean was all-consuming.

When six light-periods had passed and Korad showed no sign of recovery, Tera called Amanok to join her in working on Ilean's language.

"Vohren and I have agreed to try a meld, Amanok. Perhaps the three of us can find a way to get around Korad's grief and restore him to consciousness. We suspect he suffered some brain damage when he nearly drowned."

"You tempt me, Tera. We have come very close. I can hardly bear to pull myself back from you, but it is too much. Three-body problems are bad enough. Three-body complex systems must be impossible."

"In some cases."

Amanok couldn't help smiling, loving her faith. "It has never been done, Tera. How can we expect a three-way melding?"

"Because it is natural to us. Call it rare luck, call it whatever you will, but don't reject it on that basis."

Vohren was waiting.

Vohren and Tera's concern for Korad and love for Amanok expanded into his whole being as they saw the full measure of Amanok's past life open up before them. All his accumulated memories of being on Ellason filled their minds. Long years of lonely, difficult work on a huge, strangely lit, alien planet had nurtured a deep respect for endless water and the ellls' highly selective intelligence.

Gradually Amanok moved into the memory Tera and Vohren shared. He retreated at the knowledge of their first consummate mating, but Tera bade him linger, until he accepted the fact of her shared life with the other. Timidly he moved back into Vohren's early years.

Tera relaxed as Amanok dropped his reserve. Their shared grief for the terror the ellls had suffered at varokian hands threw them together into an irrational, emotion-filled state. Their minds fused with a soul-fulfilling mental embrace, and their thoughts became one.

Vohren's consciousness embraced them both. Soon his light good humor had them all laughing with joy, and for a precious moment they celebrated their mental union.

Their light mood could not last long, however, for their minds were too full of Korad's grief and the ellls' horror. Tera and Amanok had only to look into Vohren's eyes for the memory of the sonic attack to rise between them like some demon out of a living hell.

Tribunal

The varoks sat in judgment on their kind,
Determined still to see their minds unchanged,
While grief for actions cruel
Reduced young genius to his bed,
Alone, from life estranged.

The Directorate stood around the conference room dressed in full bracing, knowing this debate would prove long and difficult.

"Tehr Adkarian, you are accused of destroying laboratory property—"

"The mesh net was a torture chamber," Tera interrupted.

". . . and setting free valuable laboratory specimens."

"*Laboratory specimens*? Free citizens of Ellason? Members of Ilean's school? Ilean is our guest and instructor in Elllonian."

Director Mah Harahk paused so that all of Tera's spontaneous comments could be recorded. Her emotional state was also noted. Tekram was visibly disappointed to hear that no irrational anger was found in her mood.

"I apologize for prolonging this hearing," Tera assured the Directorate, "but please note—our choice of words reflects our different views."

"You are also accused of life-endangering sabotage," Mahar added.

"Then accuse me, also," Amanok said.

His statement was noted, then ignored.

"I object to the phrases Tehr Adkarian uses to describe our work,"

Tekram said. "We knew that ellls suffer when taken from their schools. Therefore, we arranged to house an entire school underwater, not in the laboratory aquarium, but in the ellls' natural water, where we could observe their behavior as a school."

"You were not studying those ellls in natural water." Tera fixed Tekram with her glare. "Elllonian schools range great distances along the coasts of Ellason. They habitually move at high speed. They don't huddle in steel nets and foul their own water. Captivity means the subjugation of the ellls' precious senses to ugly and painful sensations— and the loss of life-joy. Learn that phrase well, Tekram. *Life-joy*. It is the essence of the elllonian spirit. You had no hope of talking with the ellls when their life-joy was gone."

"There is no talking with ellls," Tekram countered.

"You still don't understand what I mean, do you? Let me give you another example. Your amplified words of doom, broadcast into their gardens uninvited, disrupted their entire pattern of daily schooling. Your so-called educational warnings actually constituted a noise attack—an intolerable intrusion on a species that relies on sound for its sense of sight and well-being—an intrusion that generated such confusion that all sense of life-joy was lost. It provoked the ellls to defend themselves in the only way they knew how. They tried to cut off the source of the sound. They attacked varoks who tried to install or repair the devices. The attacks were justified defense. How were we justified in torturing one school with captivity? How were we justified in disrupting with a lethal sonic attack a huge, remote school? The intentions of that school were peaceful. That was Ilean's school—our teacher's school."

Tera swallowed her anger as she spoke, leaning into the support of her mental union with Amanok and Vohren.

"Before the judicial councils of Varok," Amanok said, "we accuse the Directorate of the Varokian Observation Laboratory on Ellason with violating the Interspecific Codes."

Tera's hope rose.

All the varoks but Tekram took the charge seriously. "The ellls do not fall under the protection of the Interspecific Codes," he said, his unlined face held rigid.

"The exact violation is of no concern." Mahar spoke as if the impasse could be broken. "Our purpose has been to instruct ellls in the ecology of Ellason as we understand it. We have seen its balance change dramatically in the last Varokian year. We have also found it necessary to protect our personnel and this laboratory from elllonian attacks. However, we will examine the elll Ilean. If we find, Tera, that your evaluation of the elllonian mind is accurate, then we will concede a mistake in judgment—under duress."

"Our accusation remains as stated. This Directorate has ignored the competent judgments of Amanok and myself at a great price to the ellls. I have petitioned Ahl Vior that this Directorate be banned from Ellason."

The Chief of Cognizant Life, Amanok's immediate supervisor, shook his head sadly, but stared at Amanok impassively as he spoke. "Aman Okrahlan, you acted against all good judgment, against your own pronouncement of punishment, and in an irrational state when you authorized Kor Adtalorian to take a land rover for himself and to search out ellls alone. The lad could have met his death."

"Amanok is not on trial here, and Korad did not meet his death," Tera said. "He accomplished what we have tried for decades to achieve. With an open mind, he met an elll on her own ground. He was accepted—while we failed, blinded by our heady assumptions of varokian superiority and the necessity of control. Amanok's judgment in sending Korad out alone was inspired by his intuitive knowledge of ellls."

"Nonetheless, you have directly disobeyed the intentions of this Directorate by releasing the school of ellls, Tehr Adkarian." Mahar's voice did not hold much conviction. "You are instructed to leave Ellason on the cruiser returning to Varok. You are asked to resign your post as Specialist in Elllonian Communication. Furthermore, as the law requires, you are forbidden further access to ellls."

"Nonsense." Tera actually smiled. "You don't believe in what you are saying, Mahar. Your orders are meaningless. This Directorate is accused of Interspecific Code violations. Your credibility is nil. We challenge your claim that protective measures against the ellls required their torture. *Torture*, Mahar, in the name of protection? Your literal opinion of our objections will not hold. That attitude is what destroyed our work here. We are on Ellason. We must be flexible to withstand its great mass. We must be adaptable to understand the beings who live here." She saw that he agreed with her, but his mind was set. "At least you cannot deny me access to the communications link with Varok."

She caught Amanok's eyes, then Vohren's, and found the support she needed in their approval.

Mahar looked around at the varoks for more comment. There was none. "This hearing is adjourned."

"Our point of view will win at the Councils of Varok," Tera said.

"Perhaps it will," Vohren said. "I hope for your sake, Tera, that the varoks on Varok have absorbed more elllonian qualities than some who have spent years on this planet."

That's the secret of Ilean's song, isn't it, Amanok? Tera easily joined both minds. *Vohren, her song contains unheard qualities that our insulated souls have longed to adopt. The ellls put us more in tune with ourselves, less afraid of what we are feeling. That is why we have pursued them for so long, and so desperately. The great-fish must have finally realized that we needed to hear the ellls' song for ourselves. It had to happen the way it happened between Korad and Ilean. Only in a natural experience could the elll allow the varok to hear her song, could the varok allow himself to hear it.*

THE UNHEARD SONG

While ellls went mad with pain, and varoks then
Bound up their minds in rigid reason's girth,
Two youths, too keen with life
To let such horror rule their time,
Destroyed the set with mirth.

Soon after the hearing, Korad came out of his grief. When he sat up and smiled at her, Ilean exploded with joy, singing and eating and pushing food at the exhausted youth until he begged her to calm down so he could find her mind.

Ilean's elllonian memory of happy moments with the varok Tera reflected real progress in developing the Elllonian language. Nothing in her thoughts suggested she knew about the space cruiser's attack.

Korad was both relieved and worried that she had not been told about that tragedy. Believing he would cushion the truth with his love, he wanted to be the one to tell her. But not yet.

He decided to consult Tera before he told the elll about the spaceship's attack. Perhaps the Directorate would have estimates of how many ellls were killed. Surely the great-fish would have brought some news, and probably a furious reprimand.

Before he could tell her, however, the Directorate demanded an interview with Ilean. She was weak and dried-out from her over-zealous nursing duties, so Korad, exercising his youthful wisdom, insisted that she should wear lifters for the long walk to the conference room.

Gently, he eased her broad delicate feet into his lifters and strapped them around her ankles. "There," he muttered in Elllonian. "If the hum of those machines on your feet doesn't convince the Directorate that their varokian-style interview is a waste of time, nothing will."

"The lifters are not really necessary," Ilean sang. "I can stand on the moss beaches near the shallows for nearly a moon-light change." She had trouble affecting the monotone of their new spoken language, though she now found some limited pleasure in its logical precision.

"A varokian conference room floor is not as soft as a moss-covered beach, Ilean. Come on now. Lean on me while you try walking with the lifters. Remember, go easy."

In spite of his warning, Ilean's first step brought her knee up to her chin, and she fell over backward.

"Easy. Easy." Korad laughed as he reached down to help her up. "Pretend that your feet are as light as plumes."

Ilean giggled and tried again. This time the controlled effort of her thigh brought her knee up to her waist.

"Use even less effort. Here we go now, down the hall."

The elll marched gingerly down the long hallway, and the lifters took the burden of Ellason's gravity off her feet, but her knees kept dancing to different heights.

She began to chuckle. Her knee-weakening mirth made her lose concentration, confounding her efforts. Her knees flipped upward. She lost her balance. Korad caught her. She overcompensated in the other direction. By the time she and Korad arrived at the opening to the conference room, they were hysterical with laughter.

One look at Tekram's stern face brought Korad under control, but not Ilean. To her it was hilarious—the vast difference between her mood and the varoks' puzzled expressions, frozen on their faces, their stiffly braced bodies standing in a rigid circle around the empty color-less room. She laughed until great tears rolled down her velvet cheeks. The straighter the varoks stood, the louder she laughed. She lost her balance again, and Korad, thoroughly embarrassed, looked around for some way to redeem the situation. He failed to catch her. She grabbed for him as she went down, forcing half the Directorate to move out of their way.

"A *leelll-ll*" she sang out, enjoying the spontaneity of the slap-stick with all the infectious power of her elllonian sense of humor.

Tera recognized the meaning of Ilean's joyful shout, and she too be-gan to laugh. Soon the meaning registered, with some shock, in all the varoks' minds: '*a lleell-ll*,' literally 'you female,' an expression in sonics meaning 'let's go' was also used during a mating grab at high speed in the water.

Amanok and Vohren joined Tera in full release. Their delight at the youths' impropriety spilled over to the others. Even Laktal and Mahar smiled in sympathy.

Then all the varoks' moods changed to wonder, as they watched the elll. She was obviously very anxious to have Korad understand her mirth and join in her life-joy. He looked too upset. She couldn't have that. She pulled Korad into her arms and rolled back and forth on the floor singing out her love for him:

> *Dear one—stiff, brown walker—*
> *Walk into my mood.*
> *Love me here before your elders.*
> *Mark their wond'ring smiles.*
> *Melt away with tears of joy*
> *The worry from their masks.*
> *Make them part of Ellason,*
> *Make them love the ellls,*
> *Show them how we live the now*
> *And leave the past forgotten.*

Every varok in the room saw her love for Korad and read her good intent.

"Ellls are creatures of the present." Her mind was full of the conscious idea. "Ellls don't live on sensations no longer felt. Now is the time for love between our species."

Korad gently took her hands in his and kissed her beneath the chin, elllonian style. "Ilean, it is affirmed," he said in Elllonian. "To know the mind is our way. You have spoken to our minds. Now it is our turn. We will promise our good will to you in water—in your way."

No one in the room disagreed.

Tera offered her a hand and spoke in halting Elllonian. "We understand now our blindness. Apologies are not enough. We promise not varokian ways but essentials of elllonian life, water and moments. You teach us now what we have not seen."

"We have gathered here in hopes that we might try joining you in water, Ilean," Mahar said in Varokian. Korad translated as Mahar continued. "We had to be shown how much we have assumed. We can now begin work on dissolving the real differences between us."

Ilean surprised the lab Director by walking up to him and pushing her nose under his chin as a tad would its sponsor. Then she and Korad led the others to the lab aquarium.

"We shall have a varokian school," Ilean sang as she dove into the sea tank.

Some of the varoks dove into the water, where they joined Ilean in the ritual of adjustment as best they could. Only Tekram refused to participate. The stimulation of Ilean's pressure signals and electro-organ discharge was intense, and many had to leave the pool. They tried again, and some were able to contribute to the adjustment with one arm or with feet dipping into the water so they could be pulled out momentarily for relief.

Many of the sensations and mechanics of schooling were impossible to translate, so the varoks absorbed much of their understanding by close patch contact with Ilean's mood and literal thoughts. As expected, the ultrasonic and pressure signal functions of the school were the easiest to understand, since they came originally, not from Ilean's experience, but from the great-fish teachings Ilean repeated for them.

Before long, even Tekram was forced to admit that he had overlooked too much in elllonian culture. It had been misjudged by varoks—the sonic code, the enormous ultrasonic memory, the knowledge coded and stored in the library, the power of poetic expression and improvisational art, the technology known but ignored, the importance of the garden as an organic part of the school, the significance of the increasing number of loners—all had been clouded with varokian assumptions.

When a Varokian light-period had passed, the varoks rested from Ilean's intense instruction. Mahar offered her a hand to help her out of the water. "We must go to the joined schools." He spoke as if he wanted confirmation from her, and Tera translated into Ellonian. "Perhaps, with you to introduce us, we can begin to make amends."

Korad leapt out of the water and stared him down. The youth's demand for silence caught the Director's attention, and Korad reminded him silently that Ilean did not know of the attack on the schools.

Ilean looked back and forth between the two varoks, wishing she could read minds as they did. She realized Korad did not like talking about the joined schools, but it couldn't be avoided now. Mahar was right in wanting to contact them.

"I'll be glad to introduce you to the schools," Ilean said, "but first I'll have to adjust to their new pattern. I don't know who was killed by the cruiser's sonic attack and who might have been left behind with the great-fish."

Korad cried out. "Who told her? I should have been the one. Who told her?" He pulled Ilean into his arms to comfort her, but found nothing to comfort. Her memory was full of overheard conversations about the cruiser attack—conversations overheard in Varokian. She had quizzed Tera and now understood more meaning in the sounds of varoks. There was no grief, no bitterness about the attack. It was done. The dead were dead. The great school would heal.

"You have learned much Varokian—or understood varoks—in a very short time, Ilean," Mahar said. "We will never again underestimate the intelligence of ellls. Now we had best look to Tera's judgment. I can't ask her to retract her charges against the Directorate, but I think she will agree that we had better find the joined schools as soon as possible."

Without a word, Korad grabbed Ilean's hand, and they dropped back into the water. Tera was still there. She motioned for Vohren and Amanok to join them. Tekram hovered near the water, listening as the other five worked through another light period, giving shape to their dreams of a reconciliation between ellls and varoks.

A School Gone Mad

All hail, good friends, we bring you songs of hope.
Why don't you stop? What strange disease has turned
Your thoughts to lethal fire?
What mad design has bent your minds
And left all life-joy burned?

The elll Ba-ohl raced for the surface when he spotted Sa-el's large school emerging from the currents of Altoon. He led Navell and Melo and the others in a leaping chase along the sands of Ellrin, excitedly broadcasting their presence and asking that Sa-el's larger school stop and adjust to them.

No ultrasonic response came from Sa-el's school. It moved doggedly on in a straight line, as if it were running blind.

"Listen Ba-ohl," Navell cautioned. "Another school is coming toward us from the Eastern Rocks. Sa-el's school must have been listening for them."

"The librarians," Ba-ohl cried. "Hurry!"

The wind had pushed the mist into black clouds, and the currents were strong and difficult to anticipate. Ba-ohl glided at high speed just under the surface, but he saw that the librarians would reach Sa-el's greater school before he did. It couldn't be helped.

"Whatever we do, we had better not send Sa-el or the librarians into a temper."

Navell agreed.

– Δ –

Sa-el watched the librarians with eyes hard as obsidian. As the schools joined and traded tales, he said nothing—but those who swam near him picked up the tremor of his anger when he heard of the library's destruction. The tremor passed through the schools with growing ferocity. The ellls' tempers, kept on edge by their wounds, grew quickly explosive, until both schools seethed with anger aimed at varoks.

"The varoks must be driven from the sands," Sa-el shouted in impassioned sonic monotones. "They must be driven from Ellason."

The librarians took up the chant, and slowly it drowned out all distractions. Before most of the ellls realized what was happening, the adjustment to the librarians was made on the basis of the chant, so that the massive school became one unthinking entity driven by one goal—revenge.

– Δ –

Ba-ohl and Ilean's friends came too late. They felt the strange obsession in the narrow intensity of the school's pressure patterns and tuneless song. Its repetitive ugliness was chilling, its simple tones and unphrased melody like the cry of a wounded *lohn* bird.

They searched in vain for Duregal, and when they found Sa-el, they lost all hope of turning the school. He was the center of the school's existence, its disciplinarian and counsel, the sponsor of its intense purpose—and he was mad.

Ba-ohl saw only a glimmer of recognition in Sa-el's eyes. A flash of lethal anger surfaced when he tried too hard to distract Sa-el from his chanting.

There was nothing to do but follow the great school down the coast into the Northern Shallows. Navell and Melo learned that Duregal had been killed, that the school had been attacked with vicious sonic blasts from a Varokian space cruiser.

They tried several times to approach the librarians. What had turned them to revenge? They had heard Korad's song of love for ellls. The librarians had nearly followed Ba-ohl, as part of a school devoted to a new relationship with varoks.

Their final answer came from a librarian who had tutored Ilean. "Isn't it enough—the pain you see all around you? This school lives no life-joy. It exists as proof of the evil that drives varokian minds. The aliens must be prevented from stealing more life-moments."

Navell called Ba-ohl and their friends to the shallows, and they watched Sa-el's school move swiftly away.

"He will drive them on until they starve," Ba-ohl said, "or are destroyed by the varoks they attack."

"Yes," Navell said, "but the librarians are quite sane. They will see that the school rests and eats. Sa-el is nothing more nor less than the heartbeat of that pitiful mob."

"It's not over yet, Navell."

"This is the beginning of a new kind of school. Two schools have joined in one purpose, and that purpose will fire them to do battle with other schools for the food they need. It is a kind of madness. Sa-el and the librarians have created a reality larger than any of the schools alone. The old civilization of stable gardens and small, open schools is over, Ba-ohl."

"We had better gather the ellls of the Great Basin. They must help us stop Sa-el."

"Some of them might defend varoks." Navell spoke with little hope. "It's worth a try."

– Δ –

"These are the latest satellite scans." Tera placed a collection of infrared print-outs on the desk next to the controls of the large glider, as Amanok maneuvered it through the islands of the Viortahk. "They indicate that an unusually large school is moving directly toward us on a steady course. Normally, schools don't travel so fast in one direction for so long."

Amanok continued to sort through the infrared scans as Tekram watched over his shoulder. "Where did those ellls go after they passed the great-fish caves?" Tekram asked. "Ask Ilean if we should try to intercept them in the rocky shallows or in the deeps."

Tera turned away to consult Ilean. "How can we ask them to stop? We need time, not a major confrontation."

After some thought, Ilean decided Sa-el would take the shortest route to the lab. Surely he would be eager to talk to the varoks before any more tragic misunderstandings occurred. "The school will come through the rocky shallows after they feed at our old gardens," she said. "We can meet them there."

Tekram frowned but didn't argue.

The Varokian glider and its crew stopped and waited, watching the infrared shadow of the school move toward them.

Ilean was obviously excited to be in her home waters with Korad. She towed him to all of her favorite haunts. Then she gave him and the Chief Observer of Cognizant Life, Okarian Telrak, a detailed tour of the wildly flourishing garden.

When they sighted the large school coming into the garden, Tera reviewed again the song she had composed in Elllonian. It told of varokian grief at the death of ellls, of mistaken thinking by varoks that had led to their imposing torture. It told of the deaths of varoks and varokian fear.

Ilean praised the song for its beauty, but she worried that ellls would think that varoks had no life-joy left.

"I'll add another verse celebrating the new language," Tera said.

"I didn't mean to ask for compliments," Ilean laughed, "but that would give our song language a happy ending. Sa-el will like it. And Ba-ohl. I do hope Ba-ohl has found the greater school."

The starlight cycle was just ending when Tera noticed the view on the infrared screen. "The large school is gone!"

Amanok reviewed the life-indications, tracing the marks with his finger, while Tera ran the scanner gradually from north to south.

"Two smaller schools are nearby, but yes, the large school is gone." she said. "Just gone!"

"Try a deeper setting," Ilean suggested. "Maybe they have gone back to the garden to eat."

"There they are." Amanok found a rapidly moving signal. "Two hundred meters, Ilean."

"That's too deep for the garden," Ilean said.

"By Harrahn. They're moving fast." Tera was alarmed. "They are already well past the garden and moving into the Viortahk."

"They seem to be making a run for the lab, and trying to avoid us," Amanok said. "What do you think, Ilean?"

"They might have been warned away from us by other schools."

"I don't like it," Tekram said.

"You don't like it either, do you Ilean?" Amanok said. "Have ellls been known to seek revenge if there is a continual stimulus to keep it alive?"

"Like the terrible inside pressure I used to feel when I couldn't school properly. I would strain against something invisible, a cage that bound me from inside. Sometimes I would get so angry at that awful blinding that I would smash other elll's eggs when I found them. I hardly knew what I was doing. Like Sa-el's school. I don't think they know what they are doing. We must stop them before they reach the lab."

An End to Revenge

Sing Ilean. Sing Korad. Cure the ellls.
Heal mad minds and save their will to live.
Drive home the wedge of love.
Then as you watch your life dissolve,
Forgive us all. Forgive.

"Ba-ohl. Slow down," Navell cried. "You will kill us all, moving at this pace. We are already in the Viortahk. Sa-el's school has not yet passed the Rocky Shallows." The gold-fringed elll coasted to a resting glide and shivered. "On the other hand, I would rather die of torn back-fins than freeze to death. We had better keep moving, just a little slower, please."

Ba-ohl rolled over on his back and coasted until Navell joined him. "We'll go through the rocks off the western shore of the varoks' bay. Sa-el won't expect our approach from that side."

"Our approach," Navell repeated, with a grimace. "What then?"

"We will delay Sa-el long enough for the great-fish to arrive. Their mud-turtle nets cover a wide area of the west Viortahk. When we feel the school coming we will set the nets in their path."

"We are only six schools, Ba-ohl," Navell said. "Six schools of all the ellls of the Great Basin, in waters once rich with love of life. Has Ellason lost its song? Must all who live, hate to live?"

To his vast surprise, Ba-ohl heard a faint "no" in answer to his tirade. It came from the rocks of the West Viortahk. "Come to us here," a school's call sounded. "Hurry. You are not alone."

It was the released captives.

– Δ –

"Korad," Amanok called. He watched the wind throw the hair back from the young varok's face as the glider pursued Sa-el's school over Varoks' Bay. "I want you to read my mind, thoroughly, Korad. I want you to know every thought of admiration I have had for you, every honor my intuition has given you. I recognize you as my superior in elllonian affairs."

Korad protested vehemently, but Amanok commanded a stop to his thoughts.

Do me this honor. Amanok spoke with his mind, for the speed and the wind made talking difficult. *Believe and accept what I tell you now. I will return to Varok with the cruiser, when this ugly business of chasing ellls is done. I am retiring to my homestead there.*

With Tera? The boy couldn't keep the question from leaping into his mind.

No, alone. Tera will live more at peace with one mind than with two. I will recommend to Mahar that you become Director of the Elll-watch. You must re-define and rename your job when you and the ellls have had time to rediscover each other.

Amanok looked up as the lab came into view. Beyond the shimmering blue-gray of the water, the stark clay bricks of the varokian structure rose above the flat Ellasonian landscape, ominous evidence of alien invasion.

Ilean saw that the vision struck Korad with peculiar poignancy.

"I've never seen myself so alien to Ellason before, Ilean," he said. "I loved the planet too well."

Amanok grabbed Korad about the shoulders, and his voice shook with emotion, but he stayed rational. "Never forget that you are a guest here, Korad—an unwelcome guest. Look." He pointed to the west, where the sea was laced with white. "There they are."

"Two schools on the scanner now," Tera announced. "One is moving toward us from the West Viortahk."

"Can we overtake Sa-el's school?" Ilean asked.

"I think so. We've got them sighted." Tera spoke into the ship's intercom. "Home in on the ellls' signal. Full speed." She turned then to

Ilean, her kindly blue eyes ringed with sorrow. "What do we do when we meet the ellls?" she asked.

"We sing. We sing your song, Tera."

Tera gave Korad a wry smile.

"Ilean is serious," Korad said. "We should sing in the very midst of the school."

"In the water?" Tera laughed. "You're not serious."

Korad held her eye in silence.

"Of course, if we can manage."

"We'll be on them in a minute," Korad cried. "The two schools have met, Ilean. How are we going to stop them?"

"The beach will soon stop them, if we can't." She enjoyed the chase, anticipating no serious trouble.

As she stared out over the water, watching the converging patterns of the ellls, Ilean suddenly realized that the two schools were really three, and that they were not meeting in normal adjustment.

White eruptions of water began to mar the ocean's surface. Leaping, turning bodies of ellls struggled against each other as they cut back and forth through the cold waters.

"It's Ba-ohl's school and the captives we released," Ilean screamed. "They're attacking the larger school!"

Before Korad could stop her, Ilean disappeared into the water.

– Δ –

She hit the water at a clean angle and swam beneath the converging schools. Where was the source of anger sustaining the battle?

One of her former tutors, a librarian with a long tail of head plumes, rolled past her, swimming upward to attack a rough-looking elll, who must have been one of the varoks' former captives. Ilean followed the librarian, calling in ultrasonic the sound of the lost. Surely he would stop and heed the universal command. In normal times, a school would turn away from whatever it was doing to search for a lost tad.

The ellls who heard Ilean's desperate call suspended their anger just long enough to feel the odd pressure of three swimming varoks in their midst. Then they heard the strange, gasping song-like sounds the varoks made.

One librarian dove at the varokian intruders, but his attack was knocked aside by Ba-ohl and an elder of the librarians, who had made sense of the varoks' song.

"The varoks grieve for the pain they have caused ellls," the elder translated into ultrasonic. "They offer relief from physical pain, relief from life-moments no longer optimal in huge schools; they offer love and knowledge. And," he added with the encouragement of several ellls of Sa-el's school, "in their clumsy attempts at singing in water, they have given their lives into our hands."

The elder's voice gave many ellls, nearly one-quarter of the school, cause to withdraw from the conflict. They would not break the trust of helpless lives.

Others who heard the varoks' continuing song were fascinated by the beauty of the song's meaning, and that it came from alien throats.

Many former captive ellls recognized Amanok and their rescuers, Tera and Korad. They clustered around the varoks, who were now struggling to stay afloat, and supported them with the gentle motion of their back-fins.

Sa-el led the greater school out of range, on toward the lab. Desperately, Ba-ohl's school threw themselves in their path.

– Δ –

Korad could see the temper of the conflict change for the worse. Blood darkened the water as Sa-el lost patience and struck out with his ready *al*-shell, killing a former captive who dared to question him.

At the sight of their companion's brief agony, rage fired the ex-captives, and they slashed out at Sa-el, barely missing his neck with their lethal shells. Like a giant ripple, violence spread through the school, throwing up dark wells of blood as it moved outward, until the entire sea of ellls was lost again in fury.

Left behind, Tera, Amanok and Korad climbed aboard the glider. Tekram was quietly setting improvised acoustic bombs ready for firing. Korad angrily shut them down.

"What have you done? What have you done?" Tekram screamed when he saw that the devices were useless. "We can't stand by and watch this carnage!"

Tera lashed out with frustration. "So you would add pain and loss of life-joy to the carnage? Don't you understand what you are seeing, Tekram? Ellls do not attack unless they are sure to make an instant kill. There are no wounded ellls afloat in the water, only large pools of blood from those killed—or living, leaping, infuriated ellls. They are fighting for their right to know us, Tekram. The captives who understand us want to understand more. Don't destroy that trust again by inflicting pain."

"But the friendly schools are very small," Tekram argued. "They will be decimated. We must help them."

"We can help them by interrupting the chain reaction of anger that is running through the school," Korad insisted. "Ilean will give her distress call. Then we will go to them with our song, like we did the others. Ellls don't prefer anger. Believe me, Tekram."

Korad dove into the water and waited for Ilean to leap three times toward him, as a signal to begin the song again.

"There she is." Tera cried.

The strategy worked. Some ellls heeded Ilean's call, found the varoks by their song, and kept the aliens safely insulated from the murderous rage still flaming Sa-el and those maddened by pain.

"We will never stop the entire school this way. What is keeping this mood alive?" Ilean dove away from Korad, determined to confront Sa-el. Surely her old friend would listen to her.

Cautiously, Ilean worked her way under the ellls still locked in battle. Blood darkened the water in sickening streaks, and sharp shell edges slashed out from every direction.

When Ilean failed to return, Korad sang out for her, diving as deep as he dared. There was no answer. He sang out again and again, but still Ilean did not appear. Soon he was forced to surface. He rested in the water, taking in great drafts of air, when an elll brushed quickly past him.

"Ilean has gone into the center of anger," a librarian said in sonic code.

Korad panicked. He called for Ba-ohl and Navell. When they heard his call, they came to him.

"We've got to go after Ilean," Korad repeated, until they understood him. Together they dove for the center of the melee, taking the determined varok with them.

"Defend yourself," Ba-ohl told the varok, and he pressed an *al*-shell into the varok's hand. "Some of these ellls are mad with pain. They will kill a varok on sight."

Directly below they heard Ilean's cry. The ellls dove to her, leaving Korad to catch a breath.

He was about to dive again when he saw the massed fins of a fleet of great-fish encircle the struggling schools. With a surge of joy, he dove, singing out as best he could under water, while he worked his way toward Ilean's blue figure just below.

The great-fish joined the school with pressure patterns and songs that soon brought calm to many of the ellls.

– Δ –

Ilean was not yet aware of the great-fish when she found Sa-el. He was locked in battle with the large elll Cavall of their former school.

"I'll take those." As she quickly dove past the two ellls, Ilean knocked apart their arms wielding sharp shells. "We are done with shell knives, Sa-el."

The opponents looked after her, momentarily bewildered.

"Listen now, just above you." she cried. "Follow me. Korad, the varok of my school, sings a new song for us all." As they surfaced, she met Sa-el's eyes hopefully, but the inflamed look she saw there terrified her.

"Traitor," Sa-el screamed in his tortured sonic voice. "Traitor to the life of Duregal." He lunged at Ilean with a powerful stroke and grabbed her around the neck.

Korad saw the attack. His song ended, and he dove onto Sa-el's back. The startled Sa-el turned to fight off the varok, and Ilean tore away. Korad held Ba-ohl's shell knife ready in his hand, but when he met Sa-el's eyes, he paused in his thrust. In that instant Sa-el turned the shell toward Korad and plunged it deep into the varok's neck.

"Aeyulll! Aeyulll! Aeyulll!" Ilean's screams for help pierced the school with horror as she followed Korad's dying form to the bottom of the sea.

Ba-ohl and Navell spun past Sa-el, killing him with swift blows to his neck.

The great-fish were everywhere. The waters fell quiet. For one lost moment the ellls felt severed from all life-joy. They hung suspended in mid-water feeling nothing, hearing nothing but the faint, pleading song of the varoks on the surface and the soul-tortured wailing of the desperate loner, Ilean, far below.

Korad's Way

Thus Korad left her with a soul grown strong,
Determined still while facing death to free
The growing minds of ellls,
And with the varoks find a way
To forge their destiny.

All hail the loners' legend: Ilean,
The blind, the slow, a traitor to the past;
She turned the future on.
She sang her song as strangers met
And found their lives recast.

For many moon-light changes after the battle, for Ilean's sake, the ellls of the joined schools stayed in the shallows near the laboratory. They had never seen an ell grieve for someone who no longer lived. They honored her for finding the answers they had lost. She would form the nucleus of all fears and arguments, serve as liaison to both great-fish and varoks, focus pressures that tore them between logic and instinct.

They understood that Ilean's return and adjustment to the school would be difficult. She was a loner. In some ways, only Duregal, Sa-el, Ba-ohl, and the varok Korad had been her school. Now, with Sa-el and Korad suddenly gone, and with Duregal cruelly taken by *eefl*, Ilean had found her small inner school reduced to one. The gap left in her life-moments would be too large for Ba-ohl to fill.

– Δ –

Amanok had been the one to follow Ilean and carry her away from Korad's body. Ba-ohl had followed them back to the laboratory.

Amanok saw the young male boldly approach the dock, soon after the glider's motor died. Ba-ohl was exhausted from the rapid chase, but he pulled himself onto the dock and walked through the crowd of varoks waiting to greet Ilean, as if he were unaware of them.

Ilean looked up from where she huddled in Amanok's arms. Ba-ohl laid a gentle hand on her shoulder, and she turned to him with a sob as they slipped into the water.

Like a shroud, the water's surface smotherd Tera's hope. Korad was dead, and now Ilean was gone.

Only when Tekram prepared to follow the ellls in the small rover was Amanok jolted back to enough awareness to stop him. "Keep these waters silent," he commanded, staring at Tekram with all the force of repressed disdain. "For as long as ellls are willing to swim this bay, keep your rovers to the land."

"Ilean will come back," Tera told those who doubted, but they saw her mind and knew she doubted, too.

"Amanok." Tera motioned for Vohren and the others to stay behind while she came to him. As she feared, he was deep in irrational grief. "Let me share it," Tera whispered. "It is half mine. It need not destroy you. Let me help you carry it." She knelt beside him and struggled to enter his mind, but he was far beyond her reach, lost in the deep trap of his love for Korad.

With Vohren's help, Tera took Amanok to his space at the laboratory, but he could not be kept within varokian walls. He wandered to the dock and stood there looking out for Ilean, while the moonlight tulips turned the waters of the bay from deep navy to royal blue to brilliant aqua and back to deep navy again. Tera could do nothing to help him.

– Δ –

Ilean dreaded going back to the laboratory with Korad gone, but her elllonian nature saved her from mind-numbing grief, and she soon realized that she could not leave his work unfinished. Ba-ohl and the great-fish Orlegh and Harrahn accompanied her through the Viortahk, then she swam up the channel toward the dock alone.

She came to Amanok quickly when she saw him on the dock. They retreated to the lab aquarium, and there she swam with him for three light cycles, while he gradually came out of his grief.

When Amanok was fully rational, he broke his respectful silence. "There is an elll that swims beside the dock, Ilean, and an older elll that comes for him time and time again, but he won't leave."

"Ba-ohl. He knows my work is here. He knows I must make my school here. Ba-ohl will have to join me here, if he wants to school with me."

"We could rebuild the channel between the lab and the bay, so you could come and go more easily. You could do some schooling there, if we make the entrance more inviting to other ellls." Tera and Amanok came to the idea together.

"Yes," Ilean burst out in Elllonian. "Yes, that would solve everything. Then the schools could come here for instruction and exchange. It is so hard to find words for things I don't know—for the ultrasonic memory, for pressure talk. I must finish the language. If you would build an opening to the sea—an inviting place—the ellls could help me finish Korad's work."

"We'll do it, Ilean," Tera promised. "You will have all you need to make ellls comfortable here."

"I must tell Ba-ohl and Navell. They can help us choose mosses to line the aquarium. Come with me, Amanok. You don't have more grief left in you, do you?"

She couldn't know that his grief would not heal as hers would. Korad's loss left a gaping wound in his life, a loss felt forever. At the same time, he saw in Ilean the completion of his life and fulfillment in hers. He took her hand in his. "Let's go find Ba-ohl."

– Δ –

Tera wept openly as she bade Amanok goodbye, her total mind and Vohren's locked into his for the last time. She stood beside Vohren at the boarding entrance of the space cruiser, and they made one last plea, knowing it was hopeless: "When Ellason weighs too heavily on you, Amanok, come home to us on Varok. Don't deny us your last days."

Amanok smiled at the thought, but not too sadly. "My bones belong to Ellason; you know that, Tera. They will mix with Korad's and become shells for mud-turtles. I won't have it any other way."

"Then I will come back to you again. My work is here."

"But your mind is on Varok. You have much work to do with the ellls still held there. Have you persuaded any here to return with you?"

"Only some of the librarians."

"But that is quite an accomplishment, Tera. They will soon fill the archives of the Concentrate with the history of Ellason."

"If they choose to do so. There is my challenge. How do I translate a pseudo-visual echo-location memory based on underwater Ellasonian topography into a written history?"

Amanok had to laugh.

"I will always need your help, Amanok."

Vohren stood silently by Tera's side reaching out to him.

"You tempt me, Tera, Vohren, but you know I won't be coming to Varok. I loved Korad too well." Amanok thanked Vohren silently for his patience. "I can do nothing but continue Korad's work here with Ilean."

Tera opened her arms to Amanok. Then she was gone, and he stood with her touch still within, not really seeing her board the cruiser, not seeing the cruiser disappear into the high mists.

The silence of Ellason soothed him, and the muted clicking of the mud turtles beneath the dock rewarmed his heart. He turned back toward the laboratory, walked along the dock to the new entrance opening into Ilean's underwater study center, and found her waiting for him amidst a crowd of ellls. They were debating the most logical way and the best sounds to transliterate into Varokian the pressure signal for "The best way to prepare shore-pool lightning bugs for a meal before sleeping."

– Δ –

In the Varokian year 3632 *ir*, Ilean and Ba-ohl, Navell, and both great-fish, Harrahn and good-humored Orlegh, set out from the laboratory to travel the warm, glowing seas of Ellason as a mixed school. Their purpose was to teach to all ellls the new language, Elllonian, and the fine arts of planetary sustainability.

They succeeded very well. Many ellls came to the varokian laboratory for instruction, and many went on to Varok to study at the Concentrate. Varoks were welcomed as students of Ellason in all corners of the watery planet, while the population of ellls, determined to secure the quality of life-moments for all, kept watch to reproduce within the limits their planet prescribed.

THE END, AND A NEW BEGINNING

Afterword

At the time of this story, in 1503.6 *ir* (65,900 BCE Earth), Ellason was far too dim and far away to be detected by anything living on Earth. We varoks, however, had recently discovered the huge planet, called it Ellason, recognized it as an internally heated planet of radius 9000 kilometers orbiting Sol in a long, eccentric orbit. We invaded it, and carried some ellls back to Varok—much to our shame, and our good fortune.

Now we know that the varok Aman Okrahlan (Amanok) left for his progeny this enclosed manuscript, to publish or not, as they saw fit. I see fit—but I am not acting alone. I have consulted with the Council of Masters, the great-fish Allahn, and the Oran-Grey-ElConn Family.

Orserah, matriarch of that prestigious mixed family, was most enthusiastic about this project. Though of greatly advanced age, she made me feel most welcome at their home so I could meet her adopted human daughter and granddaughter, the first human beings on Varok. Tandra and Shawne read the full text aloud to the ellls of their family, Conn and Stringer, who joined them in insisting I waste no time finding a publisher on Earth, as well as on Varok and Ellason. With such watchers over my shoulder, I dare do nothing but guarantee that the text presented here is exactly as I found it, in the "attic" of the Aman family's ancestral home on Varok.

When the language called Elllonian was well seeded in the burgeoning new elll-varok culture, the ellls sang of Amanok, called *Al Ba-ohl*, Star Plumes. They sang of his love for ellls, a love so great that the souls of ellls, lost in the battle of Varok's Bay, covered his head with the silver light of Ellason's stars.

There came a time when many scholars, both elllonian and varokian, argued that a new calendar should begin with the year of Korad and Ilean. That year was clearly the beginning of a new existence for two species whose cultures were rapidly merging.

The calendar was never changed. The scholars decided—envisioning a Varok paved with moss and laced with channels of water to suit ellls—that it was in everyone's best interest to define some reasonable limits to adaptability.

Therefore, though sorely tempted to clean up some of the more embarrassing episodes, I left them alone. My pen stayed in my pocket; I sat on my transputer. Such restraint created a terrific itch in the upper lobe of my left patch organ, but I did no editing. I followed the author's wishes, whose Preface to the narrative is here faithfully reproduced.

— Aman Telariahn (Amantel), 4226 ir (2059 AD, Earth)

HISTORICAL NOTE

In 9930 BCE, when Ellason made its infrequent approach to the orbit of Neptune, it went unnoticed by *Homo sapiens*, except those who had encountered a few ellls visiting Earth, as described in the tale called *The View Beyond Earth*.

When those enlightened humans rode out to Varok, they discovered that it too could suffer problems similar to those on Earth (recorded in *The Webs of Varok*).

Then, as Ellason returned to perihelion again in 2070 CE, it triggered some human angst on Earth recorded in *The Alien Effect*.

Its perihelion also inticed a mixed family of humans, ellls and varoks out to Ellason, where they encountered more trouble recorded in *Shawne: An Alien's Quest*.

APPENDICES

A. Principal Characters

Varoks

Durable but sensitive bipeds, emotionally fragile, senses easily over-loaded. Open minds with a mood reading ability. Instinctively focused on the long-term stability of the planet Varok. Strong hormonal links triggered by mental compatibility.

Amanok (Aman Okrahlan) - the ageing director of Elll-Watch on El-lason, a reknowned philosopher and intimate friend of Tera.

Korad (Kor Adtalorium) - an "untamed," brilliant young male on his first professional assignment to the Varokian Observation Laboratory on Ellason.

Tekram (Tek Raman) - director of Species Welfare on Ellason, opponent of Tera's sympathetic approach to ellls.

Tera (Ter Ahrkarian) - director of Ellasonian Studies on Ellason.

Ellls

Aquatic, playful, be-finned bipeds, native to Ellason. Emotionally volatile, loaded with sensory input, with logic-driven minds focused on moment-to-moment experience.

Ba-ohl - a young male of Ilean's school of ellls, lovingly devoted to her well-being.

Duregal - Ilean's sponsor, responsible for her upbringing, having chosen her egg for hatching.

Falll - angry female of Ilean's school, opposed to Duregal's indulgence of Ilean, afraid of cooperating with varoks.

Ilean - a young, nearly mature, disabled female just becoming aware of her physical and cognitive limitations.

Navell - a kindly elder of Ilean's school.

Sa-el - a young male, inclined to extreme reactions and school leadership.

GREAT-FISH

Marine mammaloids native to Ellason and immigrants to Varok. Larger than Earth's dolphins, with prehensile fin-tips. Respected for their wisdom. Recognized experts in holistic analysis of interactive living systems.

Orlegh - tutor to Ilean and advisor in her disability as a "loner." Her unique awareness means she can serve as a much-needed link between ellls and varoks.

Haralahn – master of philosophy and religious theory. Native of Ellason, descendant of the intellectual with the same name. Author of *Reflections in Blood-stained Water* after the history recorded as *The Unheard Song* by Cary Neeper. See book *An Alien's Quest*.

B. Glossary

adjustment. Intense schooling of ellls, in which strong pressure signals, electro-sensing, magneto-orientation and ultrasonic messages are rapidly exchanged underwater so that accommodation may be made for the absence of a member of the school or for the addition of a new member or visitor.

aeo-o. Elllonian expression of intense pleasure.

aeyul (aeyull, aeyulll). Elllonian expression of intense pain.

ahlrialka tree. Huge spreading, plant-like growth on the hot acid plains of Varok; it produces dense, tasty reproductive burls.

alahranon. The colorful, swirling mists that surround Ellason, whose surface is almost totally covered by warm oceans.

aloon. Elllonian noun, usually used with affection to mean something like "wet slob" or "water bum."

alyakah. Varokian word for a mature, well-integrated female who would be desirable to any creature as a mother or wife.

arl. A large, brilliantly winged, moth-like creature of Varok, eaten by ellls and varoks and considered a delicacy.

brilln. A tiny, brilliantly-plumed water bird of Ellason.

challall weeds. Delicious, rigid, leafless plants which grow on the low hills of Ellason.

consummation. Total mind-link, achieved by varoks who have no mental reservations between them so that complete subconscious mind-scanning can occur.

dankah. A potent, intoxicating tea, made from the Varokian plant of the same name.

deacuh. Elllonian noun for isolation, quarantine, or loneliness and torture, all of which are synonymous in the minds of ellls.

directorate. Full title: Laboratory Directorate. The council of varoks that makes policy decisions for all varokians on Ellason.

el eggs. The large, blue eggs laid by elllonian females.

Ellason. A self-heated planet of Sol with gravity equivalent to about twice Earth's. Its orbit is three times as far from Sol as Pluto. Continental masses on the warm, black giant are small, and the deep, dark seas are enormous, glowing with ruby-red warmth near the heart of the planet.

elll. An adaptable, aquatic, life-loving species of Ellason, equipped with a formidable array of sensory organs.

Elllonian. The system of throat sounds laboriously devised by the varoks and ellls to be spoken in the varokian audible range in order to facilitate communication between those two species.

Generalist. Abbreviated as *G.* An earned varokian designation signifying the acquisition of thorough, detailed knowledge in a broad area of related studies, as, for example, physics, chemistry, astronomy, and geology from the area of physical sciences. Between Specialist and Master.

Gurahn. Mythological beast designed by the great-fish to represent the total experience of the planet Varok.

hedonic glands. Sensory organs whose stimulation gives pleasure and sexual stimulation to ellls.

integrated. An elllonian concept to describe the state of being when an individual of another species becomes a part of the elllonian school in a way that implies total acceptance of the ellls; in general, to accept oneself as no different from others.

la l lea. Elllonian; title of the tender mating duet of the ellls; literally— have a mating with me.

leel la oon. Elllonian; literally—female, you do water (swim, woman).

llaoon grass. A soft marsh grass of Ellason.

ll-leyoolianl. A species of creative great-fish of Ellason who perceive the significance of experience and express it in a manner most easily understood by their communicants, often by modeling clay represen- tations of their ideas as progressions of complex symbols.

lohn bird. A plump, football-shaped animal with large webbed feet, stubby wings, a ridiculously small, bill-less head, and a coat of deep red and pink parasitic moss that drips with a heavily perfumed liquid. One of two species on Ellason capable of flight.

L'Ran. The Elllonian word for the blue star-planet, Earth.

Master. Abbreviated as *M.* Highest honorary recognition by varoks of expertise in a broad area of study, with some understanding of all knowledge, demonstrated by wisdom and restraint in integrating and applying the acquired concepts to real problems.

Mutilation. The period of time in Varokian natural history in which the varokian species mutated from magnificent and normally sensual winged intellectuals to unduly sensitive bipeds incapable of experiencing emotion rationally.

oeln. Edible fish, large and gray, with cool arrow-shaped patterns visible to ellls as dark lines in the infrared environment of Ellason.

-oon. Elllonian suffix implying water or wetness.

pallonions. Ellasonian credits. A promise of postponed payment in goods or services whenever requested. Agreements are honored and enforced between all members of species capable of keeping promises.

pallons. Elllonian unit of measure, about twenty-three meters, the length of an elll's arcing leap over the water from a fast swimming start. The similarity of this word to the word *pallonions* is probably a result of the ancient ellls' sense of irony and humor.

patch organ. Round, featureless plate of tissue behind the ears of varoks that detects low frequency electromagnetic signals, often voltages produced by mental and nervous activity of nearby organisms.

reading. Sensing another individual's mood, emotion, or trend in thought. One function of the varoks' patch organs.

release. The ability to experience emotion and to function rationally simultaneously. An ideal state achieved rarely by varoks and only with the aid of a consummate partner.

school. Any number of ellls who inhabit a particular environs or locale and who relate by schooling. The ellls' normal social structure.

schooling. Functioning collectively and sharing awareness as if a group were one individual.

Sonarplate Apraxia. A debilitating disease affecting the hexagonal plates of ellls, caused by a viral-like agent. Untreated, it disrupts sonar meshwork function, hence ultrasonic reception and communication.

Songs to Life. Ancient varokian poems written anonymously during the Mutilation. The first verse of the poem translates as follows:

Though long denied Life's gracious gift of flowing free,
In currents wild and lifting down, thrown tumbling,
Lifted up, thrown down, and swept without control,
Our minds unlocked, in gray mists bright with crystal hue,

Though elegance denied and flight subdued,
We find Life's beauty in her gifts
And take her favors where they fall.
Though all our visions racked our minds with pain;
Though sound grew dense and ruined quiet senses;
Though mind-filling silence became unknown and unknowable;
And new life came to us, imperfect yet yearning for consciousness,
Heavily distorted, torn by savaged genes
And thrown upon misery to writhe in horror for years denied;

Though Life came not with joy or promise,
But used us for her mindless purpose–
Or too mindful—none can know—
We still survive, thankful for new strength,
Molecules still conscious in forms perhaps wiser.

Specialist. Abbreviated as *S.* Varokian designation for those acquiring specific knowledge in one field of study, such as physics.

tracking. Sensing and imitating the precise muscular movements of another individual, one function of the varoks' patches (in conjunction with spinal nerves).

udan. Varokian style bidet–toilet.

Varok. A dense, barely habitable, hidden satellite of Jupiter.

varok. The dominant intellectual species native to the planet Varok, formed by mutation from winged forebears, having lost their ability to fly and to tolerate emotion rationally.

Varokian Concentrate. An institution of Varok open to qualifying individuals of any species who are admitted as students to acquire—by high-speed microvolt implantation into the memory—established fact, non-interpretable information, and thought techniques. The integration and application of this knowledge is acquired through continuing studies, leading to the designations *apprentice*, *specialist*, and *generalist*.

wet-sweater. A shirt made of the most moisture-retaining, softest, and most delicious of Ellasonian mosses, kept alive by periodic moistening and feeding.

C. ELLONIAN-ENGLISH DICTIONARY

PRONUNCIATION

á	*a* in same (rare)
a	*a* in farther
b	*b* in bubble
c, k	*c* in cauldron (rare)
d	*d* in dawn
ee	*ee* in flee
e	*e* in met
f	*f* in few
l	*l* in let
ll	deeply exaggerated *l* in lot
lll	*l* in lot with tongue curled up and over
m	*m* in moon
n	*n* in moon
oo	*oo* in moon
o, oh	*o* in gone (rare)
p	*p* in poor
ss	*s* in pass
u	*u* in cut
v	*v* in vow
w	*w* in wonder

ARTICLES AND NOUNS

Elllonian has no grammatical gender.

All articles can be represented by "e."

The plural ending is "1"; that is, a deeper roll of the tongue
     is added regardless of singular pronunciation.

The possessive is formed by adding "b."

The objective is formed by adding "le."

ADJECTIVES

Comparative is formed by adding "l" to the positive.

Superlative is formed by adding "ll" to the positive.

The adjectival present participle is formed by adding "ah"
     to the verb root.

The adjectival past participle is formed by adding "t" or
"l" to the verb root.

PRONOUNS (IN SPITE OF VAROKIAN OBJECTIONS)

Personal Pronouns:	*1st Person*	*2nd Person*	*3rd Person*
Singular	l, la, or lle	l, la, or lle	l, la, or lle
Plural	ne	ne	ne

Demonstrative, Relative, Interrogative, Indefinite Pronouns: All
such forms can be represented by "e" or "ek."

INTERJECTIONS

aeo—o	Exclamation of pleasure.
aeyul (ll) (lll)	Exclamation of grief, horror, loss of life—joy.
uleoon	Affectionate farewell, literally: have a wet mating.

VERBS

Conjugations are limited to adding the following endings to the verb root:

	1st Person	2nd Person	3rd Person
Present	e	a	o
Past	em	am	om
Varokian Future	ee	ae	oe

ÁÁ

ácuh, adj.	Alone.

AA

ad, v.	To accumulate.
adl, v.	Filled.
advan, v.	To convince.
ahl, n.	Large underwater tree.
akl, n.	Friend.
al, n.	Star.
alahranon, n.	Mists of Ellason, especially those swirling and colorful.
aloo, n.	The deeps, deep water, especially far offshore.
aloon, n.	Water being, Water bum.
altoon, n.	Deep forest, thick water plants.
anu, prep.	Down.
anu, v.	To begin.
ayan, prep.	Beside.

BB

ba, prep.	In the back.
bak, v.	To let.

Ba-ohl, n.	Head planes.
bayon, adj.	Welcome.
be, adv.	Now.
bel, adj.	High.
bol, adv.	Far.
brilln, n.	Tiny, brilliant water bird.
broon, n.	Sound.

Cc

can, v.	To work, to garden.
challall, n.	Delicious, leafless plants that grow on low hills.

Dd

da, adv. and adj.	No.
danl, v.	To harvest.
davel, adj.	Dark.

Ee

e, prep.	Of.
eh, adv.	Where.
ek, def. art.	The.
eyah, pron.	Itself.
eyahka, adv.	Forever.

Ff

fahno, n.	Breath.
fan, v.	To leap.

Kĸ

k, conj.	And.
kahla, n.	Stranger.
kohl, v.	To have.

Lʟ

1, pron.	I, myself.
1, v.	To be.
la, pron.	Me.
lak, adj.	Full.
le, la, lo, v.	I am, you are, he is.
lea, n.	Mating.
leall or leel, adj. n.	Male.
lelel, v.	To roll.
lel-ohl, n.	Hip plumes.
leoo, v.	To live.
leoon, n.	Love.
lohn, n.	Plump egg—laying bird of Ellason's shores.
lok, adj.	Rich, sweet.
1'Ran, n.	Earth.
llaoon, n.	Soft marsh grass of Ellason.
lle, obj.pron.	To me.
ll-leyoolianl, n.	Great-fish.
ll-ohl, n.	Brow plumes.
lloo, n.	Underwater cave (of great-fish).
llov, v.	To school.
llovas, n.	School.

Mᴍ

| malelelea, n. | Female sponsor, mother. |

Nɴ

ne, pron.	Us.

Oᴏ

o, v.	To do.
oeln, n.	Fish, edible, large, gray with arrow patterns.

OOᴏᴏ

oon, n.	Water.
-oon	Suffix implying water or wetness.
oonl, n.	Fish.
oowaml, n.	Waves.

Pᴘ

pa, n.	While.
pallon, n.	Unit of length, based on an ellls water leap, about three meters.
pallt, adj.	Expensive.
pallta, adj.	Priceless, exquisite.
pem, adj.	Like, similar.

Sꜱ

save, adv.	Away.
savoll, n.	Stranger,
sazvolta, adj.	Strangerness.
sens, v.	To wait.
sensoe, v.	He will wait.
ssro, v.	To strip, to pare.

Uᴜ

u, v.	To go.
ue,ua,uo, v.	I go, you go, he goes.
ull, adj. n.	Cold, killer.
uom, v.	To send away.
uuyanvan, v.	To sleep, to go beyond knowledge.
uvan, v.	To argue.
uyan, prep.	Beyond.
uven, adv.	Furthermore.

Vᴠ

v, v.	To care. (Also va.)
va11, n.	Light.
van, v.	To know.
vanal, n.	Wisdom.
vaniel, n.	Knowledge.
vano, v.	He knows.
vaom, v.	You come.
veln, v.	To see.
von, v.	To tell

Yʏ

ya, prep.	To.
yav, v.	To join.
yavolla, adv.	Together.

D. The Legend of the First Loner

This text was found in the reconstructed Library of Ellason, circa 3705 *ir* (Varokian Calendar), probably an early Elllonian translation of the great-fish "Epic Presentation."

Too far from Earth, unseen by human eyes,
There rode a verdant world
With silent lands 'neath thirty moons
And sentient life within its heavy seas —
Fair ellls with webbed hands.

In days gone by, where days do not exist,
Beneath the deeps where varoks dare not range
And human search still fails,
Within the seas of Ellason
There lived an elll thought strange.

She longed to chase the lohn birds through the moss,
To find the stars before the dawn's renewal,
To hear the sighing mists,
To see with mind and know with heart
The world beyond the school.

The school, the throbbing lifeblood of her kind,
Was wracked with pain, and not for her alone.
Oh Ilean, speak truth.
Is not an illness shared by all,
The ancient ways o'er thrown?

Though ellls were born to swim the warmest deeps,
One sought the misted rocks and shallows rife
And valued solitude.
A mind apart, she longed to know
The deeps and mists of life.

Where Ellason's long tides creep into dark,
She crossed dry land alone to fill her mind,
But failed among the rocks
Without the gentle throbbing press
Of signals from her kind.

When strangers come to worlds they do not know,
They act upon raw guesses made in haste —
Though all intent be good.
The world perceives naught but the wound
And good intent's laid waste.

"Come, Ilean, the school throbs hollow now
"Without you here, where all our hearts reside.
"Your place cannot be filled."
She knew their pain and grieved for them,
But rode the loner's tide.

Where wave and terror mix too well with stone,
She saw her life-joy gone and welcomed death,
Until a stranger came
To seek the heart of Ellason
And breathe an elll's sea-breath.

"Come, hear my voice. Come know my every thought,
"And through your mind your heart will be my guide.
"Our lives must soon be joined.
"We cannot let this chance go by
"And fail, while worlds collide."

The great-fish found her in the varok's grasp
And took her from that lethal devotee
To safer, healing arms—
To ancient hollows drawn with moss
Beneath the warm-red sea.

"I see myself," the varok told the youth.
"In you my rage is harnessed once again.
"For Ellason, go forth.
"Go find your elll, and wisdom too,
"Within the great-fish den."

The varok trusted none,
Although he knew that great-fish see the whole,
The parts for what they mean in fine relief.
How could they understand an elll
Whose life was edged with grief?

The great-fish taught her more than senses five
Convey to varoks viewing waves with dread,
Confined to live on land.
They showed her paths that few ellls know
And none would choose to tred.

When fate gave anger's vent its awful chance,
The broken ellls let vengeance fire their zeal;
Thus violence split the school—
For gentle hearts, once torn by hate,
Are rarely known to heal.

The varoks clung with fear to plans undone—
The patterns of their minds so etched in stone,
Entrapped in all by pride,
They could not credit ellls with this:
A vision not their own.

Her dullnes to ellls' bounding sounds that see,
Her deafness to the high-pitched calls that rule
Had left her mind undone.
Thus blinded as no elll had been,
She saw beyond the school.

The water moved the weeds in dances wild.
Waves filled with blood, tossed high, bedecked with grief,
Fell crashing round her soul.
The school was split; the tide was turned;
The sea cried disbelief.

Upon the rocks she found a comfort strange,
A mind that knew hers well, yet could not say
What dwelt within its own.
As one, they sensed the edge of doom
And ran from danger's way.

There is no helping one who paints his face
With lies, and robs the truth of all its worth —
Or heedless, mocks it sore.
There is no friend in those who cheat,
Denying faith's rebirth.

The young companions saw how life was good.
They knew the joy that caring love compels.
As one, they nurtured hope
And dared to probe the secrets held
Within the hearts of ellls.

What end so fair is worth a trick so foul —
To take a free-born soul and close it in
For purposes ill-found?
What good can come from trust betrayed?
Why now can't love begin?

On secret ahl-leaves, precious to the ellls,
The varok searched for clues to link their lives,
But found instead their lack.
Their differences multiplied
And mocked the sealed archives.

They traded gifts of self—far more than love—
And put themselves aside to learn the new,
To sing for all in turn
A new-found song of trust in life,
With verses written true.

Are those less true who take the traitor's name?
Can means be all that matter in the end
When visions overlap?
Whose cause is locked in rigid thought?
Can truth be traitor's friend?

"Stay my hand, so I won't trespass here.
"An unintended danger leaves its scar,"
The varok told the elll.
"I'll bend your songs to shape your tongue,
"And fathom who you are."

I thought I knew the depths of fear, until
I saw a strange new people throw away
The history of their race
To keep it out of alien reach,
Secure from sore display.

If in the mind's true bent an angle sharp
Distorts the straight line flowing toward our youth,
Then where can trust be found?
The line is spoiled; the dent is firm
'Til forged again in truth.

What horror now. To look in tortured eyes
And fail to stop the pain of those defiled,
To understand too late
That though communion is at hand,
It won't be reconciled.

Their fear made masks of faces raw with doubt.
Then gave them nerves of steel—a devil's gift
That stoked the fire of grief—
As into blood they plunged their hands
And set their souls adrift.

The tragedy of tragedies is this:
When good will, taken wrong, its good intent
Left broken on despair,
Turns full upon itself in flight,
Destroying all it meant.

The gentlest of ellls, confined in time,
As one pure moment follows blind the next
By senses overdrawn,
Are soon o'ercome by moments' loss,
Their flooded souls perplexed.

From too much time eternal shot with grief
I heard a cry of hope from alien tongue
That told me I was free.
"Just free?" I cried. "What good is that?
"When all my life's unstrung?"

When reason lost the battle for their minds,
And varoks desperate sent the ellls in flame
To horrors never meant,
They closed their minds upon themselves
To question not their aim.

"Though all your thoughts were centered here in mine,
And we saw more than I alone could see,
I could not know your soul,
Until we shared a grief that tore
Away reality."

The varoks sat in judgment on their kind,
Determined still to see their minds unchanged,
While grief for actions cruel
Reduced young genius to his bed,
Alone, from life estranged.

While ellls went mad with pain, and varoks then
Bound up their minds in rigid reason's girth,
Two youths, too keen with life
To let such horror rule their time,
Destroyed the set with mirth.

"All hail, good friends, we bring you songs of hope.
Why don't you stop? What strange disease has turned
Your minds to lethal fire?
What mad design has bent your minds
And left all life-joy burned?"

"Sing Ilean. Sing Korad. Cure the ellls.
Divide mad minds and save their will to live.
Drive home the wedge of love.
Then as you watch your life dissolve,
Forgive us all. Forgive."

Thus Korad left her with a soul grown strong,
Determined still while facing death to free
The growing minds of ellls,
And with the varoks find a way
To forge their destiny.

All hail the loners' legend: Ilean,
The blind, the slow, a traitor to the past;
She turned the future on.
She sang her song as strangers met
And found their lives recast.

E. Bibliography

Books that continue to enlighten us in our ongoing search for meaning and long-term solutions to current dilemmas on Earth

America the Unusual by John Kingdon. Worth Publishers, Inc. (Bedford/ St. Martins), New York, 1999. A readable summary of why Americans can be so fiercely independent, hate government and fear regulation more than Europeans do.

Are We Smart Enough to Know How Smart Animals Are? by Frans De-Waal. W. W. Norton & Co., New York, 2016. If you substitute "Aliens" for "…How Smart Animals Are," you would have the theme central to the *Archives of Varok* series and the exploration of human identity reflected in religious thought in *An Alien's Quest*.

Betrayal of Science and Reason: How Anti-Environmental Rhetoric Threatens Our Future by Paul R. and Anne H. Ehrlich. Island Press, Washington D.C., 1996.

Billionaires Ball: Gluttony and Hubris in an Age of Epic Inequality by Linda McQuaig and Neil Brooks. Beacon Press, Boston, 2012. The authors remind us in great detail that we are not aware of changes in the law that have triggered serious inequality in American well-being.

The Copernicus Complex: Our Cosmic Significance in a Universe of Planets and Probabilities by Caleb Scharf. Scientific American/Farrar, Strauss and Giroux, New York, 2014. A vibrant, readable and enjoyable history of astronomy, with a comprehensive overview of the current finds that suggest answers to the "ultimate" question: "Are we alone in the universe?"

A Cubic Mile Of Oil: Realities and Options for Averting the Looming Global Energy Crisis by Hewitt D. Crane, Edwin M. Kindeemah and Ripubaman Malhotra. Oxford University Press, Inc., 2010. A detailed study of how to provide and distribute energy worldwide without endangering Earth's future.

Deep Future: The Next 100,000 Years of Life on Earth by Curt Stager. St. Martin's Press, New York, 2011. The author begins by noting that climate change may cancel the next ice age — which would give us all a better chance of survival.

Doubt and Certainty by Tony Rothman and George Sudarshan. Perseus Books, Reading, MA, 1998.

Enough Is Enough: Building A Sustainable Economy in a World of Finite Resources by Rob Dietz and Dan O'Neill. Berrett-Koehler, San Francisco, 2013. Recommended undergraduate text. The authors describe with concise, yet precise clarity the *why* and *how* of converting to a steady state economy like Varok's, complete with index and notes for sources.

The Gene: An Intimate History by Siddhartha Mukherjee. Scribner, New York, 2016. A fascinating review of how science answers difficult questions and challenges us with future options for moral integrity.

Good Natured: The Origins of Right and Wrong in Humans and Other Animals by Frans De Waal. Harvard University Press, Cambridge, MA, 1996.

The Honor Code: How Moral Revolutions Happen by Kwame Anthony Appiah. W. W. Norton, New York, 2010. The story of how shame was needed to make lasting widespread changes in social behavior.

How Nature Works: The Science of Self-Organized Criticality by Per Bak. Springer-Verlag, New York, 1996. The definitive book clarifying the role of mathematical chaos related to complex systems.

Just Six Numbers: The Deep Forces That Shape the Universe by Martin Rees. Basic Books, New York, 2000.

Leadership and the New Science: Discovering Order in a Chaotic World by Margaret J. Wheatley. Berrett-Koehler, San Francisco, 1999.

The Meaning of It All by Richard Phillips Feynman. Perseus Books Group, Reading, MA, 1999.

Mistakes Were Made (but Not by Me): Why We Justify Foolish Beliefs, Bad Decisions, and Hurtful Acts by Carol Tavris and Elliot Aronson. Houghton Mifflin Harcourt Publishing Company, New York, 2007. A must-read about cognitive dissonance and why we are all more or less guilty of refusing to face facts when they challenge our beliefs.

The Mystery of Capital: Why Capitalism Triumphs in the West and Fails Everywhere Else by Hernando de Soto. Basic Books, New York, 2000. The answer is straight forward, but its intricacy is detailed in the long history of America and Europe--their needs to develop and enforce universal public records of property so that assets are made accessible, reliably, hence "fungible." There must be universal trust in transactions of every kind. A highly praised book.

Rare Earth: Why Complex Life is Uncommon in the Universe by Peter D. Ward and Donald Brownlee. Springer Verlag Copernicus, New York, 2000.

Thinking in Systems by Donella Meadows. Chelsea Green Publishing, White River Junction, VT, 2008. A masterful summary of the inherent complexity of nature and how to manage its interlaced systems, which are often driven by a lack of boundaries, by delays, non-linear reactions, and problems of addiction, low performance or escalation.

Books focused on growth, in order of publication date

The Limits to Growth by Donella H. Meadows, Dennis L. Meadows, Jorgen Randers, and William W. Behrens III. Universe Books, New York, 1972.

The End of Affluence: A Blueprint for Your Future by Paul R. and Anne H. Ehrlich. Ballantine, New York, 1980 (First published in 1974.

"Population, Plenty, and Poverty" by Paul R. and Anne H. Ehrlich. In *National Geographic*, Page 914, Vol. 174 No. 6, 1988.

Our Angry Earth by Isaac Asimov and Frederik Pohl. Macmillan, Tom Doherty Associates, New York, 2018 (first edition November 1991.

Betrayal of Science and Reason: How Environmental Rhetoric Threatens Our Future by Paul R. and Anne H. Ehrlich. Island Press/Shearwater Books, Washington D.C., 1996.

The Ostrich Factor: Our Population Myopia by Garrett Hardin. Oxford University Press, Oxford, 1998.

Eco-Economy: Building an Economy for the Earth by Lester R.Brown. W.W. Norton & Company, New York, 2001.

Plan B, Rescuing a Planet Under Stress and a Civilization in Trouble by Lester R. Brown, W.W. Norton & Company, New York, 2003.

Ecological Economics: Principles and Applications by Herman Daly and Joshua Farley. Island Press, Washington, D.C., 2003.

Outgrowing the Earth: the Food Security Challenge in an Age of Falling Water Tables and Rising Temperatures by Lester R. Brown. W.W.Norton & Company, New York, 2004.

Hot, Flat and Crowded: Why We Need a Green Revolution and How It Can Renew America by Thomas L. Friedman. Farrar, Straus and Giroux, New York, 2008.

The World in 2050: Four Forces Shaping Civilization's Northern Future by Laurence C. Smith. Dutton-Penguin Group, New York, 2010.

World On the Edge: How to Prevent Environmental and Economic Collapse by Lester R. Brown. W.W. Norton & Company, New York, 2011.

The Great Disruption: Why the Climate Crisis Will Bring On the End of Shopping and the Birth of a New World by Paul Guilding. Bloomsbury Press, New York, 2011.

Deep Future: The Next 100,000 Years of Life on Earth by Curt Stager. St. Martin's Press, New York, 2011.

The End of Growth: Adapting to Our New Economic Reality by R. Heinberg. New Society Publishers, Canada, 2011.

Supply Shock: Economic Growth at the Crossroads and the Steady State Solution by Brian Czech. New Society Publishers, Canada, 2013.

Enough Is Enough: Building A Sustainable Economy in a World of Finite Resources by Rob Dietz & Dan O'Neill. Berrett-Koehler Publishers, Inc., San Francisco, 2013.

The Future: Six Drivers of Global Change by Al Gore. Random House, New York, 2013.

Tipping Point For Planet Earth by Anthony D. Barnosky and Elizabeth A. Hadly. St. Martin's Press, New York, 2015.

Half-Earth: Our Planet's Fight for Life by Edward O. Wilson. W.W. Norton & Company, New York, 2016.

Our Angry Earth by Isaac Asimov and Frederik Pohl. Macmillan, Tom Doherty Associates, New York, 2018 (first edition November 1991).

F. A History of the Archives

3631 *ir* (**Earth 5000** BCE) - Events recorded in *The Unheard Song*.[1]

3634 *ir* (**Earth 4962** BCE) – Amanok writes his memoirs.

4225.8 *ir* (**Earth 2020** CE) – Tandra Grey born on Earth.

4228 *ir* (**Earth 2047** CE) – Shawne Grey born on Earth.

4228.3–4228.4 *ir* (**Earth 2050–2051** CE) – Events recorded in *A Place Beyond Man*,[2] revised as *The View Beyond Earth*.[3]

4228.4–4229.5 *ir* (**Earth 2051–2064** CE) – Events in *The Webs of Varok*.[4]

4229 *ir* (**Earth 2059** CE) – Aman Telariahn (Amantel) publishes Amanok's memoirs as *The Unheard Song*.[1]

4229.8–4230 *ir* (**Earth 2068–2070** CE) – Oran-ElConn-Grey family events recorded in *The Alien Effect*.[5]

4229.8–4409.7 *ir* (**Earth 2068–4202** CE and beyond) – Biological Events recorded in *The Alien Effect*.[5]

4230 *ir* (**Earth 2070** CE) – Events recorded in *An Alien's Quest*.[6]

---

1. Penscript Publishing House, 2022. 2. Charles Scribner's Sons, 1975. 3. Penscript Publishing House, 2014. 4. Penscript Publishing House, 2012. 5. Penscript Publishing House, 2014. 6. Penscript Publishing House, 2016

Carolyn A. (Cary) Neeper, PhD raised her family in the US Southwest with her husband and a friendly menagerie of dogs, fish and fowl. An avid proponent of sustainability and steady-state economics since the 1970s, she studied zoology, chemistry and religion at Pomona College and medical microbiology at  the University of Wisconsin–Madison. Cary paints landscapes and animals in acrylics, including the cover art for *The Archives of Varok* series.

THE ARCHIVES OF VAROK

In an alternate 21st century Solar System, Earth learns that we have neighbors too intelligent, too nosy, and too near to ignore. . . .

The View Beyond Earth

Two offworld species, disturbingly human and altogether alien. Microbiologist Tandra Grey finds new hope for an ailing Earth and her own future when she makes first contact. Revised and updated from Neeper's 1975 classic, *A Place Beyond Man* (Charles Scribner's Sons).

The Webs of Varok

Silver medalist, Nautilus Book Awards 2013; Finalist, ForeWord's Book of the Year Awards 2012. Tandra leaves Earth for the ancient sustainable culture of Varok, with its promise of stability for her young daughter. But a genius with a hidden talent sets his eye on Varok's wealth — and Tandra's alien soul-mates.

The Alien Effect

Raised on the Jovian moon Varok, Shawne returns to Earth to help her devastated home planet build a new civilization — one that can thrive for millennia. She and her mixed family face unexpected lessons in love and personhood, unaware of the long-term consequences of their collision with life on Earth.

An Alien's Quest

Only two decades after first contact, even Earth's people know of Haralahn, the great-fish spiritual leader on distant Ellason. Shawne seeks his guidance in a quest for meaning that draws everyone she loves away to the Kuiper Belt and into a genetic mystery on the watery home planet of the ells.

The Unheard Song

In this Archives of Varok prequel, a humanoid invader and aquatic native struggle to communicate in their race to ensure peace and a sustainable future for the wild seas of Ellason.

www.ingramcontent.com/pod-product-compliance
Lightning Source LLC
Chambersburg PA
CBHW022039240626
47154CB00007B/2481